# Killing SLOB

Book 1 of the *Unlikely Heroes* series

Written by

## Aileen Chorley

Copyright © 2018 by Marailla Publishing

# A Touch of Genius

"Osiris, we are making our approach."

"They're not answering, Captain."

"Stop panicking, Skinner. You want to stay on my team, you develop a sodding backbone."

"Sorry, Captain. It's just... they're not answering, Captain."

"I repeat; Osiris, we are making our approach."

"D'you think they've gone on a coffee break?" Johnson postulated.

"Don't be stupid," the Captain barked with derision. "It's against regulations to leave the control point unmanned."

"Captain, they're not answering," Skinner repeated like a demented parrot.

"Pull yourself together, man."

"Sorry Captain. I-It's just that hunk of metal looks awfully close."

"Copy that," came a timid voice at last.

Captain Brash turned to Skinner with a condescending, scornful smirk.

The smirk soon faded. Space was disappearing. The doors were still not opening. Skinner struggled to keep his lips together and the words spilled out. "They're not opening the doors, Captain!"

"Osiris, open the landing bay doors," Brash demanded.

"OK, just a jiff," came a flustered reply.

"They're not opening the doors, Captain!" Skinner shrieked. "We're coming up fast!"

"OPEN THE BLOODY DOORS!" the Captain screamed.

"The red button. The one right in front of you. The one marked 'landing bay doors'."

"Oh yeah. I couldn't see for looking."

"OPEN THE BLOODY DOORS! NOW!!"

Martha put her magazine down and looked up. She was hugely put out that this... nincompoop had got the job she was promised and all because she was the Admiral's daughter. It was a grave injustice, so grave an injustice she was dammed if she was going to jump up and press the blasted button for her. "Well, press it then. Now."

A dainty, timid finger nudged the button, retracting quickly as if avoiding some contagious disease.

Seconds later, an almighty clatter reverberated down in the landing bay. Metal scraped on metal... angry, remorseless, skin-searing and very, very long. Martha cringed and buried her head in her magazine. The Admiral's daughter - known affectionately as 'little dove' to her father, Jenna to herself, and 'that bloody moron' to most others - peeped at the wreckage down below. The craft had come to rest, lying on its side like a dead insect. Jenna bit her quivering lip as a bedraggled and stupefied crew wandered out onto the floor. They looked like ghosts in a world between worlds. One of the ghosts became highly animated. A strong lean man with loose dark hair made violent sweeps with his arms, before his fists ploughed into the side of the wreck. Even from where she stood, Jenna could hear the foul obscenities. As he turned around, her heart nearly stopped. It was Captain Brash, the ship's hunk, the one all the girls gazed at adoringly. He was much older than she was, thirty-three, but he was drop dead gorgeous. Why did it have to be him?

Sinking down in her chair, she chewed her fingernails, glancing at Martha for support.

Martha looked up. "You only had to push a bloody button. How hard can that be?"

"They appeared from nowhere," Jenna protested. "Until you flipped that switch, I didn't hear anything."

"That switch should be flipped on at all times when a craft's out. I already told you that."

"I... I forgot..."

Lazily, Martha pressed the intercom. "Emergency crew to landing bay. Level..." She tilted her head, assessing. She smiled to herself wickedly. "Level 1 emergency." *Maybe she'll spend time in the lock-up for this.*

"I want her head!" Brash roared to the Head of Operations as an emergency fire crew was looking for a fire and a team of medical personal was trying to put them on stretchers. "Who was it!"

The Head of Operations scratched the side of his mouth. "Jenna Trot."

Brash gawped at the man. "The Admiral's daughter...? They put *her* up there....?"

"She only had to push a button."

"And she couldn't even do that, could she!" Brash scraped his hands through his sweaty dark hair, forcing himself to calm down. "You need to speak to the Admiral. Get her on laundry duty or something, get her in the kitchen, get her off this bloody ship!"

Arranging his spectacles, the Head of Operations looked at Brash seriously. "You think I'm going to put my neck on the block? Remember what happened to the Navigation Officer? He's serving time in some remote outpost now, god help him."

"The man let his tongue run away with him. He said, and I quote, 'if that bloody imbecile doesn't leave my sector, we'll end up in the belly of a black hole!"

"Yes, yes, I remember. Though he had been under a lot of pressure. Apparently, his wife was having an affair with the guy that got the job he wanted. The guy that looked like a cross between Mr Universe and some legendary rock god. That's got to hurt."

"Exactly. So, you've just got to be diplomatic."

"Diplomatic? The Admiral thinks his girl's got untapped potential. Can't and won't accept that the spawn of his loins could be anything other than great in some way. He'll let her kill the lot of us before he admits the truth. The man's determined, I'll say that for him."

"But she has to go," Brash said, clenching his bruised fists, staring hard at the shredded metal beneath his feet. Suddenly, he looked up. It was a touch of genius.

# Get it in Writing

Brash and his crew were silent as they ate in the cafeteria. For one, they were still a little shaken but more than that his crew were worried about saying the wrong thing. Brash was in a steaming mood.

Skinner couldn't keep his mouth shut. He had a lot of nervous energy and it always spilled out through his 'loose flapping gob', as Newark liked to call it. "At least, we're still in one piece."

The scathing look Brash gave him made his insides liquefy and severed the connection with his mouth.

Brash threw back his beer. "Skinner, I want you to check the electrics tomorrow. Newark, check the bodywork. Graham, check the hy-"

"Maintenance will do that, surely?" Graham asked.

"They're not getting their hands on my bloody ship. If any of them were any good they'd be on my team. You know I only pick the best."

This was true, as far as Captain Brash was concerned. Skinner was a jelly-bellied toad, but he was a technical genius. Flint wasn't technical or brave, but he had an amazing ability to learn new languages. He spoke about fifty. His brain seemed wired to understand them. Maybe it compensated for the fact that he was a boring misfit. As tedious as he was, Brash needed someone like him in case they ever did come across undiscovered intelligent aliens. He still held the hope they were out there. His mission and his purpose could not be in vain. Of course, they had come across other forms of life. Flint had spent half an hour trying to communicate with a large worm-like creature. At last, they decided it was unintelligent. That, or Flint wasn't as good as he claimed to be. They'd come across all manner of unusual creatures but none of them humanoid, and most little more than pondlife.

The rest of his team, Johnson, Graham and Newark, were technically proficient, brave and trained to be deadly. Yes, his team was a good team, worthy to have him as a captain.

"We'll be out of commission for a while," Brash spat angrily.

"We could get in some pool," Skinner jibed.

Brash didn't respond but his crew sensed their Captain's anger was simmering down. At last, they felt able to voice their own.

"She should be locked up for this," Johnson vented with an unladylike sniff.

Brash nodded thoughtfully, draining his glass and calling out for another.

"She could have killed us all," Graham put in, staring at the table, soberly.

"I think I've got whiplash," Skinner said. "Can you claim for that?"

"Pity she's the Admiral's daughter," Newark ruminated, his brain trying in vain to find some way around that unfortunate fact.

Flint had nothing to contribute.

All eyes looked up, all staring in wonder over the Captain's head.

A delicate little cough made the Captain's eyes widen. His face turned a furious red and his body stiffened. Newark looked almost excited.

"Err... I just wanted to apologise for the... err... incident earlier," the Admiral's daughter said in a flimsy voice. *Incident!* Brash fumed. "Daddy's been very understanding but I feel just awful."

Brash drew in a deep breath then turned to her with a pleasant if contorted-looking smile. Newark was positively pumping, the anticipation almost too much for him. Johnson was viewing the pretty blonde Barbie doll with disdain. If she wasn't the Admiral's daughter, she would have got up and knocked her out.

"These things happen," Brash said in a voice approaching congenial. The crew's eyes fixed on him as if they had found the new life they'd been looking for. Newark, however, knew what was coming and could barely contain himself.

"Please, my dear, don't torture yourself," Brash continued. "We all make mistakes. I expect it gets tedious sitting at that control point all day and I can see you are a girl that craves adventure. A mind like yours must get stupefied into inaction. It's a shame you aren't on my team. There's so much to explore out there. Never a dull moment. Anyway, don't you trouble yourself. We're fine."

The crew stared at him, incredulous. Newark was still waiting.

The Admiral's daughter looked on the verge of tears. "Oh, Captain, I knew the kind of man you were. Big and brave and... so very, very, kind. Course, when you started punching the ship, I thought-"

"Shock. Just a reaction, my dear."

"Yes. Yes, of course." Smiling like a little girl, she lurched forward and hugged Brash. The man had to prevent himself throwing her off and punching her lights out. His control was such that he even managed to pat her back.

At last, Jenna Trot drew back, smiled at him happily then skipped off.

The crew stared at Brash. Newark was still waiting for the punchline and getting a drowning sense of disappointment.

"You want her on our team...?" Graham asked, feeling like he'd stepped into a parallel universe.

"Of course not," Brash grumbled, brushing his clothes as if brushing her off him. He looked up at them. "The girl's a liability and nobody will do anything about it. So, she'll join our team but unfortunately she will die in action."

The crew smiled and nodded. Newark's world made sense again and he decided he could wait.

"Daddy, please. You know how bored I get on this spaceship and Captain Brash is *so* nice. You really should promote him. I'm sure he'll look after me."

"Absolutely not. It's too dangerous and you are too... delicate, my little dove."

"I'm not delicate. I can be strong and brave," she said, sticking out her chest.

The Admiral just laughed. Then he placed his hands on her shoulders and said, "You have many gifts. I know you haven't found your niche yet but this... this is not for you. Trust me. I'm your father."

"Well, if you won't let me do this, I'll just mope. I'll sit in my bedroom and mope. I probably won't eat and I'll waste away."

The Admiral smiled fondly and shook his head, indulging her little whim, knowing nothing would come of it. So, he was surprised and even proud when, after a week of her sitting in her room, moping and not eating, she showed no signs of giving up. Considering there was more fortitude to her than he had previously imagined, he finally relented.

"No, I'm sorry, sir, but it's too dangerous for her. I would never put your daughter in danger and we never know what we're going to be up against out there. I couldn't live with myself if..."

"I understand your concerns, Captain, and, truth be told, I'm not happy about this myself. Yet, it's what her heart's hell-bent on. And the last thing I want as a father is to hold her back. See, the thing is," the Admiral said, leaning forward, elbows on the desk, fingers crossed, "I know she's got a good brain on her shoulders. She's just not..."

"Found out how to use it?"

"Exactly. So, while she's...."

"Trying to find out how to use her brain?"

"Yes. She needs something stimulating."

The Captain pursed his lips. "I appreciate your dilemma, sir, but she doesn't strike me as..."

"Strong, brave?" He shook his head. "I'm not sure she is. Her mother was delicate too, God rest her. But... maybe there's more to her than I imagined and, if this is what she wants, who am I to..."

*Not give her what she wants?* Brash thought contemptuously.

Brash let out a pained, reticent sigh. "I'm afraid if anything happened to her, sir, I couldn't live with myself. I know it would be stimulating and challenging for her, and I'm sure it would be character building. In fact, it could do her the world of good. But it's too dangerous, sir. We never know what we're going to be up against. I mean, a lot of the terrain is treacherous, poisonous plant-life, and I can't tell you how many weird-looking creatures we've killed. Some of them are just plain ghastly. You don't have time to think. You just shoot. Flint nearly got shot last month. Got caught in the crossfire, trying to communicate with one of the creatures. I would strongly advise against this, sir."

The Admiral sighed. "Captain, I'm afraid it will be an order. If you take all reasonable steps to ensure her safety, which I'm sure you will, I will not hold you accountable."

*Bingo,* thought Brash. His daughter was toast.

Brash sighed heavily. "Very well but may I have your assurance that you won't hold me personally accountable."

"Of course."

"In writing?"

# Turned on its Head

Their craft was up and running. They had a new member of the crew but try as they might, they couldn't seem to kill her. Their first excursion to a desolate planet was a complete disaster. Brash, having got a read-out of the terrain, instructed his team to fan out to search for plant life, having picked an area of steep ravines and craggy inclines for their newest recruit. *'We tried to hold onto her, sir. Newark's inconsolable.'*

"Do I have to go on my own?" Jenna asked, gazing around at the jagged landscape and yellow sky.

"We're all going off alone," Brash replied. "Don't worry. There are no signs of animal life here."

She looked at him uncertainly and he perfected a concerned, fatherly frown. "If you don't feel up to it, we can take you back to the ship. I'm sure your father can find you something else to do."

She straightened. "No, I'll go."

She trudged off alone but the infuriating thing was that she came back. Brash was certain she'd have slipped and fallen, maybe cracked open her helmet. He'd been banking on it. Disappointing as it was, he had to let this one go.

The next excursion was more intense. It was difficult to describe the monstrous, rabid-looking creatures that came their way. No-one should have tentacles on their foreheads, Brash thought with pure hatred as he unleashed hell. The laser weapons took the enemy down easily and, as more of them fell, the Captain turned his weapon on the Admiral's daughter. But the girl was fucking charmed. She stumbled and fell just as he fired. The second round hit the enemy who got in his way. And on the third attempt, his weapon failed. Newark stepped into the breach, going berserk on the enemy and firing the odd blast her way. Again, she managed to evade his fire, stumbling and falling like some clumsy spaced out moron. When *she* fired her weapon, it was anybody's guess who she'd hit. The crew ducked and dived out of her way as they tried to take out the aliens. They were lucky to survive the day.

"Get that weapon off her!" Johnson shouted.

"You get it!" Graham shouted back. "I'm not going anywhere near her!"

As the last alien body fell in a blue gooey mess, Johnson grabbed Jenna's firearm.

Brash looked around, scanning the surrounding hills. They were covered in some sort of blue vegetation. The grass beneath him, if grass it was, was an odd shade of blue too. Strangely enough, the sky was green. Everything seemed back to front here. The air was breathable and that didn't make sense somehow. He searched for movement but couldn't detect any.

"She's bloody lethal," Newark remarked, coming up to him.

"She's like a damned cat," Brash said, staring at her, bemused.

"Why don't we just cap her now?"

"It's got to look like an accident. The Admiral will send an investigation team down here. I don't want to be strung up for this."

"OK, well, shoot her now, dump her near the aliens. Job done."

Brash turned to Newark, his opinion of the man declining. "We want it to look like she was caught in the crossfire. That investigation team are good. The biometric scanners would pick up the fact that all those aliens died before her. Then they'd want to know why."

Newark racked his brains, searching for a way around this.

Letting out a defeated sigh, Brash turned to Trot. She was sitting on the ground, sobbing and quivering like a little girl.

"She looks a mess," Johnson said, coming over.

"Yeah," Brash replied, almost sympathetically. "We'll not kill her today. Wait until she feels better. Where the hell's Skinner?"

"I'm here, Captain," Skinner shouted, looking suspiciously near to the craft.

Brash would have thought more on the matter if he wasn't aware of Jenna Trot's eyes boring into him. Did she know they were trying to kill her? No, that would require deduction.

The next outing proved no more fruitful. The air, again, was breathable and they didn't need their suits. The crew were like kids on holiday when they found a breathable planet. This one, however, not so much. There was a foul stench in the air and they realised it was coming from what appeared to be a carpet of slimy green snakes. The slippery creatures were everywhere.

"Get some samples," Brash instructed, upon which Newark drew out his firearm and began chewing up the carpet. Johnson and Graham joined in.

"Get some live ones!" Brash yelled.

"They look poisonous!" Johnson shouted. "We can't chance it, sir!"

Newark turned his weapon on Trot but she had already run off back to the craft, unable to endure the carnage.

"Stop firing!" Brash yelled. The Captain was livid. "Newark, what the hell were you doing!"

"Johnson's right, Captain, they look poisonous."

"What the hell were you doing firing at Trot!"

"Trying to kill her, sir."

"Are you insane! Remember what I said about the investigation team! How can she be caught in the cross-fire when you're firing downward, you bloody moron!" *God, had he always been this imbecilic? Killing Trot certainly seemed to bring it out of him.*

Rubbing his forehead, Brash turned to Flint. "Flint, pick up a snake."

As they got back to the craft, Flint nursed a swollen, purple hand. Though the snake was dead, the poison appeared to have seeped through Flint's skin. It had taken five minutes for the hand to balloon up. The Captain, feeling mildly guilty and making a mental note to bring protective gear next time, looked at Flint's hand and thought of Trot. How much of that stuff would it take to kill a person? He ran through the possibilities in his head... *'She must have fallen, sir, knocked herself out. Those things were all over the place."* He shook his head. The investigation team would figure it out. The angle of impact, pressure applied... If you didn't know better, you'd swear they were fucking psychic. No, it wouldn't stand up to scrutiny. Besides, the Admiral's voice was booming in his ears. *"What was she doing on her own, Brash!"*

They fared no better on the next planet. Brash could find little excuse to finish her off. There were no aliens, no harsh terrain, no hills, nothing. He thought about ripping her helmet off and saying she'd done it herself, though of course that was just desperation talking and he hated to think of himself as desperate.

The next time they set out, Brash became mindful her furtive looks. *Did she suspect them? Of course not. If she did, she wouldn't have come out with them. No-one can be that stupid. She would have run off to daddy and they'd all be banged up.*

As they touched down, he found himself viewing her curiously.

Jenna followed the crew out, inhaling deeply. The air was thin but breathable. The way the light shone on the red rocks filled her heart with a new-found lease of life. She looked down at her feet touching red soil. It was an odd feeling, almost spiritual. She'd been on that spaceship for years now. This was the only reason she was still coming out with this group. Her view of the good captain and his crew had changed considerably. She viewed them as a gang of gung-ho hooligans set on annihilating anything that crossed their paths. If she wasn't so desperate to get off that spacecraft, she would have told her father about them.

Crouching down, she observed a small insect scuttling through the grit. As she watched its meagre progress, her heart went out to it.

A heavy booted foot came down and squashed out its life.

"What did you do that for?" she shot angrily.

"It's an insect." Johnson shrugged. "That's what you do."

"Why?"

Johnson stared at her as if she was stupid. "Because that's what you do."

"Could have been intelligent," Flint remarked distantly.

"Give me a break. You going to talk to insects now? With giant worms, you were scraping the barrel."

"Flint's right," Jenna asserted, "you don't know anything about it. Monstrous tentacle creatures looking threatening is one thing but squishing insects is just plain nasty."

"*Ooooh*... You'll be telling me to hug trees next."

"We don't know how intelligent alien trees might be," Flint put in, considering this.

"Give it a rest, Flint."

Jenna stood up straight. "What are we doing here exactly? You say you're here to find and communicate with intelligent life forms but all I've seen is you massacring them!"

"So, your philosophy is die first, ask questions later?"

"Maybe they just move fast. Maybe they were coming to welcome us."

Newark laughed. "You really are as stupid as everyone says."

"Newark," the Captain bellowed, coming over. "Apologise at once."

Newark, seeming to remember he was talking to the Admiral's daughter, straightened up and apologised.

Jenna stared at Newark. "What do you mean? Everyone says I'm stupid...?"

Newark fought the compulsion to say, 'Duh!'

"Don't listen to Newark," Brash said, his eyes boring into the man. "Come on, we'll do a quick recon."

He walked off, Jenna staring after him.

Newark caught up to Brash. "So, what's the plan then, Captain? How are we going to kill her? Find a hill? Push her off?"

Brash turned to him. "You're actually enjoying this, aren't you?"

Newark looked caught off guard. As he wasn't prone to self-reflection, he had no idea how to answer.

"We're not murderers," Brash insisted. "This is just a necessary evil."

"OK. So, how are we going to do it?"

Brash sighed.

"Captain," Johnson said, coming up behind them. "Trot's gone back to the ship. Says she doesn't feel well."

"Damn," Newark complained. "She's really dragging this out, isn't she?"

"Well, that's that then," Brash said. "Johnson, tell Skinner to babysit Trot. The rest of us will look around."

Jenna wasn't too happy to see Skinner come aboard alone. The man was aptly named. He was, indeed, skinny. His eyes flitted over her as he sat down. She shivered. The weasely man turned her stomach. She'd noticed his eyes running over her a few times now.

Wiping a hand through his short brown hair, Skinner gave out a nervous laugh. He wasn't very good at talking to women unless he was drunk. Johnson didn't count. She was practically a man. Jenna looked up at him but said nothing. His eyes flitted away. He got up and started checking instruments that didn't need checking.

The rest of the crew boarded the ship sometime later. As they did, Brash felt Trot's eyes on him.

"How d'you know those tentacle creatures weren't intelligent?" she piped up.

"What tentacle creatures?" the Captain asked, staring at her.

"You're still harping on about that?" Johnson complained. "We're in the past here, Captain. She can't seem to let it go."

Brash walked up front and buckled himself in.

"How do you know?" Trot pressed. "Intelligence comes in many ways," she said bitterly.

"They were animals," he answered coolly as he began flicking switches. "Instinctive. No rational thought. We were just a meal."

"So, they were hungry. Doesn't mean they can't think."

Brash turned to Jenna, observing her closely.

"If they could think," Newark butted in, "they wouldn't mess with laser weapons, now, would they?"

"Yeah," Graham said, "and if they're clever, they won't mess with them again."

Newark and Graham high-fived and Jenna viewed them with disdain. Brash watched Jenna watching them, and his curiosity was piqued. For a brief second, he saw a two-dimensional person, not the one-dimensional caricature he had imagined. Unsettled by this, and hating to be thrown off course, he turned his back on her and started up the engines.

As the ship broke free of the planet, Brash listened to the banter behind him. But what was louder was Jenna Trot's silence. It pestered him as they made their way back and he found himself reconsidering the necessity of having to kill her. For one thing, it was proving harder than he had imagined. They seemed to have spent more time figuring out how to end her than fulfilling their mission. Yet, if they didn't kill her they would be stuck with her. And she *was* pretty useless. He'd also need to get her weapons-trained. Friendly fire isn't so friendly when you're on the receiving end of it. What was he thinking? He'd been committed to killing her and he hated to change his plans. He felt very conflicted.

Behind him, Jenna Trot's eyes roamed around the crew, studying them properly for the first time. She appraised Johnson. The woman's mousy hair was tied back in a messy ponytail. She was slim and good-looking with unusual grey eyes, but her arms and legs were powerhouses of muscle and, at the moment, she was trying to pick something out of her ear. Newark and Graham were jabbering loudly about nothing. Graham had dark hair, like Brash, but he was leaner, less manly. He kept turning to Johnson, trying to involve her in the conversation but Johnson was too busy with her ear. Newark's mouth was a constant stream of obscenities. Every other word seemed to begin with F. He was more strongly-built than Graham with messy, light brown hair that looked like it was never combed. He spotted a bit of dirt on his jacket and wiped it away, losing track of the conversation in the process.

Sitting at the other end, in a world of his own, was Flint. Flint was a bit of a puzzle to Jenna. He rarely spoke, rarely seemed tuned in. His ice blonde hair fell over his face as if hiding it. He could have been as tall as Brash but it was difficult to say as he never stood up straight. He was quite thin, almost as if he didn't look after himself. His face might have been considered handsome if it wasn't so... distant.

Skinner was sitting up front with Brash, as fidgety and animated as ever. With the exception of Brash, they were all in their twenties but older than she was. Apart from Flint, she hated the lot of them and hate was not something she was accustomed to.

She drew her attention away from them and stared at the floor for the rest of the journey. She didn't look at anyone as she disembarked.

"Perhaps you'd prefer a different assignment," Brash said as tactfully as possible. "Maybe this job isn't suited to you."

"No job's suited to me," she said quietly. "I suck at everything."

The truthful moment of self-reflection took Brash by surprise. A few weeks ago, he wouldn't have thought her capable of it.

"Ain't that the truth," Newark said under his breath and Brash punched his arm.

Brash turned to watch her walk away. The desolate line of her shoulders brought out something in him he didn't know was there. An odd kind of pity. It didn't sit easily with him, so he pushed it down. Like energy that can't be destroyed only changed, the feeling turned to anger. His crew, sensing this, suddenly found other places to be. Newark, being the last to see sense, bore the full brunt of it. As Newark walked away, Brash started to view the man in a different light. Newark, the boldest, most daring of his crew, was beginning to look like an insensitive idiot. And if that was the case, what did that make him? He had picked him, after all.

Brash thought a good night's sleep would put everything back in perspective. But it wasn't a good night's sleep. He tossed and turned and when he awoke in the morning, everything had turned on its head. He had lost all desire to kill Jenna Trot. He wasn't sure who Newark was, wasn't sure who Jenna Trot was, and as he stared at his own reflection in the mirror, he wasn't even sure who he was anymore.

# Close Calls

Brash watched Newark stuff three rashers of bacon into his gob all at once. The stuffed mouth then began to talk. "Where's Goldilocks this morning?"

Brash didn't answer. He watched Newark pick up his coffee, wondering how he was going to cram that in too. Newark managed it effortlessly and the sounds that emanated were disgusting. Brash pushed his plate away.

"Not hungry, Captain?" Newark asked, already reaching over. Yesterday, Brash would have knocked the hand away, might even have grabbed Newark's collar and hissed at him threateningly. He wasn't at his best in the mornings. Today, he let it go.

"Why d'you eat as if food's going out of fashion?" Brash asked in a deadpan voice.

Newark thought about this then shrugged.

"He was one of ten kids, Cap," Johnson said.

Brash looked at her. "Ah..."

"I was the runt of the litter," Skinner quipped.

"Figures."

Graham and Johnson were gauging their Captain's mood. He didn't seem quite himself.

"So," Johnson asked, "how long before we reach the next planet, Captain?"

"Two weeks," he answered distractedly. "But that's Marios Prime."

Marios Prime was an inhabited planet, a known inhabited planet with known inhabitants. Nothing new to discover there. It crossed a known trading route and, as Osiris' mission was not just to seek out new life but to transport goods, they would be stopping off there. Brash found this delay extremely aggravating and though the crew perfected morose, frustrated looks, inside they were secretly ecstatic. They enjoyed their jobs but they were not as committed as Brash. And they always got shore leave. One of the downsides was taking Flint – he was needed to translate. One of the upsides was that Flint was a scream when he got drunk. Flint came whether he wanted to or not. Flint got drunk whether he wanted to or not. And watching him with a hangover was almost as gratifying.

"The next planet after that will likely be weeks off," Brash lamented. He rubbed his forehead. "I overheard the Chief Engineer telling the Admiral that the hyperdrive was looking dodgy. If the old git doesn't get it fixed, we'll end up heading back to Marios Prime."

The crew again joined in the lament, inwardly thinking that Christmas had come.

"Surely, he'll get it fixed?" Johnson asked with feigned concern.

"Dodgy isn't the same as had it. He hates spending money."

"Where *is* Goldilocks this morning?" Graham asked, looking around. Even when they weren't on a mission, they had to report for training.

Brash stared at Graham. "D'you think she knows?"

"Knows what?"

"That we've been trying to kill her," he whispered, glancing around.

"No, sir. How could she?"

Newark laughed. "If you ask me, her head's as empty as a... as a..."

"You alright, Captain?" Johnson asked.

"I just get this feeling about her... Like she knows what's going on..."

"No, Captain, she's clueless."

"That's the thing with stupid people," Newark considered. "They have this way about them until you start to question whether they really are stupid. But, you see, it's just your mind playing tricks on you. That's the power of stupidity."

All eyes looked at Newark. Brash tried to figure out if that was extremely clever or extremely dumb.

"Excuse me, Captain Brash," a voice said behind him. "The Admiral would like to see you."

Brash's eyes widened. The Admiral never wanted to see him. Was the gig up? Did the pig squeal? Was he in a whole heap of shit? Johnson, Graham, and Skinner were staring back at him. Newark was stuffing toast into his mouth and Flint was on another planet talking to an alien creature.

The Admiral was located on the top deck which gave Brash plenty of time to think his way around this. The lift was pretty slow, the craft being an older model and not the sleekest. In fact, it reminded Brash of a gigantic aubergine. The top level, however, was plush. The vending machines always worked there. Brash grabbed a drink and slugged it back, before entering the Admiral's quarters.

"You wanted to see me, sir?" Brash asked, his sweaty hands clenched behind his back.

"Ah, yes," the Admiral said, rising to his full height, his imposing body dwarfing Brash by inches. The Admiral turned to look out of the window –

a painting of a window with a beautiful landscape. "I want to talk to you about something of quite a serious nature."

"A serious nature?" Brash stuttered, despite himself.

"Yes," the Admiral said, turning back around, his dark eyes descending on Brash. An escape plan flashed through Brash's mind. He'd take the escape pod. His craft would never get through the landing bay doors. What about his crew? Stuff the crew. "The science department has made a complaint." *Science department...?* "Although your primary objective is to seek out intelligent life, you were also instructed to bring specimens of lower lifeforms for study."

"Yes, sir?" Brash asked, a little dazed. "And we have done that."

"Um... Mutilated, unrecognisable carcasses was not what they had in mind. They want to study the organisms alive, if possible."

"Sir, some of the lifeforms in question were highly hostile. It wasn't possible to bring them back alive."

"I understand. But it seems... a little like overkill. It looks like they have been butchered, Brash. I've seen myself and it's not a pretty sight." The Admiral placed a hand under his nose.

"Yes," Brash agreed, regretfully. "Some of the crew get.... a little carried away, sir. Particularly Newark. He's very... enthusiastic. I'll have a word with them. Thank you for bringing this to my attention. Is that everything, sir?"

"Not quite. There's also the matter of my daughter."

The Captain's spine stiffened. "Your daughter, sir?"

"Yes. I want to know how she's getting on."

"Oh... She's not said anything then. I mean, has she not spoken to you about it, sir?"

"When I ask her, she says that she's loving the job but... she seems a little distant to me."

"Ah, well, that's the constant change in atmosphere she's experiencing, sir. It takes a bit of getting used to, especially for those of a... delicate composition."

The Admiral nodded thoughtfully. "Yes... She is delicate. I never let her have shore leave, unless, of course, I can accompany her. You get such dubious characters in these trading posts."

Brash nodded in agreement. He was thinking of his own crew after a night of drinking. "So, you sometimes take her ashore, sir?" he asked conversationally.

"Well, I haven't done as yet. I'm a busy man, Brash," he asserted, almost indignantly.

"Of course. Of course." *The poor cow's never been off the ship...? God, that's harsh.*

"But it just occurs to me now that maybe you could take her. She's no doubt toughened up a lot these past few months and with you to escort her, I'm sure she'll come to no harm."

"Err…"

"Excellent. That's agreed then. She'll be overjoyed."

"Daddy, do I have to go with Captain Brash?"

"I thought you liked the man. You were singing his praises not that long ago."

"I do, I do but…" She scratched her head. "It's the Captain's time off. I'm sure he doesn't want to be saddled with me. I'd feel more comfortable going with someone else."

"Like who?"

Jenna racked her brains. There was no-one else. She didn't have friends and all the sectors she had worked in had been short-term arrangements. A searing pain stabbed her heart. They all thought she was stupid. At the time, she had told herself that the job wasn't for her. She'd been encouraged by the staff to find something more personally fulfilling. They had been so helpful in this and as she left everyone had been so nice to her. Only now was the cold truth hitting home. They were desperate to be rid of her. She was a useless, incompetent misfit. How could she have been so ignorant of this…? Well, she wasn't now. Newark's remark had opened a gateway she couldn't close. As for her new job, she was trapped in no man's land. As much as she despised Brash and his crew, going out on their unproductive, sometimes sick missions was the only escape she had. But she was damned if she was going on shore leave with them.

"I have some friends who are going ashore," she lied. Forcing a bright smile on her face, she added, "A group of girls have invited me along with them."

"Girls?" her father asked dubiously and she scrambled for more.

"A couple of chaps said they'll come too, just to keep an eye on us."

"Chaps?"

"A couple of their husbands." *Please don't ask for names.*

Finally, her father smiled. "It's so good to know you've made friends. You know, I think this caper with Brash and his crew has been good for you. It's given you confidence."

Nodding vigorously, she smiled. When her father left, she broke down and cried.

# What were the Odds?

Flint's eyes rolled back in his head.

"Another!" Newark called out and Johnson handed him one. "Here, hold his mouth open." Graham prized Flint's mouth open as Newark poured the beer down his throat. Flint coughed and spluttered then lurched forward and puked all over Newark's boots. "Ah, Man...!"

"You never move fast enough," Graham managed between his laughter.

"Fuck you."

"I'd rather you not."

"I 'ucking 'ate you 'astards," Flint muttered, his head swimming.

"What was that, Flint?" Johnson asked, leaning in and pulling his head back.

"I ont u ill u..."

"He's speaking alien now."

Flint endeavoured to add more strength. "I... want... to... kill... you," he said in the determined breathy voice of a dying man.

Johnson slapped him on the back. "I love this guy when he's drunk."

Skinner was staggering around the bar, sleazing up to any female he could find, slurring his words and breathing all over them. The crew heard the words, *vile cretin* being yelled before Flint fell off the chair and landed on his face.

Brash walked in and looked around. "Get me a beer, Graham," he said, looking down at Flint on the floor. "Christ. Can't you think of anything better to do?"

"The bastard puked on my boots," Newark complained.

"Pick him up. Find him somewhere to sleep it off."

Newark and Johnson hauled Flint up and dragged him out of the bar. They dunked his head in a water trough, at which Flint let out a pained, muted cry. Then they looked around them. Spying an old, boarded-up building, they kicked open the door and threw Flint in.

"Cab ulza tshk a daka," a voice said behind them and they turned to face what Newark affectionately termed the indigenous little freaks. He couldn't remember their actual name. It began with K. The creature standing before them was a scrawny and ugly excuse for a humanoid - big, pointed ears like an elf; small, stubby nose like a pixie; bright orange hair like a troll; and a rotund belly that made him look bloated. To Newark, it was Disney gone wrong.

"Cab ulza tshk a daka."

The pair of them glanced at their translator, who lay sprawled out behind them.

"Canta speaka linga," Newark said slowly, raising his hands helplessly.

"Come on," Johnson said, "he's probably just being a nosey... whatever he is."

The two of them turned their backs on the alien and wandered back to the bar. The alien shook his head, shrugged his shoulders then went to get a drink too.

Brash was onto his second beer and staring at Skinner, who was trying to chat up a male Kaledian. Skinner was going to have a sore jaw in the morning. He surmised that Skinner had been knocked back by all the human inhabitants and was now just scraping the bottom of the barrel. Brash cringed as Skinner's hand rubbed up and down the bony arm. He could have stopped it, of course, but he was of the firm belief that you learned lessons the hard way. Besides, he didn't like Skinner much.

And there it was. Skinner hit the deck so fast he must have got whiplash. Stupid arsehole, Brash thought, shaking his head.

"Another, Cap?" Johnson asked cheerily.

Brash looked around the bar at the conglomeration of various species knocking them back. Aliens liked to get wasted too. Some things were universal. Brash shook his head. "No, I'm off. Make sure everyone gets back to the hotel. The shuttle leaves early and I want you all aboard."

The Captain walked out into the night and looked around him. The scruffy little bar was in some run-down backwater but the beer was cheap and it took a lot to get thrown out. Moving back toward the centre, he glanced up. It wasn't completely dark and there was a greenish twilight glow. He'd been to Marios Prime a few times. The inhabitants called it Kaledia. It was a reasonable-sized planet but only a small portion of it was inhabited. Most of it was said to be wilderness or wasteland and he'd spent many a drunken hour listening to tales of enchanted parts and strange occurrences. What total tosh! He sometimes wondered if Flint embellished the tales he translated.

Wandering past classier outfits that he wouldn't be seen dead in with his crew, he gazed around at the cosmopolitan metropolis that was Jakensk. It was a busy hive of activity and weird repulsive eating houses. He'd rather eat some of the things they'd shot up in the field than puke up what they served here. The hotel was the only place he'd dine.

Turning onto a quieter street, he ambled along with a strange sense that something was missing in his world. When he used to come to places like this he'd hook up and he had no trouble getting the ladies, but he couldn't seem to muster any enthusiasm for it now. An odd feeling was taking hold of him... like he was on a road to nowhere...

His maudlin thoughts were interrupted by a strange sight further down the street. The girl's arms were wrapped around her middle and she looked around warily. If he wasn't mistaken, he could swear it was the timid form of Jenna Trot. What was *she* doing here? The Admiral had told him that his services would no longer be required. He never mentioned that his daughter would still be coming here. He wondered who she was here with? Who did she know? And why had she refused to come with him? Though he'd had no desire to bring her along, the snub was in no small way aggravating.

As she veered into a side street, he walked to catch up. The street, more like an alley, was dark and empty. Did this girl have no sense of self-preservation? It was apparent now that she was alone. She seemed as out of place as Maria von Trap in a nightmare. Though to Captain Brash, Maria von Trap would be the nightmare. Yes, some films endure centuries.

He hung back, taking his time. Trot's arms clasped tighter; she looked around fearfully. As he watched her, he thought she cut a sad and lonely figure. In fact, it seemed to emanate from her in waves. He had never experienced such levels of sensitivity and he wondered if there was something wrong with him. He was overdue for a check-up, he knew that. His thoughts were interrupted by something moving in the shadows. Three men emerged from a side alley and his hackles rose. Their sights set on Jenna Trot. Whispering to each other, they loped forward in a pack. Brash felt irrationally protective. Could he take them? Yes, he could. They'd rue the day they messed with a member of his team!

Muscles pumped for action, Brash waited for them to pounce. As Jenna neared the end of the alleyway, the group went in for the kill. Brash sprang into action, charging down the alley like a thunderous harbinger of death. This was what he needed! A good old kicking would get the bugs out of his system! Some part of him felt like a knight of old, rescuing the damsel in distress - he seriously needed a doctor but he couldn't think of that. He was swept away on a new-found high.

Then it all came crashing down. Skidding to an abrupt halt, Brash gazed at the avalanche of bricks and slate and all manner of shit descending on the enemy. Looking up, he saw a partially collapsed wall and roof and couldn't ascertain if that had been a mini earthquake or if the building had been on the verge of collapse. He looked back at the pile of rumble still blowing off clouds of dust, knowing full well that three dead bodies lay beneath it. He couldn't see Jenna Trot anywhere. Scrambling over the debris, he made it to the end of the alley to see the Admiral's daughter wandering down the street, completely oblivious. An odd feeling of relief flooded him.

He glanced back at the alley, perplexed. What were the odds?

# Thought-Provoking

Brash stood on that corner, wondering what to do. The girl had been lucky this time but she was ripe for the plucking... hapless, naïve and as street smart as a fly on a windscreen.

His feet decided for him and he followed after her. As he drew up alongside, she glanced at him and started, wincing in an involuntary way. Brash, picking up on it, acquired a condescending air, which he had not initially intended. "Trot, I thought it was you. I wouldn't have expected to bump into you here. Are you on your own?"

"Err... Hello, Captain. No. I mean, yes. At the moment. But I'm just making my way back to meet the others."

"Others?" he inquired, peering at her oddly.

"My... friends."

"You have friends?" he asked, staring at her, bewildered.

Trot raised her chin. "Why wouldn't I have friends?"

Brash scratched his neck. "No reason... By the way, did you hear that loud crash?" He glanced around to see a large conglomeration of lifeforms peering into the alleyway. "A few moments ago?"

Her pale brow furrowed. "Crash?"

"A humongous crash. You must have heard it."

"No... I've been a little preoccupied..." She'd spent the last two hours wandering around, trying to secure somewhere to stay. Everywhere was full and she didn't relish the prospect of sleeping on the streets. She'd received lewd comments from the odd human male, and she was sure various groups of aliens had been doing the same. The language was unintelligible but the leering looks made her skin crawl. She was way out of her depth here.

Brash studied her with wide-eyed disbelief. "So... where are your friends?"

"We got separated. I'm just heading back to the hotel."

"I'll walk with you. It's getting dark. You don't want to be out on these streets after dark."

"No, Captain. It's fine. I don't want to put you to any trouble."

The Captain tried on a smile. "It's no trouble." The feeling of gallantry reasserted itself. He wasn't used to it but it was strangely pleasant. In fact, it made him feel quite smug. "Which way?" She stared at him helplessly. "Well?"

She looked around, flustered. "Err…"

"Are you lost?"

"Err… yes."

"What's the name of the place?"

"Err…"

"Surely, you can remember that?"

The mounting tension exploded in petulance. "I don't have anywhere to stay!"

The Captain stared at her as if he couldn't comprehend what she was saying. "Nowhere to stay?"

"Everywhere's full," she snapped bitterly.

"Of course, everywhere's full. D'you know how many ships are docked up there? At least twelve. You always book in advance. Always."

"Well, I didn't know that!" Her anger threatened to spill into tears and Brash endeavoured to avert a crisis.

"OK. OK, you didn't know that. That's fine. That's absolutely fine," he said in a settling voice.

His gentle tone seemed to bring new tears. He couldn't bloody win.

Scratching his head, he looked around. "Right, well, we'd better find your friends then."

Her shoulders slumped and she looked three sizes smaller. "I don't have any friends, either," she quietly confessed.

"You came down here on your own?" Brash asked, dumbfounded. She nodded, guiltily. "On your own?" His voice was back to full strength but it brought a different reaction from Trot.

"Of course, on my own! I'm always on my own!"

"But you could have come with us?"

"You don't want me with you. Neither do your crew. The only reason I'm still on your team is because my dad's the Admiral."

He felt like he'd been caught on camera. This girl *wasn't* thick. Stuff went on in that brain.

"OK, maybe you're not a perfect fit but you are a member of my team. And a team's a team."

She wiped her nose with the back of her hand. "It is?"

"It is. Now, seeing as you've no place to stay, you'll have to sleep with me."

Her eyes widened and she stared at him in horror.

"I don't mean *sleep* with me. God, that thought had never crossed my mind. I mean, as if I would, with *you.*" The girl's eyebrows dropped and her frame wilted. "I-I don't mean you specifically. You're an attractive girl. I'm sure many men would but... I'm not up for that sort of thing." Her eyebrows shot up again and Brash saw what was written in those incredulous blue eyes. "No, I like women but..." He decided to give up. "Come on. This way."

Brash did the gallant thing and slept on the floor. But he found it hard to sleep. He was wondering what the Admiral's daughter was doing lying in his bed. Was he going soft? He sensed she was awake and he wondered what was going through her mind.

Jenna Trot was awake. She, too, was wondering what she was doing in Captain Brash's bed. The whole thing seemed surreal. She hoped she would fall asleep before he started snoring.

"What do you think of my team?" the Captain asked, taking her by surprise.

"Your team? Err... they seem like a very... efficient team, Captain."

He gave a humorous snort. "I've seen the way you look at them. You detest them all. Tell me what you think of Newark."

"I'd rather not say, Captain."

"You have my permission to speak freely. I won't hold it against you."

She drew in a breath. "Well... I think he's the vilest human being I've ever met. He never thinks before he opens his potty-ridden mouth and he thinks he's something special but he's just a low-life... sir."

The Captain swallowed back a surprising laugh. "And the others?"

"Skinner's a creepy little worm, Johnson's practically a bloke, Graham could be a better person if he wasn't around them and Flint... well... Flint lives in his own world, possibly because there's something too painful to face if he comes out of it."

Brash sat up on his elbow. He had the feeling this girl knew his crew better than he did. "You can't find anything positive to say about them?"

"I live in hope."

He was silent for a moment, soaking in the blunt appraisal. It was the truth, he realised. Recently, he had been looking at his crew differently, as if things were seeping into the edges of his awareness. And now he had to accommodate a new truth. This girl was not all she had, at first, appeared. Yes, she was incompetent at everything she tried but there *was* a kind of intelligence there. How had it gone unnoticed for so long?

"And then there's me," she continued in a quiet voice. "The useless one. Daddy says I haven't found my niche. The truth is, there is no niche for me..." A long silence followed. "Good night, Captain."

He heard her roll over and felt touched by a moment of poignancy. He lay back, considering her words. Maybe it had something to do with her father. The man was over-protective in the extreme. Maybe it was because no-one would ever be honest with her. Perhaps they overlooked her mistakes, so she couldn't learn from them. Maybe it had something to do with her simple, basic nature. Or maybe her brain just wasn't wired up for practical things. It was puzzling, thought-provoking. But what was more thought-provoking were the thoughts he was having. He wasn't accustomed to using his brain in this way.

# All tied up

Waking up in the morning was awkward. They shuffled around each other and Brash let her use the facilities first.

"The water's a murky green here, by the way," Brash said helpfully. "Don't worry, it's harmless."

"Right. Thanks."

Brash was feeling gallant again. He waited patiently and didn't get irritated by how long she took.

"Captain Brash," she said as she came out, "you won't mention this to my father, will you? He doesn't know I came here alone."

No way was he mentioning this to him. The old git would overlook how Brash gallantly came to the rescue and concentrate on the spending the night in the same room part. It wasn't so long ago that he might have had something to worry about.

"No. As far as I'm concerned, none of this happened."

"Thanks. What about the crew?"

"Shit."

As luck would have it, the crew were still laid out when the two of them made their way to breakfast. Jenna looked around the dining room. The bright orange walls didn't go with the chintzy tablecloths, *at all*. Portraits of Kaledians hung on the wall. These ones had white hair. The tables were quite high, no doubt to accommodate large bellies.

They sat down together for a good old hearty breakfast of bacon and eggs. The bacon, of course, didn't quite taste like bacon and the eggs were enormous but at least they had tried.

"Another tip," Brash said, leaning over the table. "Never eat the local food. It's..." He cringed and shook his head.

Jenna laughed and Brash noticed how it transformed her face... sort of lit it up. Indeed, her blonde hair lit up in the daylight. He stared at the side of her head as she looked out of the window. He wondered how old she was. Twenty-one, twenty-two?

Graham emerged first, looking slightly the worse for wear. The sight of Jenna Trot brought him to life.

"Just bumped into her," Brash explained. "She's been here with friends." Graham gawked at that statement and Jenna turned away, offended.

Newark and Johnson got the same story and exhibited the same reaction. Skinner could barely see straight and kept rubbing his jaw.

After Newark had eaten three people's breakfasts, Brash looked to Johnson. "Where's Flint?"

"Crap."

"You didn't bring him back?"

"We forgot, Captain."

"We're lucky we ended up back here ourselves," Newark put in. "We were totally wasted."

Brash rubbed his forehead. "Christ-sakes!"

Skinner, anticipating a hurricane, braced himself for impact. His head was too fragile. Brash, however, just stood up and said, "Let's go get him."

The crew followed him out into blinding orange daylight. Jenna watched as they put on shades. Another thing she didn't know, she reflected miserably.

She trailed behind, wondering why they weren't wearing their weapons belts. They looked almost naked without them. "Haven't you forgotten something?" she asked and they turned to her. "Your weapons?"

Newark gave a derisory snort and shook his head. Johnson and Graham glanced at each other.

"What?" she asked.

"You can't bring weapons here," Brash explained without derision. "If you bring them, you have to leave them where you disembark."

"Yeah, and if you do, they go 'missing'," Graham said, making quote marks with his fingers.

"Scaly blue or green fingers get a grip of them," Newark spat, making a twisting motion with his hands as if snapping those scaly blue or green fingers.

"Oh," Jenna said as they walked on.

Foul smells drifted out of various restaurants. Jenna peeked in a window to see one of those funny-looking creatures with the big bellies tip its head back and wolf down something she was sure was wriggling. She shuddered.

In front, the crew were regaling stories of the previous night. Brash, who was only half-listening, kept glancing back at Jenna. She had to keep running to catch up with them.

The buildings got grottier the further they went and Jenna looked around warily as they reached their destination.

"You left him there?" Brash asked.

"Sleeping like a baby, Captain," Johnson assured him.

"Well, at least you shut the door." Johnson and Newark exchanged a glance. "Come on, let's get him."

The door opened effortlessly. Johnson was sure they'd kicked it off its hinges. The room was in darkness and Brash fumbled for a switch as the others, apart from Skinner, followed him in.

As the switch flicked, a large room lit up and a bizarre sight hit them. Flint hung suspended from a metal hook, his whole body trussed up in rope. The fear in his bloodshot eyes told Brash he was still alive. At least eight Guthrins – humanoid-type creatures with green skin, who Newark referred to as Martians - were pointing weapons at them but the thing that drew their eyes was the creature standing in the rear doorway. Newark's legs buckled at the sight of it. It was abhorrent. Ranting that no such abomination should exist, Newark reached for his non-existent weapon, wanting to blow it to kingdom come.

The creature itself regarded Newark with mild interest. Tilting its disproportionately large head, it observed him under aggressively protruding brows. But that was not what had upset Newark. No, it was the disgusting, sticky-coated proboscis that leapt out of its face, affording a hideous view of the horrors within.

"It's grotesque, Captain," Newark shrieked, brought to his knees by the level of ugliness.

"Newark," the Captain said in a low tone. "Get up. You're going to offend it."

"Offend *it*? What the hell is that thing?"

Skinner came flying through the doorway, crashing down on the floor. Scrambling behind the Captain, he clung to Brash's jacket for dear life.

"Flint," Brash said, shaking Skinner off. "Can you communicate with them?"

Flint's red-rimmed eyes found the Captain. Many things were written in them. Fear. Physical exhaustion, made worse by the previous night, no doubt. But there was something else. Pure hatred and loathing, which seemed to fuel the power of his speech. "Yes, I can. Am I going to do anything that might help you cruel, merciless bastards? No."

"Come on, Flint," Johnson said, trying on a motherly tone but it came out obscene. "We didn't mean to-"

"Flint," the Captain said. "We need you to ask them what the situation is here." Flint just smiled in a sour, bitter way as if he'd lost the will to live anyway. "I'll promote you. You'll be second in command. You'll get to call the shots. We'll take our lead from you in the field. Anything to do with aliens, will be your call."

A glimmer of light returned to Flint's eyes, yet it was doused with suspicion.

"I'm serious, Flint," Brash said. The others assumed the Captain was lying. The Captain wasn't yet sure but looking at the state of the man, it was the least he deserved.

Unintelligible sounds came from Flint's mouth. The grotesque head turned to Flint. Harsh guttural noises came out of it and Newark wondered which part they were coming from. Flint replied as if pleading their case but it seemed to fall on deaf ears. At last, Flint's head dropped.

"What'd he say?" Brash pressed.

"You bastards," Flint said spiritlessly. "You threw me into the lock-up of the biggest gun-running, drug lord in town."

"What?" Brash looked around at the crates and boxes and realised there were even more boxes in the back room.

"His name's Daka. He was quite insulted that I didn't know it. Apparently, we'll be staying here for a few hours. Tonight, they're going to drive us into the wasteland and kill us."

"Daka," Johnson said, something becoming clear.

She and Newark shared a glance. "The creepy little freak was trying to warn us," Newark realised. He was almost touched.

Daka spoke again and the green aliens laughed.

"What did he say?" Brash demanded.

Flint spoke without looking up. "He said they might eat you but not me. I look stringy, like I'd stick in their teeth."

Newark nodded thoughtfully. Skinner had passed out. Jenna looked like she had rigor mortis. Johnson and Graham were giving Brash, 'what now, Cap?' looks, and if Brash thought he could use his translator to talk his way out of this, one look at Flint told him that was not going to happen. The man's eyes were closed. He had given up and shut down. At that moment, Brash hated his bloody crew.

Brash, Newark, Johnson, and Graham were up for a fight but the odds were stacked against them. With so many weapons trained on them, they had no alternative but to allow themselves to be tied up. Flint was taken off the hook and thrown down with the rest. The Captain, realising the hook hadn't pierced Flint's skin, reassessed his idea of promoting him.

Daka spoke and some of the aliens followed him to the door. Yet, he stopped momentarily, glancing back at Newark. Striding over, he put his large proboscis face right in Newark's. Newark was almost crying. Daka laughed as he walked away.

Four weapons were left trained on them.

"How are we going to get out of this one, Captain?" Graham asked.

"With great difficulty," he spat, glaring at Newark and Johnson with hatred.

Two hours passed. They had no plan. Skinner was a quivering mess. Newark kept straining against his ropes. Graham and Johnson were still waiting for the Captain's plan, but Johnson's attention was moving to something else. Two of the aliens had gone out to stretch their legs but the other two were whispering and looking at Trot. Johnson recognised the seedy vulgarity in those looks and though she couldn't speak alien, she could imagine what they were saying. One of the aliens nodded indiscernibly and the other, looking suddenly furtive, got up and pretended to stretch before making a grab for Trot.

"Get off me!" Trot shrieked. The Guthrin undid her ropes and tried a little seductive encouragement, which he was never going to pull off with that accent.

Brash struggled against his restraints. "Get off her or so help me!" He could do nothing but watch on helplessly as the green bastard tried to drag her to a staircase. Trot was going berserk, kicking furiously, lashing out with her free fist, scratching her nails into green flesh. She was like a wild cat and Johnson found Trot going up in her estimation.

Newark was positioned near the staircase. "Do something, Newark!" the Captain shrieked.

"Like what? I'm bound up like a mummy. You wanted to kill her anyway. I'm sure he'll do that too."

"You fucking degenerate!"

Though Jenna heard Newark's words, they hadn't been registered. She was too busy. She was experiencing a wild surge of anger. She had never wanted anyone dead before but with every fibre of her being she wanted this alien dead. More than that, she wanted him to die horribly. They were nearly at the stairs, the alien dodging the metal hook as he dragged her along. She pulled back with all her puny might, tripping over Flint's foot and falling face first. As she did, the alien was jerked back, the green head turning red as it became impaled on the sharp metal hook. Brash watched in a daze as he saw what unfurled next. Jenna stood, gawking at the sickly sight. The other alien fired at her but his weapon jammed. Trot picked up the dead guy's gun, turned to the other alien and blasted him to kingdom come. The crew watched, mesmerised. Then they ducked for cover.

"Fire at the front door!" Brash yelled.

Jenna turned and let loose. The other aliens didn't stand a chance. She'd just killed four green men in the space of seconds and Brash was extremely proud of her.

Dropping her weapon, she started untying Johnson but the knots were proving too tight.

"Get between the ropes and dig into my back pocket," Johnson said. "I've got a knife in there. I haven't been able to fish it out. Can barely bloody breathe."

Jenna managed to fish out a folded-up knife. It looked more like a keyring, it was so small. "It's sharp," Johnson said. "Just cut next to the knot and I'll get myself out."

Jenna put a lot of determined effort in as she sawed through the rope. Finally, she managed it.

"You keep that," Johnson said to her. "You need it more than me. Anybody tries any funny business with you again, you stick it up, right in the scrotum."

Jenna nodded. Once Johnson was freed, they untied the others.

"Right," Brash said. "Graham, grab Flint. Newark, grab Skinner. Johnson, Trot, grab a gun." He picked up the other two weapons. "Let's get out of here."

"Where are we going to go?" Graham asked. "The shuttle will have left."

"We'll have to lay low, try to get a message to the ship."

As they left the building, they turned right but stopped in their tracks. Down at the end, the other aliens were coming back. And there were more of them.

"Through the bar!" Brash yelled, firing both weapons. "Run!"

# Not So Great Escape

"They're dead weight, Captain!" Newark yelled as they charged down the street.

"We don't leave anyone behind!" Brash shouted. "Over there," he said, pointing. "That hovercraft!"

The twelve-foot craft, which looked like an orange, rectangular paddling pool with a frame stuck onto it, had plenty of room for all of them. Graham and Newark threw Flint and Skinner in before jumping in themselves. Brash dragged Skinner to the front and slapped him hard in the face. "Snap out of it," he ordered. "You've got twenty seconds to hot-wire this craft. Your life depends on it."

Skinner sprang into action, flinging off a panel and fiddling with the interior workings.

"They're coming, Captain!" Johnson called, taking aim.

A whole gang of weapon-toting aliens was running toward them. The rest of the crew ducked as Johnson, Graham, Brash, and Newark returned fire. Newark was aiming specifically for Daka. The facially-challenged drug lord picked up on this and fired at Newark, shouting words that translated as, 'I'm going to rip your limbs off one by one and feed them to my Okko' (dog-like thing).

The crew was vastly outnumbered. The enemy was closing in fast. In five seconds, Newark would be losing his limbs and a dog would be getting a hearty meal. Brash thought this would be their last stand but as the craft buzzed to life and lifted from the ground, he felt a renewed sense of hope. Dropping his weapon, he jumped into the front seat, pressing every button he could find. The vehicle whizzed in all directions like a balloon losing air. The crew clung to the sides, thinking that if the aliens didn't kill them, their Captain would.

"I can't read this shit!" Brash yelled.

"Go to manual!" Skinner shrieked. "Try the lever!"

Brash pulled a lever and the craft went in a straight line, reversing at speed and ploughing through the enemy. Slamming the lever forward, Brash ploughed through them again and sped off.

"Yes!" Graham exclaimed, raising his fist in the air. Newark grabbed hold of Skinner and kissed him.

"Everyone alright?" Brash called over his shoulder.

"Everyone's alive, Captain," Johnson reported.

Flint looked like a zombie, staring at the floor with hopeless despondency. Skinner was experiencing a dazed sort of euphoria. Newark and Graham were shouting abuse from the back of the craft. Johnson sat up front with the Captain but Jenna was just starting to become aware of something. Newark's words were going off like an incendiary device. *'You wanted to kill her anyway.'*

The ground fell from under her. *They wanted her dead...? Dead? Why?* What the hell had she done? It hit her at once. The landing bay incident. Thoughts flooded her. Captain Brash was harbouring resentment and was out for revenge. That was why he wanted her on his team. To finish her off. Of course. Why else?

She should have felt afraid but it was worse than that. She had warmed to Captain Brash last night and just as she was starting to feel that, maybe, she could be accepted, she realised with brutal clarity that Brash had been lulling her into a false sense of security. Sniffing bitterly, she wiped her nose with the back of her hand. Pulling herself together, she looked around at her distracted crewmates then dragged Brash's weapon over. Getting a firm grip of it, she determined not to let it go.

Brash manoeuvred through the city streets. They were only six feet off the ground and some of the taller residents had to duck and dive out of their way. Alien expletives followed after them but Newark and Graham returned fire with a few expletives of their own. Jenna viewed them with disdain.

As they broke free of the city, Brash turned to look at Jenna. Her blonde hair shone in the daylight, making her look angelic. He took in a breath, feeling extremely proud of her, thinking there was so much more to her than he had initially realised. She was holding a weapon now, ready to fight, just like a true member of his team. He would have taken the weapon off her but she had earned the right to hold it, and, at the moment, his concern for her outweighed his concern for the rest of the crew.

He turned away with a warm feeling inside, looking out over scrubby grasslands. For the first time in so long, things felt right in his world.

"Err, Captain!" Newark called.

"What?"

"They're coming after us!"

"What?" Brash turned to see another craft in the distance. "Skinner, can we make this thing go any faster?"

Skinner was staring out the back in dazed terror.

"Skinner!" the Captain barked.

The man raced to the front, running his eyes over the alien script on the control panel, his harried brain working overtime. "Try this one," he said, pressing a button. The crew were slammed into their seats as the craft ascended with nausea-inducing speed. "No, no... err... this one." The craft shot down again.

"Christ, Skinner! I thought you were a fucking genius!"

"I've got it." On the third attempt, the craft did a loop-de-loop, the crew being held in place by centrifugal force. Far behind, the aliens watched with a fascinated interest.

"Skinner!"

"It's all alien, Captain! I've never seen one of these before!"

"They're gaining on us, Captain!" Graham shouted.

"Shall we fire yet?" Newark called, his finger teasing the trigger.

"No. Save your fire. Hurry, Skinner!"

"I can get a few rounds in," Newark persisted. "They're in range, Captain!"

"No. Hold your bloody fire!"

"Wait," Skinner said in a light-bulb moment. "It's this." He turned a dial and the craft whizzed ahead, taking Newark and Graham from their feet. The ground tore by beneath them. They must have been going over three hundred miles an hour.

Newark and Graham got up. "I'm getting one of these!" Newark shouted, his voice getting lost as his skin rippled and his hair was pressed flat to his head.

"This thing can shift!" Graham proclaimed, his hair pressed flat too.

Skinner was getting his mojo back. He turned another dial. Newark and Graham's hair returned to normal and their cheeks stopped flapping.

"What did you do?" Brash asked.

"It's an electro-"

"Cut the crap and get to the point."

"It deflects the air, sir. It's a weather shield."

The blurry ground turned from green, through yellow, to completely parched and barren.

"How are we doing, Graham?" Brash called back.

"They're still with us, Cap!"

"Skinner, how much fuel do we have?"

Skinner pulled up a panel from the floor at the front. "Looks like a new fuel rod. At this speed, we've probably got twelve hours."

Johnson glanced behind her. "D'you think they're going to go twelve hours, Captain?"

"I don't know," Brash said, appearing gravely concerned.

Eleven hours, thirty-three hundred miles of barren wilderness later, the aliens were still in hot pursuit.

"They're not giving up, Captain," Skinner shrieked, holding onto himself tightly. "And I need to go."

The Captain glared at him with disdain. "Do what Newark's doing."

Skinner glanced around. Grabbing hold of the frame, Newark was pissing over the back of the craft, shouting, "Take that, alien scum!"

Skinner decided he could wait.

Captain Brash was mentally preparing himself for a battle. Jenna was mentally preparing herself to die. She would do it herself. Those green things weren't going to get a grip of her again. She'd kill Johnson too. The woman had kindly given her a knife. As she sat there, she was developing a stoic attitude to death. She didn't fit into this life anyway. Nobody liked her, nobody respected her, she wasn't any good at anything... Her one regret would be her father. *Goodbye, Daddy.*

"Look at that," Johnson said. In the distance ahead, she could see mountains, great purple hunks of rock.

"If we can get to the mountains, we might stand a chance," Brash said.

Half an hour later, they saw pockets of vegetation. Life was returning and the nearer they got to the mountains, the greener it became. They were in little mood for sight-seeing, though. The fuel was running low. Their pursuers were still on their tail.

"How long, Skinner?" Brash asked.

"I don't know," the man said, shaking. "Minutes. Twenty, if we're lucky."

"They're gaining on us, Captain!" Graham shouted. Brash looked around, wondering where they'd got the extra oomph from. Brash turned the dial but their craft had no oomph. In fact, he had the distinct feeling it was petering out. He felt a tiny jerk here, the odd splutter there. The mountains were looming large now. Brash swerved to travel down a gorge but he knew they weren't going to make it to the end.

"I don't believe it!" Newark exclaimed.

"What!" Brash yelled, trying to keep control of the spluttering craft.

"They've stopped!" Graham called out. "They're turning back!"

Brash thought he was hearing things. Johnson rushed to the back and the three of them sounded like they were having a party. The Captain's relief was short-lived. The craft was on its last legs. He needed to bring it down. There were rocks to either side of them. Rocks below. The end of the ravine was in sight but no way could they make it. It was going to be a bumpy landing.

"Hold on!" Brash shouted.

The crew were thrown around as the craft crashed down, slamming over boulders and rocks as it careered inexorably downward.

"Someone grab hold of Flint!" Brash yelled.

Johnson got a grip of him. Jenna clung onto the rail, one hand over her head as she was bumped about mercilessly. The torture seemed to go on and on but at last, they came to an abrupt stop.

Jenna looked up. The craft had come to rest at the bottom of the ravine. Looking over the side, she saw that they were sitting in a tiny stream but the odd thing was the water. It was crystal clear.

Skinner jumped out quickly and went to relieve himself, urinating in the pure water. Flint came to life and projectile vomited over the side of the craft.

The others gave themselves a moment. Jenna retrieved her gun.

Brash went over to her. "Are you OK? Any injuries?"

"I'm fine," she said in a deadpan way, unable to conceal the loathing in her eyes.

Brash looked at her oddly. "Are you sure?"

Nodding, she turned away from him.

"Pussies," Newark remarked, looking back down the ravine.

"Why d'you think they stopped following us?" Brash asked.

"It's obvious, isn't it? Weren't up for a crash landing."

Brash followed the direction of Newark's gaze. "They were gaining on us, though?"

"Which suggests they had spare fuel rods," Skinner put in.

"So, why did they turn back?"

Skinner shrugged.

Brash looked around him. "The question now is, where the fuck *are* we and how are *we* going to get back?"

# Irreversible

As they disembarked, Johnson whispered in the Captain's ear. "Trot's carrying a gun, sir."

Brash turned around, surprised and impressed by the girl's level of commitment. He'd have to train her to use that thing himself. He'd instructed Graham to give her a few hours of practice but the man said he couldn't continue as it was against health and safety. He added that he wasn't going to be held accountable for the state of the firing range.

Brash moved over to her slowly. "Jenna- I mean, Trot. I'll take the gun now."

Jenna pointed the weapon at him. "I'll keep it, Captain."

Staring nervously at the pointed end of the gun, he looked up at her. "Are you disobeying me?"

"No. I'd just very much like to keep it... sir."

"You don't know how to use it."

"I took out four green men," she stated, her eyes fixed on him steadily. There was something in her eyes that was different. Something in her voice, too. Determination, he thought. Shooting aliens had brought out a new side to her and, as nervous as he was, he had to admit it was sexy as hell. Perhaps he should encourage this.

He assessed her thoughtfully. "Very well. But flip the safety switch. The red switch on the side."

She flipped the switch and he breathed out.

"Come on," he said, glancing back at her as he led them along the ravine.

Johnson helped Flint. Newark guarded the rear. Jenna held onto her gun, turning to look at Newark intermittently. Newark started to have the notion she fancied him.

Suddenly, Brash turned around, his eyes fixed on Newark. "Newark, a word, please."

Newark's brow creased and he walked forward, the Captain leading him away from the group. The rest of the crew watched as they entered into a private discussion.

"Right, Newark. Just to let you know. We are not going to kill Jenna

Trot. That plan is scrapped. I'll inform the others later."

"Scrapped? Since when?"

"Since now. If anything happens to her, if she so much as gets a scratch... well... think wrath of the gods and you'll get the picture."

"Can I ask why, Captain?" Newark asked, feeling slightly disappointed.

"No. I'll take the rear position."

As the Captain walked away, Newark stared after him. His disappointment was alleviated by the fact that he thought he stood a chance with Trot.

Jenna, highly suspicious of the hushed conversation and the changed positions, flipped off the safety switch. She kept glancing back at Brash. Brash noticed and found himself humming a tune.

When they reached the end of the ravine, they stopped, staring out in wonder. Even Flint raised his head. It was beautiful... The ground swept downward and they had a panoramic view of a vast area of lush green land. Meadows, forests, shining blue lakes... It went on as far as the eye could see. It was like paradise lost.

"Wow..." Johnson said.

"It's beautiful..." Jenna murmured.

Captain Brash had never seen such a sight. He'd heard tales of how the earth was long ago but in his wildest imaginings, it had never equated to this. As he stared over heaven, a great weight lifted from him. There would be food and possibly, if they were lucky, civilisation. They had to find a way to contact the ship if they were going to get off this planet. At the moment, though, he was in no rush to go anywhere.

A large band of forest lay beneath them. Brash led them down into it.

The red fruits looked succulent but the crew had no idea if they were poisonous.

Brash plucked one off a tree. "Flint, have a bite of this."

"Fuck you."

Everyone turned to Flint. Brash eyed him oddly. "That's gross misconduct and insubordination, Flint."

"Bite me."

"Are you refusing to obey an order?"

"I think, 'fuck you' speaks for itself."

Johnson viewed Flint with wide-eyed wonder. She struggled to contain a laugh. Graham and Newark were stunned speechless.

"When we get back to the ship," Brash said, tight-lipped, "you'll be arrested for this."

"We're never getting back to the ship."

Brash moved in close. "We will get back to the ship. So, I suggest you take a bite."

"Why don't you take a bite, Captain?" Jenna asked and Brash turned to her. It felt like a bloody mutiny. "Unless you're scared," she challenged, looking at him steadily.

"I'm not scared of anything," he stated, holding her stare. Sinking his teeth into the juicy ripe flesh, he continued to hold her stare as he ate the whole fruit. "Satisfied?"

"Very," she replied, maintaining eye-contact.

"The fruit's fine," Brash said to the others, still staring at Trot. As annoyed as he was, he had to admit he found this new side of her very exciting.

The team stripped the branches like a plague of locusts. Johnson sidled up to Brash. "Seems like Flint's finally flipped his lid, Captain."

The Captain nodded. "By the way, the plan to kill Trot is scrapped."

Johnson turned to him. "If that's the case, Captain, I think you should tell her."

"What...?" Suddenly, it all made sense. The attitude. the gun. Newark's remark *had* gone in. How had he missed this? Fuck.

"Should we get the gun off her?"

"No. Just steer clear of her for now. I'll have to talk to her."

As they wove through forest, Brash stared at the gun in Trot's hand. He should take it off her but the only thing that was stopping him was guilt. He thought back to last night. It seemed such a long time ago. As strange as it was, he had enjoyed spending time with her, was starting to see her in a different light. He almost felt he had betrayed her in some way, which was completely irrational, he knew. Still, he felt morose as they trudged on.

Darkness was closing in. It seemed to go dark later here and Brash wondered where exactly on the planet they were. They should bed down for the night, he thought.

A violent altercation made him look up. The gun was going off, frying branches indiscriminately and Trot was shrieking her head off. Johnson grabbed the gun as Graham grabbed the girl. Trot struggled against him, kicking out furiously.

"What the hell's going on?" Brash barked, running over.

"That low-life filth just grabbed my arse!" Trot shrieked, trying to kick Newark in the groin.

"I'll vouch for that," Johnson said.

"Newark?" the Captain asked, turning to the man.

Newark scratched his head as if he didn't understand anything anymore. He opened his mouth to speak but nothing came out.

"Newark, come with me." Brash led him away and turned to face him. "Did you or did you not grab Trot's arse?"

"Err... yes, sir, but..."

"But what?"

"I thought... I thought she fancied me, sir."

Brash stared at Newark for several moments. "OK, let's get this out of the way first. Trot does not fancy you."

"How d'you know that?"

"By the way she was trying to annihilate you from existence, I'd say it's a safe bet."

"A bit extreme, if you ask me."

"She thinks we're trying to kill her. She's bound to be edgy."

"Does she? How?"

"You told her!"

The lights went on. "Oh. Yeah."

"Anyway, the days of grabbing women's arses went out with the ark. How do you not know this...?"

"None of them shot at me before."

The Captain stared at the man, incredulously. Had this man always been a complete imbecile? Had Brash been blinkered all these years? He felt he had a duty to womankind to try to get through to the man. "How would you feel if someone did that to you?"

A sleazy grin crept onto Newark's face. Brash gawked at him, his patience wearing thin. "If this happens again, you'll be on report! Do you hear me?"

Newark scratched his head and nodded.

"Keep your hands off Jenna Trot!" Brash barked, walking off.

"Err, Captain," Newark said. "If Trot knows, is it wise to keep her alive?"

Brash turned to him, staring at Newark in wonder. That was an intelligent insight. Newark had a point. But the Captain knew it didn't matter. For some unknown reason, he could not bring himself to kill her. Something about her spoke to him.

"No. She lives. If there are any consequences, I'll take full responsibility."

He walked away, realising he was performing a selfless act. Or was he...?

When he returned, he saw Jenna Trot sitting away from the group, viewing them with suspicion. Flint was sitting away from the group, viewing them with contempt. Ignoring Flint, he walked over to Jenna, knowing he had to have 'the talk'.

Trot glared at him as he sat beside her. He sensed her inching away. He rubbed his forehead, wondering where to begin. *Miss Trot,* he thought.

Make it formal and respectful and lie like shit.

"Miss Trot, I... I want to talk about... Newark's remark earlier today." He coughed, unable to look at her directly. "Let me just get in quickly that that is not going to happen. You're perfectly safe with us. The thing is, when Newark said..."

"You wanted to kill her anyway?"

"Yes." He coughed again. "Well, he wasn't being literal. I might have said in a moment of frustration, 'god, I want to kill that girl' but it wasn't a serious intention."

Flint laughed and they both turned to him.

"I have the feeling the comment has made you edgy," Brash pressed on, "and I just want to assure you that there is nothing to fear from this crew."

Flint laughed again. Brash whipped his head to him, feeling that Flint was becoming a loose cannon. Ignoring Flint, he turned back to Jenna. "So, are we... good?"

Jenna studied the Captain's face. In the past she had always taken things at face value, never questioned people's motives but her eyes had been opening lately. She was too trusting, she knew that now, and though she would love to be able to have someone to trust in, she would question first and trust later. For the Captain's benefit, she nodded but when he made no attempt to move, she excused herself and went to sit nearer to Flint.

Brash felt more than a little concerned. Would Flint rat him out? An errant thought flitted through his head. Perhaps he should kill Flint. The notion brought him up short. What was he thinking? Kill Flint? Flint had been on his team for years. He couldn't believe he'd just thought that. And why? Sure, he didn't want to be hauled over the coals for this, but he realised he was more concerned about Jenna Trot's good opinion. The truth was, he wanted to be back at breakfast in the hotel, listening to the sound of her laughter. He had gone soft and he wondered if it was irreversible.

# Going in Circles

Most of the crew were snoring. Skinner had situated himself between Graham and Johnson. Brash said he'd take first watch and was roaming around in the woods, feeling sullen. His mind was concocting scenarios in which he was rescuing Jenna from mortal danger, ending up the hero of the hour instead of the dastardly villain.

Jenna awoke with a start. She'd been trying to stay awake but realised she'd dozed off. Flint, lying near her, was staring up into the darkness. She looked around the group, relieved to see them all asleep. She scanned the trees. She knew Brash was circling like some bird of prey.

"They're not going to kill you, you know," Flint said and she whipped her head to him. She wasn't used to Flint speaking to her.

"Was the Captain telling the truth then?"

"No."

A knife pierced her heart. She had been holding onto the hope that the Brash who took her back to his hotel room, that made her laugh this morning, still existed. She dropped her head. He had lied to her.

"But he's changed his mind," Flint said.

"Why?"

"The good Captain's given you a reprieve."

"Why's he changed his mind?"

Flint turned to her. For the first time, she saw someone behind those blue eyes. "Well, that's the mystery, isn't it?" He smiled to himself then turned back to the sky. "Have you noticed how clean the air is here?"

Jenna took a deep breath. "Yeah."

"I've heard strange tales of lands like these."

"Strange tales? You mean, legends?"

He nodded, looking out through thoughtful eyes. "Doesn't it strike you as odd that those aliens turned back? They didn't want to come through the ravine."

"Perhaps they'd had enough. Or maybe they're superstitious. But if you ask me, this place looks so... wholesome."

"If something looks too good to be true, it probably is."

"Yeah," she thought despondently, wondering why Brash had changed his mind. "Are you OK now, Flint?"

He noted the sincere kindness in her voice. "Yeah, the clouds are finally lifting." He turned to her. "Just for the record, I wouldn't have killed you."

"Err... thanks..."

"And just between me and you, I'm going to kill myself tomorrow."

"What...? You can't do that!"

He smiled at her in gratitude. "I'm afraid my mind's made up."

"Why? Why on earth would you want to kill yourself?"

"I've concluded that we'll never get back to the ship. We have no tracking devices. This is a big planet. We have no transport. I think we're stuck here."

"That's rather pessimistic, Flint."

"Realistic. And I would rather die than be stuck here, every single day, for the rest of my life, with this evil shower of bastards. Yourself excluded, of course."

"But you can't, Flint! You... You don't know what we'll discover here. What about your legends? You could discover all kinds of remarkable things."

"Yeah," he said, nodding thoughtfully, "I've thought about that but I'd still be stuck with them."

"God, you really hate them, don't you?"

"It's been building for years. By the way, as I'm going to die tomorrow, I'll tell you something I've never told anyone." A strange look took hold of his eyes, as if phantoms danced before them. Jenna waited with a surge of dreadful anticipation. "It happened years ago-"

"Get to sleep," Brash ordered, kicking Flint's legs, looking at him suspiciously.

Jenna glared up at him. "What's your problem? Why did you have to kick him?"

Brash couldn't tell her what his problem was and he decided he shouldn't have to. "Remember who you're talking to, Trot. I'm your Captain."

She bit her lip. As furious as she was, she decided to let it go. She couldn't risk Brash changing his mind again.

Turning his back on her, Brash walked over to Newark and kicked him too. "You're up, Newark."

Lying down, Jenna turned to Flint. The man's eyes were screwed tight. He looked like he was in severe pain. "Flint, don't kill yourself," she whispered. "You've got me. Please don't leave me alone with this evil shower of bastards."

\*

"This looks familiar, Captain," Johnson said.

"We should be out by now," Graham remarked, looking around.

Brash was getting a bad feeling. Something crunched beneath his feet and he looked down. The ground was strewn with discarded seeds... from the fruit they were eating yesterday. The trees looked different because the crew had stripped them bare but they were the same trees.

"We've gone around in a circle," Brash said, annoyed and frustrated.

"No. We've been taking a straight course, Captain," Graham insisted. "I'm certain of it."

"Well, how the hell have we ended up back here!"

Jenna looked around her. She was sure they had been going in a straight line.

Shrugging, she left the rest of them to figure it out and went over to Flint. He'd been walking independently today and she took this as a positive sign. "How are you feeling, Flint?"

He drew a hand through his ice blonde hair, looking like he'd been on drugs and was coming down.

"Flint?"

"I can't do it."

Jenna blew out a breath. "Don't beat yourself up for that."

"No. I mean, I can't do it! Literally. I picked up Johnson's weapon this morning whilst everyone was asleep. I pointed it at my head, pressed the trigger and the damn thing wouldn't fire. I took your knife and tried to cut my wrists and... get this... it flew out of my hand. Fucking flew out of my hand! After that," he said, looking skyward, "I thought someone was screwing with me."

Jenna stared at the man. *Had* he been on drugs? Had he eaten some weird hallucinatory mushroom? Could he be psychotic? Do suicidal tendencies go with that? Was there a god and had that god intervened? The questions were endless. Whatever it was, the good thing was, Flint was still alive.

Newark was climbing a very tall tree. As Jenna watched him, she wondered again how they had managed to go around in a circle.

"Well?" Brash shouted up.

"We're not far, Cap. I can see a lake in the distance. About half an hour's walk."

Jenna turned back to Flint. He didn't look very happy to be alive, so she tried to cheer him up. "If God's watching over you, you should feel good about that."

"Watching over me? Playing a sick joke, more like!"

She scratched her head. She thought she had problems.

"You're sure it's that way?" Brash asked as Newark came down.

"Yes, Cap."

"Come on then. Let's get going."

Half an hour turned into twenty-four hours and the next morning they ended up back where they started.

"This is fucked-up!" Newark said, holding his head.

"It's like some s-spooky, f-freaky horror film," Skinner stuttered, holding onto himself and viewing the trees with suspicion. "We're never going to get out of here, Captain!"

"Pull yourself together, man," Brash shot.

"But Captain, we're never going to get out of here!"

Brash grabbed Skinner's shoulders and shook him up. "Get your shit together, Skinner!"

Tossing Skinner aside, he raked a hand through his hair as he stared at the ground, trying to figure this out. "Right," he said, grasping at straws. "Who hasn't led?" He looked up at them.

"We've all taken lead positions, sir," Johnson replied, "except Skinner, Flint and Trot."

"So what?" Newark asked.

"So, one of them should lead," Brash said.

The crew couldn't see what difference this would make but since they didn't have any better suggestions, they went with the flow.

Brash looked at the three candidates. None of them seemed suited to the position. The only thing Skinner could lead was a running in the opposite direction race. Flint could barely lead his own life, which left Jenna.

"Jenna, you're up." From now on, he was going to use her forename. He was keen to make amends.

She accepted the task without complaint. She figured she couldn't do any worse than the rest of them had.

Stepping forward, she led them through the forest. Half an hour later, they were staring at a lake.

"How the fuck did she do that?" Newark asked. He turned to Jenna. "How the fuck did you do that?"

"I just walked in a straight line."

As Jenna went over to the lake, Newark stared at her. "She's like some weird fucking Yoda or something," he whispered to Johnson.

"Right," Brash said. "Drink, wash, do whatever you have to. We're setting off again in fifteen."

Brash glanced at Trot. Pulling his gaze away from her, he looked over the land. Lush green terrain stretched out ahead of him. Colourful wildflowers dotted the scene. Someone had to live here. He took a deep breath of pure, fresh air. He had a mission to find life.

Jenna took a deep breath too. She'd dreamt about worlds like this and she couldn't believe she was standing here. If there were inhabitants, she hoped they were friendly. That would make it perfect.

As Newark, Johnson, and Graham began a water fight, Brash called time and they headed off.

"This has got to make you feel better," Jenna said to Flint. "It's so peaceful here."

He gave her a smile but it looked strained, full of barely concealed pain. She could think of nothing else to say but, "Chin up, Flint."

She looked ahead to Brash. The Captain seemed to have renewed purpose but she wondered what his rush was. If they did get back to the ship, she would tell daddy and then- She stopped herself there. Surely, this would have occurred to him. Feeling panicked, she kept her eyes on Brash. The man kept glancing back at her, no doubt with dark intentions.

Trailing behind with Flint, she kept her eyes on all of them. The Captain had to kill her, she decided. Even if she'd bought that paltry lie of his, he'd still end up in a whole heap of trouble. Daddy would have no-one talking of his daughter that way. She picked up her pace, praying they found civilisation soon.

Moments later, she was running for her life.

# Very Friendly Unfriendly-looking Creatures

"What are those things!" Skinner shrieked.

The enormous black shapes cast monstrous shadows on the ground. Huge talons and yellow beaks told Jenna they were some kind of bird. They were closing on them fast. Brash, Johnson, Newark, and Graham fired their weapons but the weapons wouldn't discharge.

"What the hell's wrong with these things!" Brash yelled, throwing the blasted weapon away.

They tore over the ground, Skinner running for gold. He was imagining being ingested whole and spat out in a pulpy mess to feed some oversized chicks. Flint fell. Johnson and Graham whipped him up, dragging him like a bag of rubbish. Jenna had never run so fast in her life. Wild shrieks came from behind, the birds no doubt sensing their imminent victory.

Jenna stumbled, landing face first on the ground. A second later, she was wrenched up. Brash was carrying her. Up ahead, the others had come to an abrupt stop.

"The land's disappeared, Captain!" Johnson shouted. "It's a steep drop! There's a river down there!"

Brash glanced behind him. "Jump!" he yelled.

The crew all jumped, apart from Skinner. Brash grabbed his jacket, pulling him with them as he leapt over the edge, razor-sharp talons missing them by inches. The drop was steeper than imagined. Their stomachs came up through their throats as they plummeted down relentlessly... like in a dream only they knew they weren't going to wake up.

Splash-down was painful.

The others swam over to them. The gigantic birds stood on the opposite bank, watching them intently. Brash knew the crew were easy pickings but the birds made no effort to come near the water.

"Stay in the river," he instructed. "I don't think they like it."

"Maybe they can't take off at such close range," Graham said, looking at the ungainly-looking beasts.

"Is everyone alright?"

"Yes, Captain," Johnson replied. "Skinner's passed out, sir, but he's still breathing."

The Captain looked at the saggy weight Johnson had hold of. "Where's Flint?"

"Shit," she said, looking around.

"He came over with us," Graham insisted, searching the river.

Jenna looked around frantically. At last, she spotted him, floating face down, the current carrying him away. She was a good swimmer – swimming had passed many boring, lonely hours - and she threw all her self-imposed training into it as she ploughed off.

"Jenna!" the Captain yelled after her.

She was going with the current, making determined progress. Flint was not going to die. At last, she grabbed hold of him, heaving his head out of the water. She had to get him out of there and she looked around for the birds. They were still standing on the bank. On the near side, there was no bank, just a sheer cliff face. She really didn't want to get out of the river but she had no choice. Within moments, Flint would be dead. One arm wrapped around him, she struggled to the bank. Dragging him out, she started pressing his chest, glancing up to see the birds waddling closer.

"Jenna, leave him!" Brash yelled. "Get back in here!"

"He's a goner!" Newark called.

She wouldn't give up. Brash watched the birds closing in on her and he cursed. Swimming to the bank, he climbed out, ready to defend his woman. He had no idea what he was going to do. The only thing he had was his fists and if he was going to die, he would die using them. He stood before Jenna as she worked on Flint, the ominous figures drawing ever nearer. "Come on, you mother fuckers!" he yelled insanely.

The large black birds tilted their heads curiously at Brash.

Flint coughed and spluttered then sat up and vomited.

The others climbed out onto the bank, Johnson throwing Skinner down.

"What are they doing?" Graham asked, staring at the creatures.

The birds just stood there, watching them. One of the birds gave a little caw. Newark tried to fire his weapon but it wouldn't discharge. Jenna grabbed hold of it and threw it in the river. "They're friendly!" she shot at him. "Can't you see that!"

"Yeah, right," he snarled. "They're just lulling us into a false sense of security."

Brash kept his position as Jenna knelt beside Flint. "Are you alright,

Flint?" she asked.

Flint didn't reply and Brash glanced around at him. "Jenna just saved your life, Flint."

"Thanks," Flint mumbled bitterly, staring at the ground and vomiting again.

"Right, Flint, get up. No sudden movements as we back away. OK?"

The crew retreated in unison but Jenna stayed put. "I wonder what they want?"

"They're birds," Brash said.

"So, they're *bird-brained?*" Newark put in.

"Speak for yourself," she remarked, edging closer to the creatures.

"Trot, get back here at once!" Brash ordered.

The birds tilted their heads and Brash watched in horror as Jenna reached out a hand to them. That hand was toast, Newark thought.

So, Newark was surprised, indeed confounded, when two minutes later the same attached hand was rubbing and tickling a big, black belly. "They're tame!" Jenna said excitedly.

The crew stared in confused wonder.

Jenna couldn't get the rest of the crew to pet them and Brash finally decided it was time to press on.

"Come on, get up," Johnson said, kicking a splayed-out Skinner.

"Pick him up, Graham," Brash instructed. "I'm not hanging around for him."

Graham threw the man over his shoulder and they walked off, following the bank, moving out onto open land. The odd thing was, the birds followed. In fact, they kept with them all afternoon, circling in the air above, landing occasionally. The little caws they made were starting to irritate Newark. "I tell you, they're just saving us up for tea-time."

"No, one goes off for a while," Graham said, "then another. I bet they're going off to hunt."

"Why are they following us then?" Brash asked.

"Because of mother fucking goose here," Newark said, pointing at Jenna.

"They're not chicks," Jenna shot, irritated.

"How d'you know?"

"Can you imagine if they were?" Johnson asked, looking around for a possible mother bird.

"A bird that size would never get off the ground," Brash insisted, checking the skies now himself.

"Maybe they just like us," Jenna suggested.

Johnson, Graham, and Newark looked at each other then burst out laughing. Brash was touched by Jenna's trusting nature. Flint and Skinner hadn't spoken all afternoon.

The crew fed off various berries, the Captain trying them out first and glancing at Jenna to see if she was impressed. She wasn't. She hadn't forgiven him for wanting to kill her but coming to her aid today was making her feel a whole lot more relaxed.

As night closed in, the birds stayed close. The land had turned to rolling mounds and Brash spied a sheltered copse in which to bunk down. As the crew settled down for the night, the birds snuggled in their own little group.

"It's just… weird, isn't it?" Johnson pondered, staring at the black lumps of bird. The rest of the crew had given up trying to figure it out. They had accepted this new reality.

"Johnson, hand me your lighter," Brash said. "We'll get a fire going."

Johnson pulled out a knuckle-duster and a knife as she searched for her lighter. "My mother always told me to be prepared," she said to Trot who was staring at the mini arsenal in her hands.

"What was your mother like?" Jenna asked.

"Scary."

Newark was throwing small stones at the black lumps. Jenna knocked them out of his hand. "Are you insane?" she said, staring at him in askance.

"They're pussies. They just sit there and take it. Look."

As Newark picked up another stone, Brash yelled. "Knock it off, Newark!"

Jenna, infuriated with Newark, walked toward Flint. By the look Flint was giving her, she reasoned that he didn't want to talk. Sitting down near Graham instead, she watched him drawing lines in the dirt with a tiny stick.

"What are you drawing?" she asked.

"Just buildings. See, this one has a slide wrapped around it. Cool, huh?"

"Yeah," she said, smiling at the man. "You should be an… architect."

"Not much call for it on a spaceship," he said, scratching the side of his mouth. "Besides, I was shit at exams." He sniffed evasively. "Can barely add up."

Jenna's brow creased. "I thought you were technically proficient? You got on Captain Brash's team?"

He looked up, staring at her for a good long moment, his eyes flicking to Brash. The Captain was still busy with the fire. "Just kidding. I aced at everything."

Johnson, who had left Brash to it, sat down next to Graham and Jenna thought she saw them share a glance.

Johnson sniffed. "I was impressed by the way you approached that bird earlier. And... err... you know, dragging Flint out of the river. That took guts." She sniffed again.

"Err... thanks."

"You know, you might not make a bad member of this team, after all."

Even though they had wanted to kill her, Jenna felt her heart swell with pride.

On finishing the fire, Brash stood back and glanced around at the giant birds. "Well, they seem very friendly, unfriendly-looking creatures."

# A Wondrous Sight

The blinding orange light didn't seem so blinding here. Jenna stretched as she opened her eyes. The crew were still asleep but Captain Brash was stroking one of the birds' heads. The bird was making cawing sounds and the Captain was smiling. Despite everything, it warmed her heart.

Jenna was suddenly aware of the fact that Flint was awake. "Oh, hi, Flint," she said. "How are you feeling?" She was getting a little tired of asking him that question.

"Fine," he said with a mirthless smile. Least he was talking to her again.

Newark came to life, looking around then looking over to the Captain. As Newark studied the birds, his fingers played with tiny stones. "You know what we should try?" he remarked. "We should try and ride those things. Be a real blast."

Jenna looked at the man then looked back to the birds. Suddenly, she got up and walked over to Brash.

"How old is Jenna," Flint mused in a faraway voice.

"Twenty-two, I think. Why?"

"How old is Brash?"

"Thirty-three. Why?"

"No reason."

Brash turned to Jenna, pleased she was seeing his softer side. She was the only use he had for it... although... he did find these creatures quite enchanting.

"Captain, do you think these birds-" It sounded stupid but she made herself press on. "D'you think these birds want us to ride them?"

He smiled, amused. "Why do you say that?"

"Well, they haven't left us alone, they keep making strange cawing sounds and I really feel they're trying to say something to us."

"So, you're saying they're an avian taxi service?"

Jenna nodded and Brash laughed. He actually laughed. Face tight, she climbed onto one of the creature's backs.

"Come down off there," Brash ordered but already the bird was on its feet. It moved then it began to run, its speed increasing, reaching full velocity for take-off. Jenna held on tight, burying her head in its feathers as its legs left the ground and they became airborne, the giant wings making furious giant sweeps. Jenna wondered if she had acted rashly.

"Come down, Trot!" the Captain shouted but she had no idea how to fly this thing.

The crew down below were standing beside Brash, staring up in wonder. "Go girl!" Johnson shouted.

"Nice one, Trot!" Newark called after her.

"Help!" Jenna yelled but her voice was lost in the wind. "Turn back," she yelled at the bird but the bird was set on its flightpath and there was no manual control.

"Right," Brash said, flustered. "Climb on the birds."

"I'm not getting on one of those," Skinner insisted.

"Newark, grab him. Come on, Flint."

They boarded the birds and, without any direction from them, the birds revved up for take-off, following after Jenna.

"I love these fucking things!" Newark cried with a dubious hold on Skinner. Skinner had passed out.

The ground whizzed by beneath them. Johnson thought she was in a sodding fantasy fiction novel. Of course, those novels were confiscated if she was ever caught reading them - her mother wasn't raising an airy-headed dreamer. Damn right, Johnson agreed, but the wind blowing through her hair made her feel like a child again. She even felt an affinity with Trot as she watched the girl fly off into the distance. She turned and smiled at Graham, who was smiling back at her.

The sun crept up in the sky, bathing the land in a new day. Rivers and lakes gleamed in the early light. The birds were covering ground it would have taken them days to cross. They noticed weird-looking creatures grazing beneath them but they'd seen so many weird-looking creatures it barely raised an eyebrow. They flew over expanses of hills, flat land... until something incredulous hit their eyes. Buildings. Gleaming buildings, soaring up into the sky. Some of them were stone, some shone like crystal but all architecturally perfect to Graham. It was a wondrous sight.

The crew looked to each other as they drew inexorably closer. "D'you think they're friendly, Captain!" Newark called out.

Brash didn't know the answer to that but they were going to find out soon enough. These birds weren't for turning around.

# Head Fuck City

As they came in for landing, Graham gazed at the crystalline structures and his heart soared. The birds touched down on a green strip of runway edged with colourful blossomed trees.

At the end of the strip, Brash could see Jenna standing before a high stone archway. She looked extremely nervous. He climbed off and ran over to her. A delegation of humanoid-looking beings was walking toward the archway from the other side. All of them radiated an inner glow. As one of them stepped forward, Newark nearly dropped to his knees. The woman looked almost human, her violet eyes penetrating, her pale skin soft and flawless. Her hair was the palest blue but to Newark, she was a goddess. The long, thin white gown she wore stirred in a faint breeze, giving Newark a hint of what lay beneath. He thought he would pass out.

The woman looked around at them all, her eyes fixing on Jenna. They stayed fixed on her and Brash noticed the ones behind looking at Jenna too. His newly-found protective streak surged up. The woman's eyes flicked to Brash. "Welcome," she said, though her lips looked odd as she spoke. "My name is Llamia. We will provide you with refreshments and place you in suitable accommodation."

"I don't trust this woman, Captain," Johnson whispered to Brash. She glanced at Graham who seemed as star-struck as Newark.

The woman looked at her with a gentle smile. "You are quite safe here. No-one will harm you." Johnson's grip on her weapon tightened. "Your weapon is useless here," the woman said.

*I don't need it to take you out, princess,* Johnson thought sourly.

The woman seemed to smile to herself as she turned and walked away. She had a quiet word with one of the others and another being stepped forward. Brash was surprised to find that this other being was a human being. He looked around sixty, with shoulder-length white hair and loose-fitting clothes.

"You're human?" Brash asked.

"Not entirely. My name is Cornelius. My birthname was Tom but I changed it. Didn't like Tom," he said, shaking his head with a gleam in his eyes. Again, Brash noticed that his mouth moved in a funny way.

Brash introduced himself and his crew. "What is this place?" he asked.

"Erithia. Not many find it," Cornelius said, his eyes flicking to Jenna. "Come on, let's get you something to eat."

Cornelius led them through a large stone-flagged courtyard, dotted with those same blossoming trees. Entering a doorway at the far end, he took them down a corridor.

"I don't trust him," Newark whispered.

"He seems very nice," Jenna whispered back.

"Everyone seems nice to you," he spat with contempt.

"Not everyone," she said, looking him up and down.

Cornelius opened a door on the right. "Please," he said, gesturing for them to go in.

They entered a reasonable-sized room with comfortable, yet classy, almost Roman-looking furniture. Ahead, balcony doors were open and Jenna walked out to see gardens stretching ahead of her.

"Make yourselves at home," Cornelius said. "Food and drink will be brought shortly."

Brash thought the man was going to leave but he sat himself down, looking at them expectantly.

As expected he was bombarded with questions.

"Who are you?" Jenna asked. "Were you born here? Are there other humans here?"

"Who was that woman?" Newark asked.

"Are you going to kill us?" Johnson accused.

"Where's the bathroom?" Skinner blurted.

"Did you tame those birds?" Jenna asked.

"How do those things get off the ground?" Graham added.

"We need answers," Brash demanded.

Cornelius glanced at Flint. Flint sat up. "You're not speaking English, are you?"

"What's going on here?" Brash implored.

"Patience, Captain Brash," Cornelius said. "Well spotted, Mr Flint. Now, if you'll try not to interrupt, I'll answer your questions. Let's see... I was born Tom Spencer. I came here as an unborn baby. My father, Bradley Spencer, a human, met my mother, Hubeen Froisk, a Kaledian, in Jakensk."

"Yuck!" Newark exclaimed and Brash hit him on the arm.

Cornelius continued, undaunted. "They'd heard tales of mysterious lands and the two of them set off on an adventure. Or were they pulled off on an adventure?" he offered enigmatically.

"What d'you mean?" Brash asked.

"Please don't interrupt. Now, where was I? Oh yes. I was born here. Yes, there are other humans here. I'm looking at them now. That woman, Llamia... she's sort of in charge. She's over two hundred years old."

"Downer," Newark muttered.

"No, we're not going to kill you. You'll have to take my word for that," he said, looking at Johnson. "The bathroom's out the door, second door on the right. Yes, we tamed the birds – they're called aruks, by the way. They live in the mountainous areas to the south, except these ones, and they do struggle to get off the ground. We give them a bit of help there. And... yes," he said, turning to Flint, "I'm not speaking English. You may have noticed that the shapes my mouth makes do not correlate with the sounds you hear." He pressed his lips together, trying to judge how they would react to this next bit. Oh well, straight to the point. "We transfer thoughts and can read minds."

"Holy Fuck!" Newark exclaimed, feeling like he'd been raped and feeling the need to voice this. The rest of the crew just stared at Cornelius.

"I speak my own language and the thoughts connected with the words, I transmit into your heads. You process those thoughts into *your* language."

"But... why don't we hear the alien words as well?" Jenna asked.

"Well, for one, I speak very quietly and what you do hear you block out. The brain can't do those two things at once. It does the thing it understands. In fact, throughout your life, your brain does an awful lot of blocking out." He smiled enigmatically. "You'd be surprised what you do not see."

"You're... psychic?" Brash asked, looking at him like he was the devil.

"Yes. We all are here."

"That's not possible," Brash insisted. "That's mumbo-jumbo!"

"And yet, here I am reading your mind, Captain Brash. You want to get back on that bird and get the expletive out of here."

The Captain was stunned speechless. Jenna found all this fascinating. "How do you read minds?" she asked.

"Um... It's all about tuning in to a certain frequency. Some are born with this gift; others must work at it. When you work with the power, as we like to call it, things progress more quickly."

Newark was lost, way out of his depth. The others were at the deep end too. Skinner, not best pleased with this non-scientific rhetoric, was struggling with another issue.

"Excuse me, Miss Johnson," Cornelius said. "Your friend wants to ask you to escort him to the bathroom. He seems rather nervous to be alone."

Johnson turned to 'her friend'. "Fuck off, Skinner."

"What is this... power?" Jenna asked.

The door opened and trays of food were brought in. Some of the carriers looked almost as good as Llamia and Newark wondered how old *they* were.

Cornelius got up. "Eat and drink. Take a walk in the gardens. We'll talk later." He left them staring after him.

"This is fucked up," Johnson said

"But did you see the architecture?" Graham murmured.

"Come on, get something to eat," Brash said, off-hand. "Skinner, go to the fucking bog!"

"I'll take him," Jenna said.

Newark tucked into the banquet straight away. The others watched him for a while then deciding it was safe, tucked in too.

When Jenna returned, she noticed that Flint was eating. Picking up a plate, she loaded it with all manner of delicious-looking food... various fruits, vegetable dishes, spicy dishes, nothing remotely repulsive.

"They might be weird fuckers," Newark remarked, "but still, this place isn't that bad."

"Two hundred years," Johnson said to Graham. "Two hundred. That's disgusting."

Graham nodded in agreement.

"You look better," Jenna said to Flint. He looked almost human again.

"It's fascinating... Communicating without speech. It's a new frontier..."

"What is it about language that you love so much?" she asked curiously.

He gazed at the wall. "It's the beauty of sentence construction, the cadence, the way certain words are emphasized – change the emphasis, change the meaning. Language has a musicality... Even if I've never heard the language before, I can sometimes work out the gist of it. Language is a language of its own..."

Newark laughed. Jenna turned to him and scowled. Raising his hands to her, he stuffed a few red things into his mouth. Almost at once, he started coughing and spluttering, fanning his mouth with vigour. "Shit, it's like acid!"

"Yeah," Graham said. "I had one of those. They're hot."

"Like LIamia hot?" Johnson asked under her breath as Newark threw a jug of water down his throat. Graham didn't hear her. He was too busy laughing at Newark.

"Serves him right," Jenna said, turning back to Flint. He was staring at the wall again, his face stiff.

Captain Brash was watching Jenna talking to Flint. She'd talked to him a lot now and he didn't like it at all. He thought he'd go and initiate a conversation.

Glancing around the room, he made his way over to her. "Quite a place, isn't it?" he began.

Jenna turned to him. "It's fantastic."

"Yes, but we have to remain on guard. The old man... seems nice but we don't know that for sure yet."

"You're right, Captain. It doesn't pay to trust people. After all, they could be trying to kill you."

He leaned into her. "I explained that. You've got the wrong end of the stick. If I wanted you dead, I'd have let the aruk take you, wouldn't I?"

"The aruk was friendly."

"I didn't know that at the time. Listen, I want us to start again. Wipe the slate clean." He touched her arm. "Jenna, I-" Brash stopped himself just in time. He'd had the impulse to let it spill out; how he felt about her, how he was experiencing feelings he never had before. Coughing loudly, he looked around. The crew were staring at him. He removed his arm. "Anyway, I think you should tread carefully here. I think we all should."

Flint had an amused gleam in his eyes. The others went back to eating.

Half an hour later, Cornelius re-entered the room. "Everyone feeling better?" he asked, congenially.

"You've been very hospitable," Brash said, viewing the man with suspicion and keeping a firm check on his thoughts.

"Good. Would you like to do some sight-seeing?"

They walked through stone courtyards, tree-lined walkways, passed buildings that looked like ancient Greek temples, and were now in a large crystalline structure, staring up at a high domed ceiling. The circular wall around them shimmered with colour, as if it was alive. Graham wandered around, his head craned to the sky, trying to work out how the building stood up. He couldn't see any support structures. And there didn't seem to be any purpose to this building. There were no higher levels, no rooms... just one vast cavernous space. Pathways ran along the floor, dotted here and there with benches, plants and water fountains.

"So, what is this building?" Graham asked Cornelius.

"The crystal creates a beneficial atmosphere. We come here to... recharge. Come, let's sit down for a while."

Cornelius led them to the centre where a circular stone bench was broken only by a gap for entry. They entered and sat down.

"So, you still have questions?" he asked.

Brash coughed. "What are these people called?"

"Erithians."

"Are there any other species here?"

"Just me and one Kaledian."

"Don't you feel alone here?" Jenna asked. "Don't you want to be around others like you?"

"There are no others like me. Humans don't tend to find Kaledians attractive."

"Ain't that the truth," Newark said under his breath.

"Kaledians don't tend to find humans attractive, either."

"But your parents?" Jenna asked.

Cornelius shrugged. "It must have been a soul connection."

"You don't look Kaledian," she said, staring at him closely. "You look completely human."

Cornelius drew back his hair to reveal large pointed ears. "My stomach's larger than average too. Can't seem to get rid of it. Why d'you think I wear loose-fitting clothes."

"Oh."

"What's the story with the Kaledian?" Brash asked.

"He arrived not too long ago. He had to leave Jakensk. Stumbled on us by chance. Any more questions?"

"Yes," Jenna said. "You mentioned a power? What is that?"

"Ah... yes. There is a power that runs through everything. Everything you see, across the universe, is part of one invisible energy... different manifestations, maybe, but all existing in the same field. Even you are part of this field. Once you recognise and fully believe this, you can learn to manipulate the field."

Mumbo jumbo, Brash thought. Skinner's scientific brain was getting insulted. "Belief isn't science," he piped up importantly.

"No, it is not," Cornelius said. "Your point?"

"That is my point."

"Your point leads nowhere."

Right, Skinner thought, I'll baffle him with science. So, he did, rattling off a brief history of time, journeying through every scientific discovery and theory and breakthrough since time immemorial. "And not once, in all of that, is there a theory of belief."

"No," Cornelius said, nodding thoughtfully. "Your point?"

"That is my point." *Was the man trying to goad him?*

Newark was yawning and stretching. Johnson and Graham were sharing fond looks. Flint had tuned out. Skinner and Brash were getting extremely annoyed.

Cornelius turned back to Jenna. "So, where was I? Yes. Everything you see is contained within this field. Up-down, left-right, matter-antimatter, and so much more that we can't, yet, even imagine. The field is an infinite well but it is neutral. It can be used for good or evil. It can be used to create wonders, or it can be used to destroy. We, here, have drawn on this power to create this beautiful land. We even use it to protect the land. A shield of energy protects us. It's a huge dome extending from the forest right down to the south."

Skinner understood shields. He'd worked with shields. "What type of shield is it?" he asked. "How's it generated?"

"By directing the power. Haven't you been listening?"

"Captain," Skinner said, sitting up straight, "I think this man is… deluded, sir."

Cornelius laughed. He stood up. "Since you have such a problem with belief, why don't I take you to the educational building."

The educational building was another crystalline structure, yet it was a proper building with rooms and stairs and floors. Cornelius lead them to the second floor. "This is where our children learn."

"And what do they learn?" Skinner asked, snidely. "How to cast spells?"

Cornelius laughed. "You really are quite funny, aren't you?"

Skinner viewed him with suspicion. *Was he taking the piss?*

"They learn many things. Maths, history, geography, technology, and things that perhaps your schools do not teach. Come, let me show you. I'll take you to the practice rooms."

They followed behind Cornelius, Newark muttering that he didn't want a tour of a school. The corridors were clean and white and the air inside felt fresh.

Cornelius opened a door and they found themselves standing behind a viewing screen, staring out at a classroom of children. All the children were standing at white tables, which had fruits set upon them. Newark and Graham shared a glance. "Snack time," Newark whispered. "How fucking interesting."

"Just wait," Cornelius said.

All at once, the children raised their hands over the fruits. Within moments, the red fruits rose off the tables. The crew watched on, stupefied. Some of the fruits starting spinning, faster and faster until they were red blurs.

"What the hell's going on?" Brash asked.

"Energy play," Cornelius replied. "Wonderful, isn't it?"

The crew were lost for words. They were witnessing something that should not be happening and none of them knew what to do with that.

They wandered out of the room quietly and were still quiet when they left the building.

"The village of the damned…" Brash murmured.

"What?" Jenna asked.

He turned to her. "It's an archive film. You can get them on Vintage. Newark and Graham watch them for a laugh. It's... Never mind..."

"How do you feel, Mr Skinner?" Cornelius asked. "Challenging beliefs can be very... challenging."

Skinner stared at him through vacant eyes. *Was* he taking the piss...?

"Why do they need children if they live so long?" Johnson asked. "Are they all as *old* as Llamia?" She glanced at Graham. Graham was looking at the architecture.

"Llamia isn't old. After four hundred years or so, the body does show signs of age. You'll see quite a few older residents here and there. The Erithians don't live forever. So, they still need to procreate occasionally. In fact, that is the only reason they would have sexual intercourse."

"What?" Newark asked, disgusted. "They don't like sex?"

"It isn't that they don't like it. They are just beyond it. They have found a greater form of connection. For them, sex would be putting their foreheads together and fusing their mental and spiritual energies. You should try it. It's out of this world."

Newark shuddered. Brash wondered what was wrong with these people. Graham and Johnson were looking at each other with questioning expressions and Jenna thought it sounded romantic.

"Come on," Cornelius said, "I'll show you the control room now. Follow me."

They followed Cornelius down the street. But as if to add insult to injury, Newark spotted an older pair of inhabitants touching foreheads.

"They're doing it in the street!" Newark exclaimed. "And they're old!"

The couple in question broke off and stared at Newark. Cornelius raised a hand to them as if to apologise. He turned to Newark. "Why shouldn't they do it in the street?" the man asked patiently.

"They're having head sex in the street. And they're old!"

Cornelius suppressed a smile. "Or," he said, "they are making a meaningful, celebratory connection that does not involve their older physical body. The part that connects does not get old. Do you understand?"

Newark just stared at him. Brash scratched his ear. "It all sounds messed up to me."

Jenna viewed Brash critically. "I think it's beautiful. Maybe you're the one that's messed up."

Cornelius looked a little proud of her. Stretching boundaries wasn't easy but she was managing very well. "Come on, we're nearly there."

Expecting the control room to be a highly technical hub of activity, they were surprised when they entered a temple-like structure and found themselves staring around a large empty room that was surrounded by pillars. The sound of running water and soft music played in the background but the weirdest thing was the two bodies lying on beds in the centre of the room.

"What are they doing?" Graham asked. "Sleeping?"

"No. They're meditating. They are on duty at the moment."

"Of course, they are," Brash said. Skinner rubbed his forehead.

"It is their job to monitor the shield. If anyone comes through the forest, they are the first to detect it. If someone arrives, they contact the aruks."

Brash rubbed his forehead now.

"The aruks collect any visitors. The four that brought you are tamed by us. They help us when we ask them to. These meditators also help the aruks off the ground."

"Using this... power?" Jenna asked.

"That's right. The aruks come from a region of steep cliffs. They don't have the same problem there. They dive off the clifftops and glide."

"Why don't you just send some sort of craft?" Brash asked, disgruntled.

"We like to keep things simple."

"And these birds just do whatever they're told?"

"We don't tell, we ask. They are made of the same energy as us. They respond well to kindness, gratitude and good intentions." Cornelius smiled. "They're lovely creatures, aren't they? Got such a cute little caw."

"I know," said Jenna.

"Now, the last stop on our tour will be the healing facility."

As they walked back out into the sunshine, Newark raked a hand through his hair. "This is one head fuck city."

# God Help Us

The healing facility was another crystalline structure. It was a little like the first, with paths and plants and water fountains, but this one had levels and rooms like the educational building.

Cornelius led them to another circular stone bench exactly in the centre. There were more people here and the crew looked around at them. Brash noticed the one Kaledian coming out of a room. He looked distinctly out of place. The pot-bellied creature kept stepping in and out of the doorway like he was doing some strange ritualistic dance. When he got to the front entrance, he did the same thing.

"What's the deal with him?" Brash asked, pointing with his chin.

Cornelius looked around. "Ah, Fraza. There he is. Yes, he has Obsessive-Compulsive Disorder. Poor thing. Now," he said, turning to Jenna, picking up on his earlier conversation, "I'm coming to the crux of the matter now. You see, most can't get through the forest. You must have a certain kind of energy to open a door. I did, as an unborn baby. And you did, Jenna, yesterday."

"What?" she asked startled. "Me?"

"Yes."

Brash rubbed his forehead. "Is that why we kept going around in circles?"

"In a nutshell, yes. The shield kept repelling you. Whoever was leading kept altering their course slightly without even being aware of it."

"And yet, we didn't end up back at the ravine?"

"No, because unconsciously you wanted to get through the forest, creating a sort of push me-pull me effect. Crazy, isn't it?"

"Oh yeah..."

"What does that mean?" Jenna asked.

"It means you go in circles," Cornelius said.

"No. I mean, what do you mean, I have a certain kind of energy?"

"Oh. It means you are using the power already."

"I don't think so," she said staring at him then looking to Brash. Power? Her?

"She got us through the forest," Flint stated, his eyes lifting to Jenna.

Skinner was staring at the floor, tuning out. His brain couldn't handle anymore. Newark wasn't listening, either. He was watching a group of jaw-droppingly beautiful females, trying to imagine what head fucking would be like. Johnson and Graham were sharing looks, doing a little head fucking of their own. But Brash was staring at Jenna thoughtfully.

"Have you ever noticed anything odd, Jenna?" Cornelius asked. "Strange things you couldn't explain?"

She shook her head.

Brash was now staring ahead. He was picturing a collapsing wall and three dead bodies. Flint was picturing a knife flying out of his hand.

"What does this mean?" Brash asked.

"Some are open channels, which means the power comes through freely. We refer to them as pure. And I sense you, Jenna, are very pure." Cornelius lent forward, his expression becoming serious. "Circumstances have brought you here but we believe you were drawn here. There is a dark force in the universe. It has been growing for some time. If the balance tips, there will be dark days ahead. Llamia has prophesized that one will come to us who could reverse this tide of events. We believe that one to be you, Jenna."

Jenna gawked at the man.

"So, let me just get this straight," Johnson said, raising a finger in the air. "You're saying that the future of the universe depends on... Trot?"

Cornelius nodded.

"God help us..."

# Needs Must When the Devil Drives

"So," Cornelius said, rubbing his hands together, "she's going to need a team and you guys are it."

"Sorry," Jenna said. "Could you just backtrack a bit?"

"To which bit?"

"All of it. I don't understand how this energy field works or how I got everyone through the forest. And… whatever it is you think I've got, I'm sure I've not got it. I'm pretty… unremarkable…"

Cornelius smiled. "That's the beauty of it. You don't have to understand it. And you've got it, alright. Perhaps it's been coming out unconsciously. You see, there is so much more to us than we realise. Unconscious motivation is ninety-nine percent of everything that happens. For most of the time, most beings live life asleep."

Skinner snorted. He had nothing else left to give. Newark was in his own unconscious-driven world with a blue-haired beauty. As the blue-haired beauty left the building, he tuned back in. "Have I missed anything?"

"Oh yeah," Johnson said.

Brash rubbed his forehead. "She needs a team? What the hell do you want her to do?"

"We'll go into details later," Cornelius said.

"We need to get back to our ship," Brash insisted.

"You need to look at the bigger picture. Save universe or get back to ship." Cornelius weighed each option in his hands. "This, Captain Brash, will be the biggest mission you or anyone has ever embarked on."

Brash was sold.

"Now, she'll need a team worthy of her. So, to that effect, a few home truths are in order. Captain Brash, let's start with you. You have been living in a very blinkered way."

"Now, hold on a minute."

"Did you know that Johnson and Graham are having a relationship, or that Graham falsified his way into his current post, aided by Johnson, of course."

"What?"

Johnson and Graham cringed. The Captain turned to them.

"Time to open up, Captain. Maybe chill a little, too. Let me get you a drink." Cornelius looked around. A few moments later, four beings arrived - two beautiful females and two equally beautiful males. Newark wondered what was in those genes. One of the males was holding a glass of what looked like beer. Cornelius took the glass and handed it to Brash. "Please, take a drink, Captain."

Brash smelled the drink. "Smells like beer." He took a sip. "Tastes like beer too." He knocked the whole drink back.

"Can I get one of those?" Newark asked.

Cornelius looked at him. "D'you know, I've got something better for you." He looked at one of the females. "Why don't you take Mr Newark for a drink more suitable to him?" he asked with a certain level of suggestion.

She nodded and Newark stood, his anticipation mounting. "How old are you?" Newark asked her.

She smiled a thread-bare smile. "In human years, I would equate to twenty-five."

"That works for me." He looked back with a grin as she led him away.

"You could use some recreation too," Cornelius said to Skinner. "You like virtual games?" Skinner nodded, his brain desperate to tune out for a while. "Mervan will take you."

Skinner got up and followed the man.

"Err, Cornelius, what was in that stuff?" Brash asked. "I feel a little peculiar."

"It's a potent herb. I believe shamans used something like it on earth. But this is an alien enhanced version. It's just a few hours of a trip."

"What!"

Brash's eyes rolled back in his head and he fell off the bench.

"We'll pick him up soon," Cornelius said as the crew all stared at their Captain.

"Do we get some recreation?" Graham asked, dragging his gaze to the man.

"Yes, Piyra, here, is going to take you to our petting zoo."

"Petting zoo?" Johnson asked, insulted. "A fucking petting zoo?"

"Yes. Your soul is crying out to pet an animal, trust me." Johnson looked at the man as if he was off his trolley.

"The Captain won't like this at all," Graham asserted.

"Believe me, when the Captain comes back, he'll be overjoyed."

"We're not going to any damn petting zoo," Johnson said, putting her foot down.

"Mr Graham, pet the animals and I'll get the chief architect to have a chat with you."

"Oh. OK," he said with a shrug.

"What's in it for me?" Johnson asked.

"Selflessness."

"Very funny."

Cornelius looked at her thoughtfully. "You always wanted a pet when you were young, didn't you? Give yourself permission to have one now."

"You trying to turn me soft?"

"No. Just trying to iron out the wrinkles." He appraised her. "OK, you and Graham get a double suite and the best grog in the house."

"Done," she said, getting up.

Flint gave Cornelius a mirthless smile. "What do I get, Cornelius?"

"A counsellor. Udren will take you."

And then there was Jenna. "What do I need?" she asked.

"A whole heap of training. We'll start tomorrow."

A few men came over to carry Brash away. "Will he be OK?" Jenna asked, looking at the Captain, concerned.

"He'll be fine," Cornelius answered with a wave of his hand. "Do him the power of good."

"Where have Newark and Skinner gone?"

"Come, I'll show you."

Cornelius took Jenna through one of the doors. Leading her down a corridor, he opened a red door on the right, marked 'virtual reality suite'. Skinner was strapped into a chair, wearing a bulky helmet, with all manner of monitoring gear hooked up to him. His stiff body was convulsing.

"Total immersion," Cornelius remarked. "Thinks he's the character he's playing. It's a little like dreaming. Completely convinced of the reality of it."

"He doesn't look like he's enjoying it."

"Oh, he's not. I should imagine it's pure hell."

"What...?"

"It's called the 'die a thousand deaths in a day' programme."

Jenna gawked at the man. "That's totally sadistic."

"Not at all. Sometimes you've got to be cruel to be kind. He'll thank me later." Jenna looked at him as if he was mad. "Listen, the man's a toad, a complete worm. Terrified of his own reflection on a dark night. But you see, once you've faced death so many times you develop an immunity to fear. In some cases, it can make you apathetic to the point of suicidal *but* in others, it can make you fearless."

"And what if he becomes suicidal?"

"We have a programme for that too."

"I don't care what it can do. It's cruel!"

Cornelius looked at her seriously. "Needs must when the devil drives. Come on, let's go and see Newark."

Jenna was shocked to find Newark locked in a room, staring at a few jugs of water on a table.

"It's one-way glass," Cornelius said. "He can't see us."

"Why is he in there?"

"He's spending time with himself. Seeing what he inflicts on the rest of us."

"How long is he going to be in there?"

"I haven't decided yet."

"He's going to be livid when he gets out."

"Yes. He's going through hopeless disappointment and disillusionment at the moment. The anger will come."

"Disillusionment?"

"You're quite innocent, aren't you?"

"Oh, he thought..."

"Newark's a long shot, I know. But it's worth a go."

Jenna rubbed her forehead. "This is not what I imagined this place to be like at all."

"Well, we do a lot of meditation here, too, if you want to join in."

"Err... no thanks."

"Maybe not. Your untrained channels are open enough."

She sat down on a nearby chair, not at all sure what was going on here. Cornelius looked at her with compassion. "Different problems require different solutions. If we had three hundred years, your crewmates would not be where they are now."

"Will they be different?"

"Skinner, yes. Brash, for a time. Newark. That's anyone's guess. Flint is a work in progress - you wouldn't believe what that man's been through. Johnson and Graham, marginally, but they'll be petting animals every day. Newark's not safe around animals yet," he added as an aside.

"It seems wrong to change people."

"We're not trying to change them exactly, just bring out their finer selves. They're in there. It's like bringing light out of the shade. But..." he said with a shrug, "there are no guarantees."

She looked up at him, cautiously. "I dread to think what you're going to do to me."

"Don't worry. Once you get into your training, you'll have fun."

Fun... she thought. What would it be like to have fun?

# Collateral Damage

Jenna awoke on silky sheets and stretched luxuriously. For a moment, she wasn't sure where she was. When she remembered, she was filled with a strange feeling of optimism.

The room was lovely, the floor mosaic, the furniture deep red with gold trim. She noticed that the light, spilling through the crack in the curtains, made the tiny tiles in the mosaic glisten.

Getting up, she opened the curtains and stared out over a patchwork of gardens. She drew in a deep breath. A whole new day was starting, a different chapter. She was someone the universe depended on. Of course, she wasn't thinking too far ahead with that. Deep down, it was incomprehensible to her that she could do anything to fix things. But right now, she was basking in unearned glory, as a fish out of water craves the sea.

The place Cornelius took her looked like a Japanese dojo. Flimsy double doors opened out onto a lake and gardens.

"This is mine," he told her. "I train in here."

"Martial arts?"

"Yes."

She looked around. "Do you feel like you belong here with these people, Cornelius?"

"Yes. I grew up here. The Erithians are an old race."

"I know. They're like old people in young people's bodies."

He smiled. "Better than being young people in old people's bodies."

She smiled then a crease marred her brow. "You said yesterday there's a part that doesn't get old?"

He looked at her, perplexed. "Why do you do it?"

"Do what?"

"Put yourself down so much?"

"Excuse me?" Had she missed a whole part of the conversation?

"You're smart, quick on the uptake, yet all your life you've bumbled your way along, almost apologising for existing."

She stared at the man. "I haven't done anything." She could feel herself getting cross now. "If I've bumbled my way along it's because I can't *do* anything! I'm useless! And the saddest part is, I managed to block it out for so long!" Her new-found high was crashing. Reality was setting back in. "You think you've got a saviour of the universe? God help the universe! If it wasn't for the fact that everyone would be dead or whatever, they'd all be laughing at me or trying to kill me!"

"That's good."

"What is?"

"Anger."

"Fuck you!"

"Excellent. We'll leave it there for today."

"What…?"

"I said we'd leave it there."

"But we haven't started yet?"

"We'll get stuck in tomorrow."

The door burst open and a very peculiar Captain Brash breezed through. He floated over with expansive arms and a wild look of wonder in his eyes. "I love you!" he said, flinging his arms around Jenna. Her angry heart skipped a beat.

All at once, Brash swung around, his arms outstretched for Cornelius. "I love you!" he called out. As he rushed over to the man, Jenna's heart took a nosedive. The older man patted Brash on the back.

"It's amazing…" Brash declared. "It's all one… Your field is alive, all-encompassing… It's all consciousness… Nothing else… You, me…" he said, gazing wondrously around him, "we're dreamed characters and nothing exists… nothing but love…"

Jenna was starting to feel very uncomfortable.

"You've just interrupted Jenna's first training session," Cornelius said in the hopes that Brash would go away.

"Training session….? There's no need for that… None of this is real… What does any of it matter…? All you need is love… That group knew it… They knew it…"

The door burst open and a livid Newark stormed through. "I'm going to kill you, old man!"

"I love you, Newark!" Brash called out, rushing over to him.

Newark's eyes widened. "What the hell have you done to him!" The sight of the Captain made his anger intensify. Nobody messed with his Captain. Missing Brash's hug by inches, he charged Cornelius.

Jenna watched, incredulous, as the great steaming lump of Newark smashed into thin air and got thrown back to land unconscious on the floor. She stared at Brash leaning over him, stroking the man's face. "I love you, Newark."

She drew her gaze to Cornelius.

"Newark will be fine," Cornelius said with a wave of his hand. "Captain Brash, why don't you take a walk in the gardens. The flowers are lovely."

Brash rose to his feet as if drawn by a magnetic force. "Flowers... Yes..." He wandered to the door and disappeared.

Jenna stared after him. "What's *wrong* with him? What have you *done* to him? I don't want him like that!" Surprised by what she'd said, she glanced at Cornelius.

"Don't worry, the walls of individuality will close around him again."

"Then what was the point?"

"You can't have a powerful experience and not be affected by it. The seeds are there now, although coming back down could be a little... tricky."

Jenna was beginning to wonder if this man knew what he was doing. "Where's Skinner?" she asked.

"Sleeping. He'll be asleep for a day or two."

"Flint?"

"He'll be in intensive counselling for weeks, perhaps months. You wouldn't believe what that man's been through."

Jenna wanted to ask but didn't want to pry. She instinctively felt that Flint had come to the right place. The others, she wasn't too sure about. There seemed to be an awful lot of collateral damage. She gazed at Newark lying on the floor. "So... you're trying to get Newark to get to know himself...?"

"God, no. I'm not a miracle worker. I'm trying to teach him restraint."

Part of the collateral damage was kneeling in the garden, staring intently at a pink flower. Johnson and Graham, realising it was Captain Brash, struggled to understand what he was doing.

"Are you alright, Captain?" Graham asked.

The Captain's incredulous eyes couldn't pull themselves away from tear-jerking beauty of nature. "Look at this, Graham."

"What, the flower?"

"It's amazing..."

"Err... yeah. Captain, I just want to explain about the application form."

"Forget it... What's a form in the whole scheme of things... It's meaningless, Graham... Meaningless..." Graham and Johnson looked at each other, confused.

"Johnson and I have been seeing each other but we didn't want... I mean, we know how you feel about members of the crew engaging in..."

The Captain's head turned, his eyes lighting up even more. Getting to his feet, he grabbed Graham's shoulders. "All you need is love... Love is all you need..." The Captain's head turned swiftly. "Ah, look at that!"

Johnson stared down at the furry yellow ball in her arms "It's a young Kook, Captain. Apparently, they grow quite big."

"It's incredible," the Captain effused, gazing at it with love.

Johnson and Graham looked at each other, concerned.

Something else caught the Captain's eye and he wandered off.

"What the fuck have they done to him?" Johnson asked.

"I don't know. But the old man's going to pay."

# Time Out

Johnson, Graham, and Newark were hanging in mid-air, arms and legs flailing wildly. Jenna gazed at them, thinking they looked like hideous marionettes.

Newark had woken up, furious, at the exact moment Graham and Johnson had charged through the doors, shouting, "You're dead, old man!" None of them got anywhere near him.

"Let us down, you evil freak!" Johnson yelled.

"What have you done to the Captain!" Graham shot. "You sick sadist!"

Newark was more creative. "I'm going to roast your balls over a steaming vat of hot acid!"

Cornelius frowned. "Is acid hot? Does it steam? Interesting…"

"You know what I mean!"

"I get the gist, Mr Newark."

"Why don't you fight us with your fists, old man!"

"I'm not fighting. You're the ones that are fighting."

"You're using your strange devil magic!" Johnson yelled. "You should be burned at the stake!"

A particularly gruesome image flashed through Johnson's mind. Cornelius shuddered. "Again, I'm not fighting. As soon as you calm yourselves, I'll let you down."

Ten minutes later, they came down to earth with a thud. Almost immediately, Newark was on his feet, storming the enemy like a raging bull. Then he was in the air again. Then on his feet.

"We can play this game all day if you like?" Cornelius said.

After the fourth attempt, Newark saw the light, remaining on the floor, glaring at the man with hatred.

"Your loyalty to your Captain is touching," Cornelius said to them. "He'll be himself again soon. Please, don't worry about him. Now, you all look in need of… a little recreation. Let's take some time out."

"Oh no," Newark said, "you're not pulling that shit on me again!"

Cornelius gave him a gentle smile. "I was just going to say we have a water park here. Swimming pools, water slides… It's such good fun. Go and enjoy yourselves. You'll find new clothes and costumes in your rooms."

Graham and Johnson really wanted to go to the water park but they didn't want to show it. Newark didn't want to go to no water park. "I want a drink," he demanded, "and not water... and not that shit you gave the Captain."

"You would like to frequent a bar?"

"Of course, I'd like to frequent a sodding bar."

"I'll come with you then."

"Oh no, I'm not going anywhere with you."

"That's a shame because my house is the bar."

"What...?"

"The Erithians do not drink."

*"Boring bastards!* I want a proper bar with women and noise and-"

"And somewhere to act as a backdrop to your roiling mood?"

*Was the man taking the piss?* Fists clenched, his body set to go, Newark stopped himself just in time.

"I'm afraid it's my house or swimming," Cornelius said.

At that moment, Captain Brash appeared in the doorway holding a bunch of flowers and a furry yellow creature. The crew stared at him, horrified.

"Ah, Captain Brash," Cornelius said. "Some of your crew would like to go to the water park but they would feel remiss in their duty if they did."

"A water park..." Brash repeated in wonder. "Yes... yes... I need the feel of water on my skin..."

Johnson and Graham's faces fell.

Newark turned to Cornelius. "I'll take that drink."

As they walked out, Cornelius turned to Jenna. "Aren't you going for a swim?"

She looked at Captain Brash then shook her head.

Jenna wandered around the city. The weird thing was, the Erithians stopped to talk to her, asking her how she was, asking her if she was enjoying her stay there. After a while, she barely noticed the funny way their mouths moved. It was such a contrast to the people on the ship. Yes, they would be pleasant to her, but now, as she watched these Erithians actively coming over, she remembered the many times her own people had veered off in other directions. Indeed, the Erithians were so friendly, Jenna was starting to feel a little uncomfortable. It was too much too soon. She headed back to the accommodation to find it empty.

The crew's rooms were situated around the sitting room they had been brought to yesterday. It was almost as if the place had been prepared especially for them. She wandered into the sitting room, staring at fresh food that had been laid out on the table. Heaping up a plateful, she sat down by the window, staring out over the gardens. She thought about Llamia and how she had prophesized her coming. She had the feeling they had got the wrong person. She felt like an imposter but, despite this, she wanted to cling to it as she had once clung to a birthday card that had been sent to her by mistake.

Three hours later, Johnson and Graham came in with wet hair and shell-shocked faces.

"Where's the Captain?" Jenna asked.

"Out of it," Graham replied wearily. "We've laid him on his bed."

"Did you enjoy the park?"

"It was a bloody nightmare."

"He was running around naked," Johnson said. "Wouldn't put his trunks on. Said the water had to touch every part of him."

"Why?"

"Some shit about not feeling life until you know you're living it."

"And get this," Graham said. "Completely naked, he dives off the highest board. When I told him that would hurt, he said some bollocks about pain not being real."

"He felt it, alright," Johnson said, turning to Graham with raised brows.

"We were running around after him all afternoon." Graham dumped himself down on the couch. "Had to stop him killing himself. You wouldn't believe the shit they've got down there. It was worse than looking after those damn pets."

"We should go to that zoo as soon as we get up tomorrow," Johnson remarked, giving Graham a meaningful look.

"*Really* early," Graham said, nodding thoughtfully. "I don't know who was more embarrassing, the Captain or that crazy Kaledian."

"Fraza was there?" Jenna asked.

"Oh yeah," Johnson said. "You don't ever want to see a Kaledian in a swimming costume, I'm telling you *that*."

"The crazy fuck kept holding up the lines," Graham complained. "Before he'd go down the slides, he kept stepping from side to side and touching his forehead. Johnson shouted, 'move you fucker' and the Erithians kept turning to *her*."

"Yeah, him and the Captain are best buddies now," Johnson said, ruthlessly biting a long stick of green.

"Really?" Jenna thought how nice that was for Fraza. Being the only Kaledian, he must feel left out.

Newark burst in, steaming drunk. "Who wants to go to the water park?"

"Fuck off, Newark," Graham said.

# The Root of the Matter

Newark emerged the next morning, feeling a little the worse for wear. The old man's beer was potent stuff. Johnson and Graham were nowhere to be seen and Trot seemed to be stuffing down her breakfast.

"Why are you in such a rush?" he asked.

She hesitated. "Got training this morning," she said with a quick smile.

Newark laughed. "The old man's backing the wrong horse with you."

She looked at him, indignantly. "What d'you mean?"

"Well, come on, let's face it, you're hardly 'saving the universe' material, are you?"

"Sometimes, Newark, you are a complete shit!" And with that, she stormed off.

As Newark tucked into breakfast, the door opened behind him. He turned to see the unknown quantity that was Captain Brash and realised, too late, why no-one else was around.

"Morning, Captain," he said, heaping up his plate quickly, thinking he'd make a fast exit.

On hearing silence, Newark glanced behind him to see the Captain wandering through the room like a wraith. He looked weird, all drawn into himself, his arms pressed tight around his middle.

Newark wasn't sure what that meant and wasn't quite sure what to do. "You... OK, Cap?"

The Captain looked up with haunted eyes.

"I thought we were getting stuck into it today?" Jenna asked, walking along a beam.

"We are."

"Walking up and down a beam doesn't feel like that to me. Why am I doing this?"

"You are centring yourself. Focus is very important. You need to learn to concentrate your attention. Plus, it will make you less clumsy."

"Who says I'm clumsy?"

"Just bits and pieces I've picked up whilst trawling through your crewmates heads."

"That's disgusting! Newark was right. It is like rape. You haven't been going through my head, have you?" She fell off the beam.

"That's exactly what I'm talking about. See how you lost focus and fell off the beam?"

"Sod the beam! Have you been going through my head?"

"Needs must, I'm afraid."

"Right," she said, crossing her arms and looking at him intently. "What are these needs exactly? You never told us."

Cornelius appraised her. Then he drew in a breath. "OK. In another galaxy, there is a ruthless.... what does he call himself...? Oh, yes. He calls himself, the God of Thunder. Or Thunder God, for short."

"You have *got* to be kidding me..."

"No, this is no joke. The name's a bit pretentious, I'll admit, but that's how he sees himself... as some raging destroyer god, set on annihilating anything that stands in his way. The unfortunate fact is, this being has a strong command of the power. And he is using it for evil. Many have already fallen under his rule; many more have died."

"How do you know about him, if he's in another galaxy?"

"Llamia can tap into the field, sense any imbalance."

"How the hell can she do that?"

"The Erithians are highly attuned to the vibrations of the field."

"And these vibrations just turn into images and words in her mind, do they?"

"Yes, that's right," he said, looking pleased with her.

Jenna stared at him. She scratched her head. "Look, if the Erithians can use the power, why do they need me? Can't they fight this... Thunder God themselves?"

Cornelius looked caught off guard. There was something he didn't want to impart yet. "I'm afraid they can't. You'll just have to trust me on that."

She viewed him critically. "Then why not you?"

"I am not strong enough."

"And I am?"

"We believe so." *We hope so*, he thought to himself.

"But you could, at least, help me."

"It is Llamia's instinct that I shouldn't go with you."

"Why not?"

"The most helpful things can often be the greatest hindrances."

She stared at him. "Or, the most helpful things can actually help."

"Llamia's instincts are to be trusted."

A huge, terrifying burden suddenly descended on her. She lowered herself to the floor. "Listen, I think you've got the wrong person. Maybe I should leave. My dad will be going out of his mind. I-I can't stay here."

"You're concerned about your dad now? It didn't bother you too much yesterday."

She rubbed her temples. "I hadn't heard the words, Thunder God, yesterday. Dark force in the universe is one thing but now it has a big scary face."

"Your father's been cocooning you for years. If you go back to that ship, you'll never get out from under his wing. You'll never be your own person and you'll never know how great you could be."

"Great? Me?"

"Yes. Look, this is exactly what he wants."

"Who, my father?"

"No, the Thunder God. He picked that name to intimate everyone and it works. Change the name, change the perception. Call him 'sick little bastard', if it helps."

"Sick little bastard," Jenna said, trying it out.

"You've got a choice to make, Jenna Trot. Do you go back to daddy and carry on the life you had, or do you see what else you can be?"

The life she had... Put like that, it was a no-brainer.

"Are you going to get back on the beam now?" Cornelius asked.

Jenna dragged herself up and got back on the beam. As the door burst open, she fell off.

"You need to come see the Captain," Newark said, panicked. "He's freaking me out."

Captain Brash was sitting on the floor in the corner of the room with his arms wrapped around his middle, staring at one point on the rug.

Jenna rushed over to him. "Captain, what's wrong?"

"You won't get a response," Cornelius told her. "He's coming down." She turned to him. "Can you imagine having vastly expanded vision, feeling vast and expansive yourself then suddenly being squished back into the narrow confining prison of yourself?"

"No. Can you?"

"Yes. Been there, done that. He'll be fine," he said with a wave of his hand. "Just make sure you keep feeding him. Might need to mash it up a little. Think baby and you'll get the idea."

Jenna looked back to Brash. She felt an enormous rush of compassion for the man and found herself stroking his damp, dishevelled hair.

"Come on, Jenna, we need to resume training."

"You're not leaving me here with him," Newark piped up.

"I shouldn't think he'll move for hours. He's in the pain stage. If he moves through embarrassment and anger, let me know."

"I'm not feeding him like a fucking baby!"

"There's a beer in it for you."

Newark paused for thought.

Jenna spent the next two hours walking up and down the beam.

"If your thoughts wander, return them to the beam."

"This is boring," she grumbled.

"Good. It means you're doing it right."

Eventually, the old man let her come down and she sat on the floor beside him.

"Thoughts hinder the power," Cornelius said.

She looked at him sadly. "But I've only just started to think about things." She felt that something important was going to be whipped away from her.

"Thoughts are running around in your head all the time, whether you're aware of them or not. Maybe you're not conscious of them but they're there, like scurrying little insects coming in and out of the cracks. Now, *you've* just started to pay more attention to things. Sometimes circumstances nudge this but it is a good thing. That which you become aware of, you have more control over. You have started to use your brain again. Why have you neglected it for so long?"

"I don't know. Maybe *you* can tell me since you dig around in there."

"I can only find what is shown. If you hide something from yourself, how can *I* see it?"

Jenna shrugged. "Maybe I need counselling, like Flint?"

"Nobody needs counselling like Flint."

Again, she wanted to ask.

"So, you're the Admiral's daughter?" Cornelius asked, conversationally.

"Yeah."

He detected a bitter note in her voice and decided to probe deeper. "What were you like as a child, Jenna? Think deeply. Close your eyes. Lie down, if you like. You must be tired walking up and down that beam."

Jenna did feel tired. She lay down and closed her eyes. Moments later, a cushion was being placed under her head.

"What are your early memories?" Cornelius asked in a soft lulling voice. "Did you fit in?"

"I never fitted in."

"Are you sure? Just relax and let early impressions come to you. What about as a very small child?"

She lay there for a time, reaching back through the years. Vague memories came up... lost, forgotten memories... The impressions were becoming stronger. "I... I think I did fit in then..."

"Make the pictures clearer, Jenna. Did you have friends?"

"Yes, children played with me."

"What is this place? Is it a sort of schoolroom?"

"Yes... Wait. Are you in my head?"

"Yes. Don't worry about that. You're nice and relaxed now... Back in the past... Nothing to worry about... The children seem to respond to you well."

"Yes..."

"Who is that girl straight ahead, the one scowling at you?"

Jenna stiffened. "That's Mara. She never liked me. If I try to talk to her, she ignores me."

"Why does she ignore you?"

"She doesn't like me."

"OK. Take yourself a little further along. Still at school. We're looking for a moment when things begin to change."

Pain took hold of her face. "The children are being mean to me. They're calling me names."

"What names?"

"Teacher's pet."

"Why?"

"Because I'm the Admiral's daughter. They're saying I think I'm better than them. I never think that. I don't want to go to school anymore. Nobody will play with me."

"Who's that girl, the one smirking at you as if she's won first prize in a competition."

"Mara. She never liked me."

"I know. Could there be some connection with her and the other girls being mean?"

"I don't know. She never liked me."

"Did the teachers know how unhappy you were?"

"I told them no-one would play with me. They talked to the other children and it got better... but then it got worse again. They had another talk but nothing ever really changed..."

"Did the teachers monitor you over the years?"

"No. There was no point telling them anything."

"What about telling your mum or dad?"

"Mum's dead. Dad was busy. Besides, that would make things worse."

"OK. Come forward now. What happened as you got older? Did you succeed at school?"

"I did OK. I didn't do as well as daddy thought I should. He blamed the teachers. It was very embarrassing. He made me take all the exams again."

"Did you do any better?"

"No."

"Was he upset?"

"Yes. He told me to ignore my grades. I was officer material and that was an end of it."

"I see... So, in many ways, it was not OK to be you, was it?"

"No..."

"How do people respond to you as an adult?"

"They're really nice to me. But I can see things I couldn't before. I'm a joke. I think they resent me."

"Ok, Jenna, sleep now." Cornelius waited until the girl's breathing evened out. He leaned closer. "I'm speaking directly to your subconscious mind." He felt the connection, felt her subconscious rise to the surface like a creature rising from the depths. "You blocked everything out? You allowed her to bumble her way along, unaware of what people really thought of her?"

Her mouth did not move. The impressions Cornelius received were strong and hard. "Of course, I blocked it out. The girl's a useless misfit. How is she expected to deal with all that and carry on functioning? I took the line of least resistance."

"Well, now you've met me. The girl was unfairly treated at school and lost all confidence in herself. She was given grossly distorted expectations from the start from an ambitious man who wanted that ambition to carry on through his genes. Her path was never his. In short, she became a self-fulfilled prophecy, bumbling and screwing up because she'd never had the space in which to fail and had the extreme misfortune to meet, in her formative years, a jealous and vicious little control freak. Add to that how sheep-like kids can be, and how anti-bullying procedures do not appear to have been in place, I'd say she was set up to be the joke she became. So, this is the deal. Release all the stored-up pain. It's the only way she can move forward."

"Are you shitting me? D'you know how much stuff's down here?"

"Every single truth, right back to the early years."

"It'll be a system overload. Can't we do this slowly?"

"I haven't got time."

"But she'll crack up."

"She's stronger than she thinks. Do it. Now," Cornelius commanded.

"No, I won't."

"You do it now, or I'll find a programme that will do it for you."

"You're one mean bastard. OK, here goes..."

# System Overload

Newark was spoon feeding Brash with little success. The stuff kept dribbling down the man's chin, making an unholy mess. Newark knew he wouldn't be doing this for anyone other than his Captain, and he definitely wasn't doing it again. He kept turning to the door, hoping for Johnson or Graham to appear but the bastards were keeping away.

On hearing the outer door crash open, he felt a renewed sense of hope. It was dashed in a second as a weird kind of wailing reverberated out in the corridor. Another door slammed shut and, confused, he got up.

The wailing was coming from Trot's room. Staring at the door curiously, he turned the handle and peeked inside. The girl looked distraught, thrashing on the bed like she was in physical pain. He had two choices: ask her what was wrong or close the door again. The second option was more appealing but he was curious to know what had happened.

"Trot?" he asked as sensitively as he could, though it came out a little gruff.

The girl spun around, eyes red from crying. Lurching off the bed, she grabbed a vase and threw it in Newark's direction. Newark managed to close the door just in time. Completely baffled, he wandered back to the Captain.

"I was fucking naked," the Captain whispered, head in hands.

Newark knew what this was. He was entering embarrassment. "Welcome back, Captain," Newark said as if the Cap had just returned from a mission.

The Captain looked up at him. "I was fucking naked...!"

Newark scratched his head. "Yeah, I heard about the water park incident."

"Incident...? It's a fucking incident...?"

"No, no, I didn't mean that. I shouldn't think anyone noticed. Least you made a new friend." The Captain stared at Newark as things became clearer. "Though, the little bastard will probably be hanging around us like a bad smell now."

The Captain's head fell and Newark thought he was sinking into pain again.

Gut-wrenching cries came from down the corridor. Brash looked up. "What's that?"

"It's Trot, sir. Don't know what's wrong with her. She's been like that since she came back."

The Captain scrambled to his feet and made his way down the corridor.

"I wouldn't go in there, sir."

Brash opened the door to find Jenna rolling around in pain. She turned to him, her eyes growing wide. She picked up a vase from the other side of the bed and slung it hard. Brash ducked just in time.

"Jenna, what's wrong?"

"You fucking murderer!" she yelled, looking around for something else to throw. Brash closed the door behind him.

"I'd let her calm down, if I was you, sir."

Brash ignored Newark. Wandering back into the living room, he fell onto the couch. He now had more things to deal with. Jenna had seen him yesterday and the thought made him want to retch. On top of that, she hated him because, from a new perspective, he realised that a murderer was exactly what he was.

Newark tried to be helpful. "I think I know what's happening here, sir. You're oscillating between pain and embarrassment."

Brash's face turned red. He shot to his feet, grabbing Newark by the collar.

"No, I was wrong, sir. You've slipped into anger."

Johnson and Graham eventually returned, feeling like they'd entered a madhouse. All manner of weird sounds were coming from Trot's room and they could hear the Captain yelling in the living room. "How could they let me do that!"

Graham and Johnson looked at each other then backed up to the door.

A wide-eyed Newark came out into the corridor, his eyes fixing them like prey. "Ah, there you are. You can deal with this shit! They've both gone nuts!" Striding past them, he left the building.

"I think the Captain's back," Johnson whispered, looking down the corridor with concern. The yelling was still going on.

They continued to back up then froze on seeing the Captain's furious face. "What the hell did you let him do to me!"

Lost for words, they let him get it out of his system but the rant seemed to go on forever and, with the wailing coming from Trot's room, Graham was getting a headache.

Trot burst out of her room, looked at the three of them then stormed off to the bathroom. That seemed to provide a break in the Captain's rhetorical rant. In fact, the man seemed to change like a switch had been flicked and he gazed at the bathroom door. Looking winded, he wandered back to the living room. Johnson and Graham looked at each other, debating what to do. At last, they tiptoed past the living room, straight to their own room, gently closing the door behind them.

They lay awake all night, listening to the silence. They just didn't trust it at all.

In the morning, the world had turned upside down. They heard Trot yelling, heard her kicking a door and smashing various bits of pottery against the wall. In the lulls, they were sure they could hear the Captain sobbing. Unwilling to believe that, they decided they were Trot's sobs, that her voice had got sore and was producing rusty sounds. Climbing over the balcony, they made their escape through the gardens.

Newark was sitting on Cornelius' veranda, waiting for the old man to come down so he could get a beer. He'd been searching around the place but couldn't find the stuff anywhere.

He had turned up here yesterday, pleading with the man to 'sort out all that shit." But Cornelius said it was better to let them work things out of their systems. After that, he gave Newark the beer he'd promised him. When Newark asked for another beer, the old man insisted he play a game for it. Newark had to sit and stare at the beer for fifteen minutes before he could drink it.

"What are we? Five?" Newark complained. "Just give me the fucking beer."

"Humour me," Cornelius said. "If you don't play, you can't have the beer."

Newark would have grabbed the beer but he knew where that would end up. With him on his arse and a smug old git smiling at him.

He played the game.

This morning his thoughts turned to the Captain. He found himself worrying about the man. No-one should be brought that low.

Cornelius arrived with a beer in hand and placed it down before Newark.

"Err, thanks," Newark mumbled. "That mind-reading shit comes in handy."

"Yes, I suppose it does."

"You're sure the Captain's going to be alright?"

"In the long run, it will do him the power of good."

"It better," Newark said with an undertone of threat. Taking a deep swig, he wiped his mouth with the back of his hand. "How long are we going to be here, exactly."

Cornelius pursed his lips. "Could be months."

"Months? We can't stay months!"

"Why not?"

"Because it's dull as sin here!"

"I don't think you fully grasp the seriousness of the situation we are facing, Mr Newark. This is bigger than you, bigger than any one of us. I told Miss Trot yesterday and I'll tell you. The evil force has a name. He calls himself, the Thunder God."

Newark laughed. "No shit?"

"Shit. He is becoming extremely powerful and we need the best we have to stand against him." Newark preened his mental feathers. "Are you committed, Mr Newark."

Newark sat up straight and sniffed. "Sure, why not. I'll chase the mother fucker back into whatever hole he climbed out of."

"I doubt it will be that simple but I appreciate the sentiment. Now," Cornelius said, placing his hands on his knees. "I need you to reformulate your relationship with Miss Trot."

"What?" he asked, confused.

"Eventually, you will be part of *her* team. You need to... show a little more respect."

"Her team? We're not her team! We're the Captain's team! Does the Captain know about this?"

"No. Not yet. And the Captain will still be the Captain but ultimately, she must have the final say, for she will be working with the power. In overall terms, it will be her team."

Newark shook his head. "Have you seen the state of her? Wait. Is that why she's upset? Because you told her about this Thunder God dude?"

"No. She's working through some other stuff."

"Look, I'll show her some respect when she stops being a namby-pamby little princess."

"That's good enough." Cornelius stood up but stopped in his tracks. "Ah, I think your friend has arrived. I'll go and open the door."

*Friend?* Newark thought. Peering into the hallway, he caught a glimpse of an Erithian woman in a flimsy dress. For a moment, he thought his luck was in. On seeing the woman leave, he sank back in his chair. A moment later, Cornelius came out with Skinner.

"Hey, you little worm," Newark said, getting up. "Where the hell have you been?"

Skinner walked around the table and punched Newark hard in the face. Newark couldn't comprehend what had just happened.

# Major Adjustment

Captain Brash stood on the balcony, gazing at Jenna Trot. He felt a deep wave of compassion as he watched her wander through the gardens like a spiritless ghost. Empathy had never been one of his strong points but he had it now in bucket loads. He wondered what she had inside that produced those gut-wrenching sobs. He suspected it had something to do with Cornelius. Cornelius had some explaining to do.

He wondered if he should go out there, walk in the garden with her. Sometimes it was hard to know the right thing to do.

After a few contemplative moments, he decided to venture outside. He kept his distance, his arms around his middle as if holding himself together. He hated to appear weak but his whole being was a quivering mess of... He didn't know what these feelings were. He'd never experienced them before. Sitting down on a bench, he gazed at the flowers forlornly.

Within minutes, a hard-faced Jenna Trot was standing before him. Her voice chilled him to the bone. "Not collecting flowers today, Captain Brash? Pink ones, I think you had yesterday. Pretty pink. Pretty pink girly flowers."

He stared up at her, wondering where that snide voice had come from. In the past, he wouldn't have stood for it. Now, he could see the pain behind the words and, instead of anger, he felt concern and curiosity. He could see the hatred in her blue eyes but he had the instinctive feeling it wasn't personal.

In the most heartfelt voice he had ever used, he said, "I'm sorry..."

She looked thrown off course but quickly resumed composure. Sneering at him, she walked away. Brash stared after her, knowing in a way he never could have before that for Jenna, he epitomised everything and everyone that had ever hurt her. It was like looking through a window.

These moments, however, would prove to be precariously rare. The old Captain was struggling to reassert himself.

"Where the hell are the rest of my crew!" Brash shouted at Johnson. Johnson and Graham had only come back because they were hungry. They stared longingly at the table.

"I don't know where Newark is, sir," Johnson answered. "I haven't seen Flint or Skinner for a couple of days, sir."

At that precise moment, Newark came through the door with a peculiar-looking Skinner. Peculiar because, for one, his spine was erect, not the usual sloped shoulders and drawn in aspect. For two, he was holding their stares. And, for three, Newark seemed to be his best buddy.

"Skinner?" the Captain asked. "What's different about you?"

"They've given me new clothes," Skinner reported, maintaining eye contact. Brash detected an arrogant look in those eyes. Graham and Johnson felt it too as the man turned to them.

Brash eyed him critically. Where was the cowardly worm he was used to? He must be in there somewhere. "Do you know what we're doing here in this place, Skinner? There's a dark power in the universe and we are up against it." Brash searched Skinner's eyes for the familiar frantic flit.

Skinner picked up a juicy red fruit and squashed it in his hand. "We'll crush them until their blood spills through our fingers."

The Captain's eyes widened.

Newark was pumping. "I love this guy."

Johnson and Graham didn't understand anything anymore. They wanted to stroke some small fluffy animals.

"I'm going to find Cornelius," Brash said, walking out.

"What the hell have you done to Skinner!" Brash roared.

"Skinner has just... died a thousand deaths," Cornelius told him. Brash looked at him as if he was mad. "It's a programme. The man needed... toughening up."

"But he's completely different!"

Cornelius scratched his neck. "Yeah, he's going through a god complex at the moment."

"What...?"

"When you've stood up to death that many times, you lose your fear of it. That has knock-on effects. In Skinner, it has made him feel invincible. He'll calm down."

"And what about Jenna? What have you done to her?"

He scratched his neck again. "She's working through some issues that have suddenly come up. Again, she'll be fine," he said with a wave of his hand.

"Have you seen the state of her?"

Cornelius nodded regretfully. "She has to overcome her past to be able to move on. That's just how it is."

"And what about me? The weird trip you sent me on?"

"It wasn't just a trip. You broke free for a time. Glimpsed behind the veil. A lot of people would pay good money for that. Even many with the power have not seen what you have seen." Cornelius assessed him. "You have to be more than you are, Captain Brash. That much is obvious."

Feeling insulted, Brash moved over to Cornelius but a sudden breeze blew in through the doors and pain gripped his chest. "What is this?" Brash muttered, helplessly.

"You have tasted the sublime. Every hint, every memory of it brings a yearning so deep, it's a physical pain."

"Why would you do this to me...?"

"Don't you want to walk through life with your eyes open? Pain is the price we have to pay." Cornelius looked at the door. "Ah, Jenna, have you come to resume your training?"

"I want you to teach me to fight. I want to kick the shit out of something," she said, glancing at Brash.

"Excellent. I'm going to teach you all how to fight."

"I think I can handle myself," Brash spat.

"Maybe. Let's teach you to handle yourself better."

The whole crew, apart from Flint, stood in the Dojo. They turned as one when Fraza walked in. The Kaledian smiled at Brash but the Captain looked down.

"Ah, Fraza, there you are," Cornelius said, turning to the rest of them. "Fraza will be joining your team."

"What?" they asked in unison

"Fraza got through the forest. He has the power, although his power is relatively weak."

"I'm not having the Kaledian on my team," Brash objected.

"It's not your team, though, is it?" Jenna shot. "It's mine and I say Fraza's on it!"

Brash stared at her. "Maybe I'll just take my crew back to Jakensk then."

"Maybe you won't, seeing as you can't get through the forest without me."

"Maybe I'll get a kind Erithian to help me."

"Maybe they'll tell you to sod off."

Their eyes locked in mortal combat. Annoyed as he was, Brash couldn't help thinking this girl was fabulous. He'd put up with the freaky Kaledian for her. But he had a problem. His crew couldn't witness him backing down.

"Captain," Cornelius said, "you are going to be up against difficult odds. Fraza can help you."

"How?"

"Fraza?"

The Kaledian stepped forward, giving Brash a genuinely hurt look. Looking around the group, he went to stand before Johnson. Scratching each ear five times, he composed himself. Suddenly, his hand shot out and Johnson fell backward, landing on her backside.

"Holy Fuck!" Newark exclaimed.

"He can do what you do?" Jenna asked Cornelius.

"He has been training," Cornelius said. "His power is weak. Yours is strong. Do you see where I am going with this?"

Jenna nodded, the possibilities swirling before her eyes.

Johnson got up, eyeballing Fraza.

"Oh, I'm very sorry," Fraza said, attempting to take her hand. Johnson jerked it away, still eyeballing him.

"He speaks English," Jenna said.

"Yes. He's like your Mr Flint," Cornelius told her. "So, what d'you say, Captain?"

"Captain, this will be a major adjustment," Johnson said with a meaningful stare.

"Oh, I don't know," Newark put in, "I quite like the little fucker, sir."

"I like the little fucker too," Jenna asserted.

"I agree with Johnson," Graham said.

"Pussy," Newark coughed.

"I say we take the Kaledian and kick some butt," Skinner decreed.

Brash rubbed his forehead and looked around his crew. This would be a major adjustment but the Kaledian could prove useful. "OK," Brash said, turning to Fraza. "But I'm the Captain, alright? We're not buddies and that day never happened. Do you understand me?"

Fraza nodded then jerked his head three times.

Brash viewed him oddly. "Why's he doing that?"

"Oh, it's a reaction to your authoritative tone of voice, Captain," Cornelius said. "It's fascinating the number of rituals and responses he has. You could write a book on it."

The Captain started to reassess his decision.

"Right," Cornelius said. "That's sorted then. It'll give him the confidence boost he needs. Now we're all getting on so well, let's fight. Newark, you're up first."

Newark smiled. At last, he was going to get his pound of flesh. Or, so he thought. The old man pulled off some crazy moves, laying him out flat on the floor.

Cornelius broke it down, demonstrating each part. Then he instructed them to pair up. Jenna claimed Brash. Johnson claimed Fraza. Newark and Graham paired up and Skinner said he'd take them both on. Cornelius took

Skinner. He wanted Skinner's new-found invincibility to have some substance before it was severely tested.

And so, it began. Their training started in earnest, Jenna trying for all she was worth to inflict pain on a reluctant Captain Brash; Johnson exacting payback on the Kaledian; Newark and Graham enjoying the release after one truly crazy shore leave; and Skinner learning to fight for the first time in his life.

As the session ended, Cornelius pulled Jenna aside. "Tomorrow, we are going to start working with the power. We are going to do some lucid dreaming."

"What dreaming?"

"You are going to wake up in your sleep."

# Lucid Dreaming

She was drawing pictures in the sand... buildings with big slides wrapped around them. Lifting her gaze, she watched the waves crashing on the shore of the lake. A snorting grunt turned her head. Standing behind her was a large pig with Newark's face. Stuffed into its mouth was a bright yellow lemon. Something about the lemon spoke to her but she couldn't grasp what it was.

Getting up, she stroked the pig's head then wandered off, trampling over unkempt grasslands. Movement in the grass caught her eye and she found herself staring at Graham and Johnson making out in the grass. "Eww! You two should get a room."

"Stop being a perv, Trot," Johnson remarked without breaking off.

Jenna turned around to find the Captain standing there, a gun in his hand, a mean look in his eye. "Do you want to die or should we have sex?"

The Captain's dark silky hair ruffled in a light breeze. His lean, strong frame stood silhouetted before a dying sun, the handsome face in shadow. Sex sounded good. She'd never had sex. She moved toward him but looked down to find herself stuck in quicksand. She looked back up but the Captain was gone. Flint was standing there, a pained expression on his face. "You'll never get out of there," he lamented.

"Help me, Flint!"

"I can't," he said, stepping into the quicksand and sinking from view.

In her panic, she called out for daddy. The Admiral appeared like a great monolith, blocking out the sun. "Of course, I'll help you, my little dove. I'll always protect you."

Gazing at the outstretched arm, she closed her eyes, held her breath then sunk down into the quicksand.

Dropping onto a beach, she found herself staring at the Newark-faced pig. That lemon was still in its mouth. There was something about that lemon...

*Wait a minute. Pigs don't have grotesque faces like that.* Grabbing the lemon from the pig's mouth, she stared at it then glanced around her. *"I'm dreaming..."*

The weird thing was, it all felt so real... not how you imagine dreams to be when you wake up. She could smell the salty air, hear the pig grunting, feel the breeze on her skin. And yet... this wasn't her body. Her body was lying down and her brain was doing all this. Wow...!"

She jerked awake. She was back on the bed, attached to equipment with Cornelius standing over her.

"That always happens first time," Cornelius said.

"What does?"

"The shock of finding yourself awake in your dream jolts you out of the dream."

"Right. That was amazing... That's never happened to me before."

"Yes, well, the induction programme helps. Remember the lemon. Next time, you'll probably remember sooner. We're going to induce sleep again. Are you ready?"

"Yes."

Cornelius went to lie on the next bed and prepared himself.

Captain Brash was running toward her naked with a bunch of pink flowers. It was a hideous sight. She turned and ran but the land was running out. Throwing herself off the cliff, she plummeted down, air rushing past her ears...

A soft pillow of feathers swept her up. The soft pillow was a large black bird. She turned to see Brash, fully clothed, gazing at her.

The bird came down to land. She climbed off and, as she stroked the bird's head, she saw a lemon lodged in its beak. Taking the lemon, she stared at it thoughtfully. There was somewhere she needed to be. Where was it?

She turned to see a little girl walking toward her. She cringed. It was Mara. Looking down, she saw herself as a child again.

Mara looked cross. "Who said you could come here? You're not allowed." Other girls were standing behind Mara now, looking cross too.

"There's somewhere I need to be," she insisted.

"You shouldn't be anywhere! Don't you know that!"

The bird squawked behind her. She turned, staring at the lemon lodged in its beak. Didn't she just take that lemon out of its beak? *The lemon...* She tried hard to get hold of something.

The bird squawked again. It had Skinner's face. *Wait a minute. Birds shouldn't have Skinner's face?* Staring at the lemon, she glanced around. *I'm dreaming...*

She turned to the cross-faced girls who were sneering at her cruelly. But now she was awake.

Walking over to Mara, she stared her hard in the eye. "Get out of my way or, so help me, I'll lay you out and pulverise every last molecule of your puny little hide." Mara's bottom lip began to quiver. She ran away, crying hysterically. "And don't ever come back!"

She turned to the other girls. "Boo!" she shouted. They disappeared in a puff of smoke.

Feeling pleased with herself, she looked around, realising this was her dream and she could do anything. Could she fly? She could try. After all, she couldn't die.

"Come on," she yelled over her shoulder, throwing caution to the wind. The aruk was running beside her and the two of them took off into the air together. "I love this dream!" she called out. They soared and banked and glided, shooting through clouds, racing over water, following the contours of hills and valleys before rising high in the sky...

The Aruk dived and she followed, touching down on the ground. She was standing outside Cornelius' dojo.

Opening the doors, she entered.

"Ah," Cornelius said. "You got here at last."

"Are you a dreamed character?"

"I am projecting myself into your dream. So, I'm as real as you are."

"Wow..."

"Wait. Stop that! You don't want to wake up again!"

Too late.

It took them another attempt.

As she entered the dojo this time, Cornelius told her to have some dull, boring thoughts ready to hand.

"The dream seems so real," she said. "My brain does all this...?"

"Yes. The best virtual reality there is. But there are some chinks. Look at that picture then look back at it quickly. You'll notice that the picture doesn't look quite the same each time."

She did as Cornelius said. "You're right. Why does it do that?"

"You've caught it off-guard."

"Wow..."

"Jenna."

"Oh yeah." She thought about her father's long speeches when the whole crew assembled for their monthly pep-talk. "So, what are we doing here, exactly?"

"I've brought you here to begin your training with the power."

"Why here?"

"I don't want my dojo ripped up. Your power is strong but it is haphazard, sporadic. It is controlled by unconscious motivations. We now need to bring it to light. So, let's begin. We'll start with the basics. I've placed a bowl of fruit on this table. Focus on the bowl, imagine the power coming through you, raising it up."

"Cornelius, I'm in a dream. I've just been flying. I think I could raise a bowl."

"This bowl is mine, from my mind. If you can raise it, you are affecting something outside yourself."

"OK." She focused on the bowl. Nothing happened.

"To affect something consciously, you have to believe you have the power. Belief is like a switch. Then you focus on that power coming through you. You are the gatekeeper. You can stop or allow. Give it a go. You've got nothing to lose."

Flying through her dream had done wonders for her ability to believe. It might be a dream but she had experienced it. She imagined a doorway inside herself opening, imagined this power rushing through, coming up like a surge of magma from a volcano. The bowl smashed against the ceiling, the table hit the wall and fruit splattered everywhere.

"Wow...!" she exclaimed.

"Jenna, don't do that!"

She awoke with a jerk and turned to Cornelius.

Cornelius smiled. "See why I didn't want you in my dojo. You need a lot of training before I can let you loose in the real world. We'll press on again tomorrow."

# Making of a God

The gangway lowered, thudding violently against virgin turf. A raft of soldiers ran out, standing in formation, their weapons at the ready.

The president stood before his delegation, nervously awaiting the imminent arrival. He had never seen the Thunder God before but the man's terrifying reputation preceded him. He'd heard gruesome tales that made the eyes water, the toes curl. Indeed, the president had been hoping, no praying, that his tiny planet would be overlooked.

Wiping sweat from his brow, the president plastered a smile on his face.

Two figures walked down the gangway, their black cloaks billowing out behind them. The thinner of the two had short blonde hair and looked to be in his late twenties, but the eye was drawn to the other man. The figure looked imposing. A black scarf covered his nose and mouth, focusing attention on the dark penetrating eyes.

Heaving in a steadying breath, the president stepped forward. "Sunni cel Siraz, Kal," he said, which translated as, 'welcome to Siraz, Lord'.

The blonde-haired man looked displeased, so the president bowed graciously. As he did, a strange constricting sensation took hold of his throat. He dropped to his knees, unable to breathe. Suddenly released from pain's grip, he looked up with a fearful, yet questioning expression.

"Take off that bloody scarf, Rotzch!"

"It's my allergies, Lord. You know how it affects me."

"The air's fine. You're overshadowing me. He was looking at you. If you weren't my translator you'd be dead by now!"

The scarf was removed. Rotzch cleared his throat, fixing his eyes on the robed man on the floor, addressing him in the man's own language. "It is *extremely* bad manners to address the God of Thunder in a foreign language. Rude to the point of insolence. The Thunder God can't be expected to know every language there is."

The president stood up to humbly apologize but when he opened his mouth, speaking that same gobbledegook, the Thunder God lost all patience.

The delegation gasped then stared in stupefied horror as their president became a hot steaming mess on the floor.

"We need a new president!" Rotzch called out. "Preferably one that speaks Hellgathen!"

Nobody seemed to want the job. Finally, one man was pushed forward.

"Do you speak, Hellgathen?" Rotzch asked the shaking man.

The man wanted to say no but didn't want to open his mouth.

"I don't think anyone here speaks the language, Lord," Rotzch said.

"Typical," the Thunder God complained, drawing in a calming breath. "Translate then."

"Now," the Thunder God said wearily and Rotzch translated. "I am here for a little... R and R." The new president's eyes flicked between the two men. As Rotzch was translating word for word, he was caught in confusion. He decided it had to be the big man. The other one just didn't make sense. "This is the holiday hotspot of the galaxy, is it not?"

The new president nodded vigorously.

"Good. I expect people will pander to my every whim for the duration of my stay?"

The man nodded vigorously again.

"If I am pleased, I may decide not to blow up your planet. I cannot say fairer than that."

The president gulped.

"Well, speak man," Rotzch said.

Nervously, the man opened his mouth. "I-I'll escort you to the f-finest hotel, Lord. It has s-spectacular views over the ocean and the most e-excellent food."

The delegation parted and the new president led the guests through them.

"The man was looking at you," the Thunder God hissed.

"Only because I was speaking his language," Rotzch assured him.

The craft was open-topped and basic, not what the Thunder God was accustomed to but he decided to let it go. Nothing was going to spoil his holiday.

The new president bowed before Rotzch as the door was opened. That was the last straw. Deadly blue eyes fixed on him and the cowering man realised too late his mistake. He began to convulse violently as if someone was whisking his insides. As he dropped down dead, Rotzch called out, "We need a new president!"

The Thunder God, however, had got past that. His wrath was huge. He'd come here for a break, and now, here he was, plunged back into work. The carnage went on until the holiday resort of Siraz was, at last, closed for business.

Perhaps part of the problem was that the God of Thunder truly believed himself to be a god. This hadn't always been the case. Venn, as he was formerly called, started off a puny little runt, picked on by his peers, despised by his parents and humiliated by his father at any opportunity. His life began poorly and he stored up a whole heap of hurt and anger. That might not have led to any problems but Venn had also started off with something else. Strange things began to happen around him, most notably at home. Doors slammed shut, furniture flew, pots smashed. The family started to believe in ghosts. Friends stopped visiting, friends started to whisper behind their backs, friends started to shun them. The whole situation was intolerable and there seemed to be no end to their misery. Until, at last, they made a startling connection to their weird little boy. The strange things only happened when he was around, so they quickly, and without hesitation, chucked him out.

Alone in the world, his bitterness grew. He knew he was different but he didn't know why. And he would have continued to lead a sad, empty life had it not been for a fortuitous meeting...

Olberax was a master of the power. An Ingui by birth, he had the misfortune to inhabit an ugly-looking body. Yes, he had arms and legs and a face, as such, but the arms and legs were like huge flabby tree trunks and the face was marred by two holes for a nose and two giant bulging green eyes. The whole thing was wrapped in leathery mucus-coloured skin. In terms of agility, the Ingui were like the sloths of the universe and this one was quite old, even for his race. Approaching two hundred years, it could be said that he'd had too much time to think. He had spent many torturous years pondering the meaning of the universe. Theory after theory consumed him but after all these years he had come to the firm and sobering conclusion that there was indeed no point. Life was utterly pointless. From this last and now fixed perspective, he saw the futility of it all... saw the many beings throughout the universe eking out pointless existences. And how many more beings to come would endure the same futility? An endless cycle of pointlessness... Thrown into a deep depression, he wanted the misery to be over but he had too much compassion to be selfish about it. The universe had to end. It was the only way, yet he was far too old and weak and the universe was far too vast. His depression deepened.

With such sorrow in his heart, he decided, at last, to end his life. But, as luck would have it, he was ending his days on Hellgathen. The potent concoctions served up there would do the job for him. And luck was definitely on his side, for as he downed his second glass, Venn walked in.

Olberax felt the strength of the power immediately. It was off the Richter scale. He turned his big bulking head to see what could have been a disappointment. To Olberax, it wasn't. It was a gift. The blonde-haired youth was scrawny, his story clearly written in his hostile blue eyes. He was a directionless, bitter and twisted youth. He'd been using this power, power that he didn't even understand, to wreak petty vengeance for every slight or insult that came his way. Rather than solve his problems, it compounded them, for it made the youth more ostracized. The boy cursed his life and every being in it. The one question that hovered in his mind like a permanent wall-hanging was, *why had no-one ever loved him?*

For the first time in years, Olberax smiled. There was so much power there, lying untapped. This boy could one day become a god. This boy could fulfil the mission that he was too weak to achieve. This boy, this brilliant boy, could end the charade forever.

Olberax bought him a drink. As he'd never had a drink bought for him before, Venn viewed the creature with suspicion but accepted the drink anyway.

A few drinks later: "I could be a god?"

"You are a god."

Suddenly, it all made sense to Venn. This was why he had to bear such suffering. Of course, he was a god! Gods were reviled by their own people, weren't they? Gods had god-like powers. Gods wreaked furious vengeance. At last, his life made sense and the universe was going to pay for it.

# An Act of Balancing

Weeks of dream training led to weeks of actual training. To Cornelius's immense relief, his dojo did not end up in tatters. The girl was coming along well, marshalling this tremendous power of hers with a determined and disciplined will. It was as if there was a pent-up spirit inside, squashed for years, dying to come out. She was, at times, still taken over by fits of uncontrollable anger, or drawn in by bursts of pain and shame. But it was all part of the process, Cornelius reflected... the death throes of the old, the birth pains of the new... It was fascinating to watch.

Her crewmates weren't quite as fascinated. Like their Captain, she had become an unpredictable item, sometimes angry and off-hand, sometimes pathetic-looking and tearful, sometimes something else. The something else came out in the dojo. Cornelius taught them martial arts three times a week and Trot threw herself into it like a woman possessed. She always wanted to pair up with Newark because she knew the man wouldn't go easy on her. Newark trod carefully at first, knowing the Captain was on his case but after taking a few hard knocks, he thought, *stuff this!*

Newark fought like a bull, charging in bull-headedly and, as the training progressed, Jenna used this to her advantage, anticipating his moves, using his own weight against him. Cornelius watched with almost fatherly pride. He was even more proud when Newark, at last, exercised a little restraint and a lot more of his brain.

Skinner was still sparring with Cornelius but was coming along well, using his muscles in a way he never had before. In a few more weeks he'd have the physical resilience to back up his new self-concept.

As for Captain Brash, Cornelius could see what was not yet evident to the rest of the crew. He was hopelessly in love with Jenna Trot. It was a factor Cornelius could do without. He wasn't sure yet if it would prove useful or not to their mission. Love clouds everything... people die for it, people get distracted by it...

Cornelius watched Brash now as they wrapped up their session. The Captain's eyes followed Jenna as she walked out of the dojo. Cornelius continued to watch as the Captain turned and walked over to him. "She's covered in bruises," Brash complained. "Aren't you going to talk some sense into her?"

"And what should I say? Please be careful, we don't want you to get hurt? We'll leave that for the big nasty Thunder God?"

The Captain glared at him. "I'll protect her from him. We all will."

"You will not be able to protect her from him. Maybe you could protect her from lesser mortals but what if she gets separated somehow? What if she needs to be able to protect herself? What if she's been protected all her life and now wants to be able to do that for herself?"

Captain Brash stared at the man, the words sinking in. "OK," he said, thoughtfully. "But can't you get her away from Newark?"

"Captain, she is not fighting Newark. She is fighting herself. All her life she has felt limited. She now has a destiny to fulfil and she's determined to be good enough for it. Newark goes harder on her but to Jenna, he is her greatest ally. The harder he goes, the more she learns."

Brash never thought he'd hear Newark referred to as her greatest ally. The analogy only went so far, though. She barely spoke to them outside of training. Brash had tried to bridge that gap on many occasions and, though she spoke, she wasn't really connecting. The old Captain would sometimes get annoyed with her; the new Captain was out on a limb, floundering in uncharted waters.

"Is that everything, Captain?"

"No. I want to speak to you about Skinner, too."

"Mr Skinner?"

"Yes. He's... Well, to be frank, he doesn't seem interested in very much. Outside of training, he loafs around like an untidy piece of furniture. He used to have a lot of nervous energy and a fast mind. When the man wasn't scared, he lived for fixing and figuring things out. His mind never stopped. But now he's like... Well, he's like Flint, only less despondent; like Newark, only less obnoxious. It's really weird not to have him jabbering away like some hyped-up druggie."

"I see. It's a process, Captain Brash. He's lost all fear of death. Now, a little of that will return in time, but at the moment he's moved through his god complex and is in a state of... apathy. Sort of the opposite extreme. It could be a reaction to many years of fearing and worrying. It will all stabilise then hopefully we'll have a new and improved Mr Skinner. You see, Captain Brash, it's an act of balancing. Hopefully, it will stabilise at a point of integration." Cornelius assessed the man. "How are *you* dealing with everything, Captain?"

"I was stroking one of Johnson's pets yesterday. How d'you think I'm dealing with everything? You've turned me into a goddam pussy!"

"As I said, it's an act of balancing. But I think I have just the thing to kick-start Mr Skinner's fine mind. Soon, I will take you all to the observatory. It's about time we got our bearings."

"You mean, a plan?"

"No. We don't have a plan, Captain."

"You don't have a plan...? What's all this been about then?"

"This has been about preparing you and your crew. And there is much work to do there, believe me. For now, though, we'll take a glimpse at the universe so you can get your bearings. The exact plan, Captain Brash, will be your department."

As Captain Brash walked out of the dojo, he felt very at odds with himself. He had always been a man of action, rising to any challenge that was presented to him. But then he had to ask how many challenges *had* been presented to him? The lower forms of aliens they had encountered didn't have laser weapons. Nothing in his job before this had required that much planning. Whatever this was, it was so much bigger than any of that. Facing armies... facing a demented god hell-bent on destroying the universe... The enormity of the task spread out before him. He couldn't calculate the number of lives that depended on them. For the first time ever, he had a severe crisis of confidence.

And with that came a startling realisation. He was as big an imbecile as Newark. Fear was not his problem; never had been. It was an over-exaggerated view of himself. The walls of his ego were crumbling around him. Who was he really? A gun-toting, alien bashing, trumped-up excuse for a man...?

He wandered down the street in a world of his own. As he quietly opened the door to their accommodation, he heard voices in the living room.

"D'you think she's got pre-menstrual tension?" Newark asked.

Johnson laughed. "D'you actually know what that is, Newark?"

"I've had girlfriends."

"What, for like five hours?"

"You can learn a lot in five hours."

"Yeah," Graham put in. "Especially, if sex only lasts two minutes."

"Well, if she's got it," Skinner said in a laid-back voice, "maybe it's catching."

"What d'you mean?" Johnson asked.

"Looks like the Captain's got it too."

"The Captain's going through some stuff," Newark said defensively. "That shit the old man gave him screwed with his head."

"Yeah," Graham agreed. "And anyway, he's coming back to himself every day."

The Captain stared at the doorway. He didn't want to be his old self anymore but neither did he want to be someone who his crew termed, pre-menstrual.

"Wait a minute," Johnson piped up. "The Captain's going through some stuff but Trot's pre-menstrual? The old man's probably been screwing with her head too. But, oh no, she's *pre-menstrual.*"

"Since when do you stick up for Trot?" Graham asked.

"Since she learned to kick Newark's butt."

"She hasn't kicked my butt," Newark protested.

"No? How many times has she laid you out already?"

"D'you want laying out now?"

"Bring it on!"

The Captain thought they were like a bunch of squabbling siblings. Thuds, bangs, and swearing came from the room but it brought no response from him. Turning around, he walked out into the dimming light. He needed to be alone. He had a lot of soul-searching to do. He needed to find some balance.

# Team Building

The crew were eating breakfast when the Captain came in with the Kaledian. Walking over to Skinner, he knocked the man's feet off the table. "Wake up, Skinner." Turning to the rest of them, he took a brief note of the many black eyes, before announcing, "I have a plan."

"What's the plan, Captain?" Newark asked excitedly. The rest of the crew waited with baited breath.

"We're doing team building today." The crew stared at him blankly. "Where's Trot?"

At that precise moment, Trot walked in off the balcony. "Team building?" she asked, brows raised, a hint of irony in her eyes.

"Outside in ten," he said, turning on his heel and leaving the crew staring after him.

They left the city, trudging out over open land like a reluctant expedition. It was bright and sunny but not orangey like it had been in Jakensk. Jenna wondered why. She looked around the green and beautiful land, breathing in the purest air.

Finding an area of flat ground, Brash got them to sit in a circle. None of them, apart from Fraza, felt very comfortable. It was a little too touchy-feely. Fraza, on the other hand, was in desperate need of friendship. The Kaledian stepped from side to side before he finally sat down. Newark wondered how the hell this little freak got through the day.

"Right," Brash said, "we're going to go around the circle and each of you will tell us your forename."

"Don't you know their forenames?" Jenna asked, surprised.

He should know. Their names would have been on their application forms. But he'd never paid much attention. The old Captain would have lied. The old Captain wouldn't be sitting in a circle with them now. This one, however, was starting over.

"No. Now," he said, "Jenna, yours is a given. Fraza, is that a forename or surname?"

"It is a forename," the Kaledian replied in his alien accent, scratching his ear incessantly. "Do you want to know my surname?"

"No. We'll stick with Fraza. Graham, what's your forename?"

"Graham, sir," Graham replied.

"No, Graham, your forename."

"Graham, sir. That's it."

"Your parents named you Graham?"

"Yeah…" He scratched his neck. "My dad was a bit of a joker, sir."

"*Okay*… Well, let's move on to you, Johnson."

"Darius, sir," she answered.

"Darius? Isn't that a boy's name?"

Johnson sniffed. "My mother wanted a boy, sir. She thought the name had some clout."

Brash stared at her, so much becoming clear. "Right, well, do… you like that name?"

"Not really, sir."

"Do you want to change it?"

Johnson looked at him. The possibility had never occurred to her. "Yes…"

"OK, then. What will it be?"

Still staring at him, she thoughtfully murmured, "Daria."

"Great. Daria, it is. Now, Newark, you're up." Brash had no idea what to expect next.

"John," Newark replied.

"Really?"

"Yes, sir."

"Good. Skinner?" Skinner was leaning back on his elbows, staring up at the sky. "Skinner? Your forename?"

Skinner's head came down. "Jeremy, sir."

Newark laughed. Skinner ignored him and went back to staring at the sky.

"And what's your name, Captain?" Jenna asked.

"My name is Lucas."

Lucas, Jenna thought. She liked that name.

"Now that's done, we're going to split into two teams and start off with some racing. For today, we'll use forenames. Jenna, Newark and Fraza, you're on one team. Graham, Johnson and Skinner will be on the other."

"You only used three forenames, sir," Johnson pointed out.

"Well spotted… Daria." The word sounded weird on his tongue. He had to force himself to use it.

The Captain pitched out the starting and ending points and the teams entered several relay races. Fraza ran like an ungainly duck but he could fair shift. The rest of the crew threw themselves into it too, apart from

Skinner, who needed to be coaxed. "Get your fucking shit together, Skinner!" Johnson yelled, shoving him hard.

"It's *Jeremy!*" Newark called out, laughing.

By the end of all the races, most of the crew were smiling and Brash smiled when he saw Newark and Jenna high-five each other. Even Skinner was being pulled out of his apathy. Brash thought there was nothing like doing child-like things to bring out the real person.

After racing, he led them to the river to set about a raft-building challenge. He was surprised by how much enthusiasm the teams showed. But then, apart from the water park, which nobody wanted to revisit, there wasn't an awful lot to do in this city. It was too wholesome. The residents seemed to get off on meditating.

The rafts were terrible and they all got wet but that didn't matter. They had fun. They laughed, they joked, and, in the crew's eyes, Fraza had turned from a weird little freak to a weird little crewmember.

Throughout it all, Brash's attention kept straying to Jenna. He found her laughter and smiles uplifting. She might not want him like he wanted her but he wanted her to have some fun. For he knew, right down to the bones of him, she had never had any before.

"Captain!" Newark said, pointing at the sky.

The Captain followed the direction of his gaze. A black dot in the distance was heading this way. It was some kind of craft.

"Take cover," Brash called.

Crouching under bushes, they stared up as the craft went by. "It's one of ours," Skinner remarked.

"The Admiral's looking for Jenna," Brash said thoughtfully, glancing at the girl, who was staring back at him.

"Surely, they saw the buildings?" Graham asked, staring up in wonder. "Why aren't they stopping?"

Brash scratched his head. It seemed the Admiral had not given up on his daughter. But if that was the case, they would have set down here, checked out the city. It made no sense... unless it had something to do with that shield.

He was drawn from his thoughts by the sight of Jenna running off.

"Come on, let's head back," Brash said, walking on ahead.

When he got back to the accommodation, Brash gently knocked on Jenna's door. She didn't answer but he heard her crying. Tentatively, he opened the door. She spun around, looking at him angrily. "You think I'm weak and pathetic, don't you? Think I'm getting upset because I want to run home to daddy!"

Brash shook his head. "No. I think you're incredibly strong. You love your father and it must be killing you to know he's worried about you. You didn't even try to flag down that craft." He smiled at her gently and she stared back at him. It was like somebody understood her for the first time.

"Well," he said, "you know where I am if you want me." He turned to leave.

"Wait."

Brash turned back around.

"I want you," she whispered.

# Getting Your Bearings

The crew sat, staring up into space. Space was all around them. The 3D observatory dome was like being suspended in space. Jenna gazed at the stars, thinking about the heavenly experience she'd had last night. *So, that was what all the fuss was about.* She discreetly glanced at Brash to find him glancing around at her. He looked even more handsome today. The soft strands of his dark hair, grown over the past weeks, teased his face and neck, giving him an edgier appearance. *Lucas...* she thought, trying out the name. With his new hair and new name, Jenna thought he seemed younger somehow. She hadn't spoken to him since last night. She'd woken up this morning to find his side of the bed empty. Was that supposed to happen after these things? She had no point of reference, only overheard conversations. *'He scarpered faster than a dose of diarrhoea.' 'Yeah, they all do that.'*

Cornelius, standing on a platform, glowed in the dark. His white clothes, he informed them, were fluorescent. He was holding a fluorescent white stick and the whole thing gave him a god-like appearance.

"This is where you are now," Cornelius said, pointing with the stick. "I believe you call it the Milky Way Galaxy. And this," he said extending his stick to the left and circling a large region, "is the area under the control of the Thunder God, who, from now on, will be referred to as SLOB."

"SLOB?" Brash asked.

"Sick Little Obnoxious Bastard. I refuse to call him Thunder God." The crew nodded in agreement. "As you can see, his area of influence is large and it is growing fast."

Skinner's mind was starting to kick in again. "To cover such an area, he must have extremely advanced technology."

"Yes. We believe he has what is called, a Super Mega HyperDrive."

"What do we have?" Brash asked, expectantly.

"Nothing."

"You mean we have a bog-standard craft?"

"No, Captain. I mean, we don't have any craft."

The crew stared at Cornelius, waiting for some sense to come out of him. "What are we going to do then?" Newark asked. "Take an aruk to the other side of the freaking universe?"

"No, Mr Newark. The Erithians are going to... open a doorway."

Skinner's slouched body hauled itself up by the elbows. "And how, exactly, are they going to do that?"

"They are going to use the power to create an opening in the space-time continuum."

"They're going to use their minds...?" Skinner asked incredulously. "Where's the science in that?"

"Are you insane...?" Johnson asked with equal incredulity.

Cornelius spoke to their concerns. "Yes, they are using their minds but only to direct the power. There is no science in the universe to explain it. No, I am not insane. You see," he said, stroking his chin and looking at them thoughtfully, "reality is not all it seems. It's... malleable at a certain level of consciousness. Space and time are constructs of this universe but..." And here was where he would lose them, "they do not exist in isolation. They exist within consciousness itself."

"He's a fruitcake!" Newark exclaimed.

"I knew it," Johnson agreed.

Cornelius pressed on. "This is how the Erithians know about what's going on zillions of miles away. You might say they're psychic but they are just tapping into the oneness of the field."

"How do we know anything is going on zillions of miles away?" Graham asked. "We've only got your word for it."

"Yes. I'm afraid, at this point in time, that's true. But when we open the doorway and you find yourselves in a distant galaxy, you'll have more than my word for it."

"Is it like a wormhole?" Jenna asked. The others turned to her.

Cornelius smiled. "Sort of."

"Is it safe?"

"Yes."

"And we don't need a craft to get through it?"

"No. You see, on a fundamental level, every point in the universe is connected to every other point. Using the power, we open a gate from one point to another. It literally is like stepping through a door."

"Then how would we get back?" Brash asked, unconvinced by this.

"You acquire the Super Mega HyperDrive. But you'll need to acquire your own craft before that."

"If the Erithians can do all this shit," Newark asked suspiciously, "why don't *they* take out SLOB?"

"They cannot do that, I'm afraid."

"Why?" Brash asked with equal suspicion.

"You've heard enough for one day."

"Why?" Brash demanded.

Cornelius assessed the man. "Very well, Captain. Because the Erithians are not from this dimension."

The crew stared at him.

"Not from this universe...?" Brash asked.

"Correct."

"That's impossible..."

"He *is* a fruitcake," Johnson affirmed.

Cornelius inhaled, assessing them all. "There is much more to reality than this one dimension. Indeed, there are many things that the brain cannot grasp. I'm afraid you will just have to trust me on this."

"What *are* the Erithians then?" Jenna asked.

"The bodies that you see are hard light representations of their more ethereal bodies."

"Like ghosts?"

"Something like that. But not. They have lowered their vibration to come here at a time when the physical universe is in crisis. They exist within the area protected by the shield... the area where their reality is bisecting yours. They have picked this point in space-time to meet me... and you."

"But they have a water park," Newark said.

"Yes."

"And children."

"Yes. They have lives in their dimension but they have no disease or war and a far greater understanding of the totality of things."

"So, they've come here for us," Jenna reflected soberly.

"Yes, and though they can help in certain ways, they cannot actively intervene. It's like a mother raising her children. She might want to give them a hand up but she doesn't want to live their lives for them. If she did, what would be the point of the child?"

"Can someone explain all this?" Newark asked helplessly.

"Yes," Jenna said, thoughtfully. "From some higher dimension, the Erithians saw what was happening here because they are closely connected to the field. They lowered their densities to come here to train Cornelius to train us to kill SLOB. They can send us through space-time but that's as much as they can do; one, because they're stuck here and two, because they can't get too involved. If they did, our destinies would not be our own and it would be pretty pointless."

The crew all stared at Jenna. Cornelius stared at her, his face brightening in a smile. "In a nutshell, yes."

Jenna looked up at him. "They came here to train you but... was SLOB even born then?"

"No."

"Then...?"

"As I have said, Llamia has the gift of prophecy but this is just her tapping into the field. Everything is contained in the field, even the future."

"But the future can't be known."

"No, you are right. The future she sees is based on present circumstances. Change the circumstances, change the future. So, in effect, what she sees is a future echo."

"Does she see us defeating SLOB?"

"This isn't known yet."

"Why?"

"Because that depends on the choices you make."

"I'm lost," Newark said.

"Do you understand, Jenna?" Cornelius asked.

"I think so."

He smiled. "You really are a clever girl, aren't you?"

No-one had ever called her clever before. She glanced at Brash to find him staring at her. The look was almost reverent.

"I'm not sure about this door thing, sir," Johnson said to Brash as they left the observatory. "I reckon we're all going to get fried."

"Maybe this story's just a spiel," Skinner pondered, "to get us to test out some new thing they've invented."

"What do you think, Jenna?" Brash asked, turning to her. All heads flicked in her direction.

"I trust Cornelius," she said.

Newark shook his head. "You trust everyone."

"Not anymore," she shot, holding onto some lingering resentment. "Besides, this power is real. You've seen it yourselves. Cornelius has been training me to use it."

"You're going there now, are you?" Brash asked and she nodded. "Can I watch?"

"Jenna, I'll meet you at my dojo," Cornelius interrupted as he walked past. "I just need to talk to Llamia."

She watched Cornelius walk away then turned back to Brash. As the others dispersed, she nodded.

They were awkward as they walked side by side through the streets, Brash wondering what last night had meant to her. Erithians smiled at them as they went by.

"They don't look the same now, do they?" Brash said and Jenna glanced at him. "Now we know they're not from this universe."

"Oh, I don't know... It sort of makes them more understandable, somehow."

He turned to her with a gentle smile. "You look at things a little differently, don't you?"

She shrugged. They fell into silence again until Brash suddenly said, "We need to talk."

Now, to Jenna, this was an innocuous comment, so it came as a surprise when Brash said, "Last night cannot happen again."

A brick fell through her stomach and she stared at him, lost.

"No, I mean, we have to be more careful," he insisted. "The crew cannot know about this. It sets up an unhealthy dynamic."

"So... you're saying we should sneak around behind everyone's backs?"

"Yes. No, I mean, we should be discreet. Meet up in private, perhaps. That's if you want to?"

She smiled. "Can I call you Lucas in private?"

He smiled back. "You can call me anything you want."

He had the impulse to lean down and kiss her but he stopped himself.

"I see we have an audience today," Cornelius said as he entered the dojo. Brash nodded his head to the man then went to sit in an ornate chair in the corner.

"Now," Cornelius said to Jenna, "we'll pick up where we left off, with the sparring, OK?"

"OK."

She and Cornelius stood to face each other, a few metres apart in the centre of the room. They braced themselves, digging their feet into the floor. Brash watched, waiting for something to happen. It never did. When Cornelius smiled and congratulated her, Brash was taken aback.

"Err, what just happened?" he asked.

"Jenna is getting stronger," Cornelius informed him.

"Right," he said, scratching his head.

"Watch this, Captain Brash. I'll offer no resistance this time."

They stood to face each other again and this time Cornelius flew back through the air, smashing against the wall. Brash stared at the cracks in the plaster. Cornelius did too. They needed a bigger room.

After that, Brash watched Jenna levitate objects like those freaky little children; he even watched her levitate herself, hanging suspended in the air like some supernatural being.

"What the crap!" he exclaimed.

Jenna fell back to earth with a painful thud.

"Keep working on that focus," Cornelius said. "Nothing should distract you."

"How did she do that...?" Brash asked, dazed.

"She is marshalling the power. In this case, directing it beneath her to lift her up. Before, she was marshalling it against me, and tomorrow we are going for a total body shot."

"Total body shot...?" Brash asked, gazing at Jenna.

"That's where the power is unleashed from every point of your being. We'll do that outside," he noted to himself.

Brash couldn't stop staring at Jenna. Jenna felt uncomfortable. She wasn't sure if this would affect their relationship. For his part, Brash needed to get his bearings. Things were moving so quickly. Doors in space, beings from another dimension, Jenna performing miraculous feats. She seemed to be taking all this in her stride but he needed time to process it.

What Brash didn't know was that Jenna was trying to get her bearings too. She'd never had a relationship before, didn't know what they involved and how to deal with them. She was experiencing a riot of feelings, the most predominant one being panic. *Lucas thought she was a freak!* The relationship was ended before it had begun. The panic turned to hurt and anger. Another thing Brash didn't know was that since her training had begun, extremes of emotion could lead to bursts of uncontrolled power. He didn't know this as his chair slammed back against the wall, throwing him onto the floor. He looked up, watching her race out through the flimsy doors.

He turned to Cornelius.

"Be gentle with her," Cornelius said. "For all our sakes."

# Remarkable Progress

"You were a virgin?"

"Err... yes."

"Really? I wouldn't have guessed."

Jenna tried to figure out if being a virgin was a good thing or a bad thing. It was definitely some kind of thing. For Captain Brash, it was an unusual thing and it brought up another question. "Have you ever had a boyfriend?"

"No," she quietly admitted.

"No?"

She felt herself getting cross. "They weren't exactly queuing up."

He stared at her, something becoming clear. "You've got some catching up to do," he said, grabbing her hand.

"Where are we going?"

"We're going to take a walk in the countryside."

They didn't do much walking. They christened their new relationship in a muscle-clenching, hair-grabbing, grass-smearing way and, for the first time in her life, Jenna felt truly wanted.

She walked into the dojo that afternoon as if floating on air. When she caught sight of Cornelius watching her, she attempted to straighten her hair. As a slight smile creased his lips, her embarrassment turned to anger. "Why do I always feel you are reading my mind?"

"I don't have to read your mind. Your clothes are a mess, there are grass stains on them and when you walked in you had sex written all over your face."

Jenna stared at him. Then she straightened. "That's beside the point. I don't want you reading my mind. It's not right."

"I don't do that unless I feel it is absolutely necessary. Now, shall we press on?"

"What are we doing today?" she mumbled, off-hand.

"Do you want to learn how to mind-read?"

"*Yeah.*"

Shaking his head, he smiled. "As I have just said, it is only to be used when appropriate, not for eavesdropping or any other gratuitous reasons.

It can take a long time to master it but if I give you the basics, you can practice on your own. If you join our meditation group, this will greatly enhance your ability."

Knowing she wasn't sold on the meditation group, he instructed her to lie on the floor.

"Now," he said, "your mind can act as a transmitter or a receiver. But it has to be in a certain state. It has to be relaxed and empty. So, relax and empty your mind. I am going to transmit certain thoughts. See if you can pick anything up."

After ten minutes of trying, Cornelius sighed. "Jenna, your relationship with Captain Brash must not be allowed to interfere with your training."

"It isn't," she insisted.

"I've just spent the last ten minutes getting a graphic re-run of your morning with Captain Brash." He shivered. "I am not a voyeur, so if you can't get past this, we need to leave it there today."

Jenna sat up. "You were supposed to be transmitting not receiving."

"My channel was open. Unfortunately, I got the adult channel."

She cringed. "Sorry. I didn't realise what I was thinking."

"That's the point. Thoughts tend to have a life of their own. Pay attention to your mind, get to know it. That will help you be more open to reading others' minds."

"What about the rest of the crew? Shouldn't they train their minds?"

"That could lead to all kinds of problems. A crew that can read each other's thoughts?"

"Yeah... I wouldn't want Newark reading my mind," Jenna reflected soberly. "I wouldn't want to read his."

"No, believe me, you wouldn't. And I'll give you some advice. If you should ever develop this ability, don't go peeping into Captain Brash's head. Your relationship would only suffer. You must only use this ability when necessary."

"You won't tell the others, will you? About me and Captain Brash?"

Cornelius shook his head. "I'm not interested in tittle-tackle. But from now on, please leave Captain Brash at the door."

So, she did leave Brash at the door. After a lifetime of inadequacy, she wanted to be all she could. Captain Brash managed to leave Jenna at the door too. After years of being a rubbish captain, he wanted to be a better one. He wanted to build a truly effective, cohesive team. His team building activities became a twice-weekly event and the crew looked forward to them. For Jenna, it was a respite from her training, a chance to forget the seriousness of their mission.

Skinner was, at last, finding his point of integration, throwing himself into activities with a fearlessness he'd never known before. The crew watched him leap into rivers without a thought for what was in there. The sight of Skinner brought a poignant reflection to Brash. He considered it sad that so many adventurous spirits were trapped beneath layers of personality. He wondered how Flint was getting on.

Newark was taking Fraza under his wing but the Captain wasn't sure Fraza wanted to be taken under his wing. Fraza's latent aggression came out in the dojo. Jenna and Fraza raced to grab Newark and when Fraza claimed him, he would throw everything he had at Newark. Newark, proud to be in popular demand, threw out words of encouragement, which made Fraza's fists pump harder.

Cornelius was becoming proud of his little fledglings. They were making progress. He started to train Jenna and Fraza together, trying to get them to use their combined power. Jenna's power was like a 150-watt bulb to Fraza's 40 watt, but 40 watts could make the difference, Cornelius told himself.

Cornelius continued with Jenna's mind training, although, much to her frustration, she couldn't seem to master it. Not one thought had passed into the corridors of her mind. Cornelius invited her to go beyond the mind to pay attention to her instincts. The girl had good instincts, though they had been overshadowed by years of self-doubt. Now, he was encouraging them to come to the fore. As they wandered through the gardens outside his dojo, Cornelius asked her to tune in to the forces around her... the heat on her skin, the breeze, the sounds of nature...

"Let's sit down," he said, leading her to a nearby bench. "Pay attention to what lies beneath. There's an energy around us that speaks to us. Tune in to it. It is one with your own energy and it whispers to you constantly. Listen to what it has to say."

"Newark's in trouble!"

They looked around to see Johnson running over.

"I'm in the middle of a session with Jenna," Cornelius said patiently.

"Newark's got his head stuck in a railing and we might need your magic to get him out. The animals have gone berserk. His face is a mess."

Cornelius drew in a deep breath then let it out slowly. Getting to his feet, he said, "Lead the way."

Johnson led them through the streets toward the petting zoo. She was jogging, the others walking at a brisk pace. Cornelius refused to jog.

"What happened?" Cornelius called to her.

Johnson dropped back. "Newark said he wanted to come to the zoo with us but he started throwing stones at the animals. We tried to stop him. Then he shoved his head through the railing to make strange faces and disgusting noises. They're biting his face now. There was no-one around to help."

They arrived to see Newark's backside sticking out. He was cursing, raging and screaming. "Get the fuckers off me!" he yelled, his bloodied hands frantically batting the creatures away.

Jenna winced at the sight of his bloody face. For the first time, she felt sorry for Newark.

"Can you get him out of there?" Graham pressed. "We've had to throw stones at them to keep them off but they just keep coming back. And they're vicious. I've never seen them like this before. I thought they were pets?"

"They are but they don't like abuse," Cornelius said. "Why should they?"

"They're that intelligent?"

"They're from another dimension, Mr Graham. Of course, they're intelligent."

"*Do* something!" Newark yelled. "They're eating me alive!"

"Jenna," Cornelius said, turning to her. "This is a perfect opportunity. Open the bars."

Swallowing hard, she turned to Newark and focused on the bars. Opening herself up to the power, she imagined two hands pulling the bars apart, directing the power into those hands. The metal creaked then the bars broke. Stunned for a moment, Graham grabbed Newark as his head came free. The pets came through too, wanting more blood. Cornelius went over to stroke them and, at last, they settled down.

Newark's face was a mess. He looked to be in a lot of pain, his eyes screwed shut.

"Newark, how are you feeling, bud?" Graham asked.

"How d'you fucking think I'm feeling?" he said, shaking.

"His body's going into shock," Cornelius observed.

"Do something!" Jenna urged.

"You do something," he said back to her and she looked at him, confused. "The power isn't just for moving things. It is an all-encompassing, all-purpose entity. You can direct it in any way you want."

Dragging her gaze away from the man, she stared down at Newark. The others moved aside as she knelt next to him. Letting her hands hover over his face, she closed her eyes and focused, allowing the power to come through, imagining it pouring into every damaged cell, healing each cell. She carried on until she heard Johnson gasp and Graham swear.

She opened her eyes to see brown eyes staring back at her. The face, though blood-stained, was back to normal.

"I fucking love this girl," a pain-free Newark cried, grabbing her arms and giving her a loud kiss on the cheek.

Cornelius watched Jenna, intrigued. She was a natural. She'd just done what it took others years to achieve.

Newark glanced at the creatures, who were paying him no attention now. "Vicious fuckers. Remind me never to do that again."

Result, Cornelius thought, his eyes returning to Jenna. She was making remarkable progress. He just hoped it would be enough.

# Good Day to be a God

The Thunder God eyed the body with disdain. "Someone get rid of that," he spat. He turned to his Third-in-Command. "Find me some candidates. I'm interviewing for the post of Second-in-Command in five minutes." He paused "Do you want to apply, Manghar?"

"Well, I would, Lord, but I've got some other, excellent candidates in mind." Bowing graciously, the Hellgathen scuttled out, trying to think of who he could sell this to.

"I'm behind schedule," the Thunder God complained, turning to his generals. The holographic map of the universe hung in the centre of the room. "Look how much I've got to do."

None of them wanted to comment.

Taking a deep steadying breath, he studied the map. "Where to go next?" He tapped his fingers on his leg. "Any suggestions?" He looked around, catching someone's eye.

The man felt compelled to speak. "This area should crumble easily, Lord," he said, pointing at the map. "As far as we can ascertain, this group of planets is fragmented and fractious."

"Yes..." the Thunder God said ponderously. "But then they're hardly challenging, are they?" He gave out a weary sigh. "Sometimes it all just seems too... easy."

The generals didn't know how to respond to that. He wanted the job done quickly, yet he wanted challenge. How could they win?

The Thunder God stared at the map for several moments. "Formulate some options. I'll look them over. You may go." He waved them away.

Turning his back on the map, he went to sit on his black leather throne, looking around idly. He wondered what the people of his home would say if they could see him now. Suddenly, he sat up straight. Why hadn't he thought of this before? Hellgathen. That's where he would go next. He'd do a little gloating and punishing before blasting the place to smithereens. He rubbed his hands together. Today was a good day to be a god.

"The little shit's a monster!"

"Hush! He'll hear you. Then you'll end up like this one." The man pressed a button and the former Second-in-Command was unceremoniously discharged into space.

"He should have had a proper funeral. No-one gets a proper funeral. I didn't sign up for this!" Serza banged his fist into the wall. "I'm thinking of going off to join the resistance."

"There is no resistance."

"None?"

"You're either with him or your dead. No-one can stand against him, you know that. He has super fucking natural powers!"

"D'you think he *is* a god?"

"No, I think he's the devil."

Serza went to stand before the window, looking out at the blackness of space. It seemed hopeless. He thought about his family on Hellgathen. He wished he was back there with them now. At least, he knew they were safe. That was the Thunder God's home planet. Even gods don't shit on their own patch.

The Thunder God's mood was dampening. Why was Manghar taking so damn long! Pressing the intercom, he yelled, "Manghar!!!"

A few moments later, Manghar came running in, dragging a Lorien with him. Loriens were ugly creatures, the Thunder God considered, flinching. Their light green flesh looked like it was peeling.

"The first candidate, Lord," Manghar announced, slinging the man forward.

The Thunder God looked the candidate over. Where the hell had he dragged him up from? The man was shaking infuriatingly. What the God of Thunder didn't know was that the man was there because Manghar had pulled a gun to his head.

"Name?" The Thunder God asked.

"Kinthz, sir."

"And if you get the job, how would you approach your new leadership role?"

"Well, sir," he said, rubbing his flaky hands together nervously, "I t-tend to go for a more hands-off approach. You know, l-let the men be a little creative. Find I get a lot more out of them that way. After all," he said with a high-pitched laugh, "we're not a dictatorship."

The Thunder God shot to his feet. "We are a dictatorship!"

"Oh, yes but..."

"You're fired!" The steaming pile on the floor lay testament to the fact that the Thunder God was being literal.

"I'll get the next one," Manghar said, darting out of the door.

The God had to endure three more rejects and, in the end, Manghar was forced to tell him the truth. "Nobody wanted the j-job, sir."

"No-one wanted the job? Why?"

"The m-men are all s-scared of you, sir."

"Well, of course they're scared of me but that shouldn't interfere with a promotion. Their one purpose should be to satisfy their god!"

"Yes, Lord."

"Do they not love their god?"

"Y-Yes, Lord."

"Not enough, obviously." He paced around, irritated beyond words. All at once, he thought of a solution. He turned to Manghar. "Every fortnight there will be a devotional ceremony. Sort it out. And get Rotzch. He's being promoted. And bring back my generals. We're setting a course for Hellgathen."

# Blinding Circle of light

Weeks had turned to months. Cornelius felt it was almost time to let his fledglings go. Jenna had come so far in her training and he felt he had taught her as much as he could. The rest was up to her. Captain Brash had become the captain he was capable of being, responding to his crew in a more mature, more responsible, more insightful way. Because of his new leadership, his crew was a more cohesive team, managing to absorb Jenna and Fraza as their own. He hoped Newark had become a little more thoughtful. Newark was an asset, he knew that, but the man had to have more foresight. Hopefully, having his face chewed off had given him some pause for thought. Yes, all in all, he was proud of his team, and a little sad now that their time here was almost over.

Jenna and Brash had managed to keep their relationship under wraps, sneaking off into the gardens after dark, or meeting up outside the city. Jenna had wanted to know all there was to know about Lucas. He had joined the corps at eighteen, coming from a reasonably humble background but driving his way up by sheer ambition.

"Did you have brothers and sisters?" she asked.

"A younger brother and a younger sister. Haven't spoken to them in years. Raima and Charlie…" His eyes took on a sad reflective quality.

"I suppose you're doing this for them," she said softly.

"They've probably got families of their own now."

"You never wanted to settle down?"

He glanced at her. "I never saw that for myself. But then I never saw any of this."

"Do you think we're going to die, Lucas?"

He smiled at her sadly. "It's a possibility. But at least, if we do, we'll die trying."

She lay back and stared at the stars. "It's hard to die when you've only just started to live."

He lent over her, brushing hair from her face. "We'll try our best not to let that happen." His lips connected with hers and he kissed her more gently than he had kissed any woman.

Jenna wondered what the women on Osiris would think if they could see her now.

Today, Cornelius had invited them to come to the observatory. They got there to find space switched off. Jenna stared at the white dome, wondering when it would start up. When she looked down again, she saw Llamia standing on the platform.

Llamia smiled at them with that strange, almost-there smile. Johnson glanced at Graham and found herself getting cross.

"It has been an honour to have you as our guests," Llamia said, glancing fleetingly at Newark. Jenna glanced at him too, wondering what he was thinking. "Cornelius informs me that your time here is at an end."

She paused for this to go in. The whole crew, even Newark, felt a strange pang of sadness. There might not have been any bars here but with Brash's inventiveness and Cornelius training sessions, they had come to settle, even if they hadn't quite realised it.

"I want to congratulate you," Llamia continued, "on your hard work and commitment." She looked at them more seriously. "You are now what this universe depends on. You must be more than you think you are capable of being. You must rise beyond even your highest expectations. The dark force calls himself a Thunder God. But there are no gods and, from a certain perspective, there are no limits... only delusions and self-imposed barriers. Tomorrow, we will open the portal and send you off with all our blessings. Please don't feel anxious about this. It is perfectly safe."

"Have you been through it?" Johnson asked, a little offhand. She received one of those infuriatingly superior smiles.

"I have travelled through similar doorways, yes." Llamia looked around. "Does anyone have anything else they wish to ask of me?"

Newark stuck his hand up and Llamia replied before he could ask. "I'm afraid that will not be possible, Mr Newark."

"Where are you sending us?" Brash asked.

"The planet is called Hellgathen, in the Spearos Galaxy. It is the birthplace of the dark force. We will be placing you just west of the capital, Akmenuth. You will need warm clothing as it will be cold there and this has been provided for you."

"Do you have any weapons for us?"

"No. You will need to acquire these yourselves."

Jenna surprised them all with the next question. "Do you have faith in me, Llamia?"

Llamia's violet eyes rested on her. "Do you have faith in yourself, Jenna?"

"Nobody's ever had faith in me before. Why me?"

"Why not? Other people's faith can only take you so far and they're just reflecting how much faith you have in yourself. Stop looking in the mirrors. Look inside yourself. Remember, there are only delusions and self-imposed limitations. Both are falsehoods. They need to be shed."

The crew were lost. Her words seemed only to register with Jenna and Fraza.

"Cornelius will come for you in the morning," Llamia said, smiling at them with such compassion it made Newark want to cry.

As she walked down off the platform, Cornelius took her place. "Rest tonight. Get a good night's sleep. I'll save my leaving speech for tomorrow."

The crew were quiet as they headed home. Jenna hung back with Cornelius. "I'm really going to miss you," she said.

"I'm going to miss you. I'll miss Mr Newark too. He made life... interesting."

"You can keep him if you like?" she joked.

He smiled. "No, I'm sure he'll come in handy."

"What about Flint?"

"Mr Flint will be staying with us a little longer."

"Won't the Erithians be leaving now?"

"Not yet. They will leave when my time is through."

Her face crumpled. "You mean when you die?"

"Yes. I'm getting older. A few more years is nothing to them."

Tears clouded her vision. "I hope I get to see you again, Cornelius."

"So do I." The old man did something unexpected. He hugged her tightly.

It was another fine day as Cornelius led them out of the city. The crew were feeling extremely anxious. Would this doorway work? What would they do when they got there? They didn't know what they were up against. They were completely winging it. The only thing they had, apart from the layers of clothes they were sweltering in, was a digital map Brash had in his pocket. It gave a layout of the universe, and a more detailed layout of the region they were, ever so soon, going to be plunged into.

All the Erithians were out, standing in one gigantic circle. Cornelius led them into the circle.

"By the way," he said to Jenna, "Flint wishes you the best of luck. He also wants to thank you for saving his life."

"He's not come out to see us off?" she asked, disappointed.

"No. He's not yet up to facing the others. And he's at a very delicate stage."

"I see. Tell him goodbye from me then."

Cornelius positioned the crew well away from the centre. "Do not move from this spot until the doorway appears," he said seriously. "Now," he said, looking around at them all, "I'll make this short. Really proud of you all. I know you'll kick ass. Mind your step when you walk through."

And, with that, the man left the circle. The Erithians closed their eyes and raised their hands. The crew looked at each other with immense trepidation. Brash took hold of Jenna's hand as the air became highly charged. A mini whirlwind sped around them, picking up leaves and bits of twig and grass. The pressure became acute. The wind intensified. They had to brace themselves against it. Suddenly, the air cracked like a whip and a blinding circle of light appeared. The crew stared at it.

"Go through!" Cornelius shouted. "Quickly! This takes a lot of effort! Oh, and bear east!"

The crew glanced at him. Brash, still holding onto Jenna, went through first until all the crew had disappeared.

The light vanished. Arms came down and Llamia turned to Cornelius. "What do you think their chances are?"

"Well, I wouldn't put odds on them."

# Tipping Point

The ground fell away. Brash and Jenna dropped three feet, landing clumsily on cold, hard earth. Moments later, bodies were falling on top of them. Brash pulled Jenna out from under them then stood up, looking around. The sky was thick and grey. Spiky, ice-covered mountains cut the skyline in the distance. Frosty wilderness stretched around them.

"We're alive!" Johnson exclaimed, her breath misting in front of her. Fraza was doing some strange little ritual but the crew paid him no attention.

"We need to find the city," Brash said.

"Which way?" Graham asked.

"East."

"Which way's east?"

"Good question." Brash got out his pocket map but there was no detailed map of Hellgathen.

"East?" Newark asked, looking around. "Was the old man taking the piss?"

They looked up as a craft flew by. It was coming from the direction of the mountains.

"That craft is flying from somewhere to somewhere," Skinner said thoughtfully.

"No shit," Newark remarked.

"As the Erithians wouldn't have us trudging over mountains, I say we follow the direction of the craft."

Brash nodded. "Agreed."

They set off, hiking over frosty moorland. They kept their eyes peeled but saw no signs of life.

"It's weird to think we're in another part of the universe," Jenna said, looking around.

"That's if they've dropped us in the right place," Newark remarked.

"Look," Johnson said, pointing. "There's a road over there."

Brash caught hold of an exuberant Newark. "We'll keep off the road. But we'll follow its course."

The road was no more than a cart-track - chewed up mud hardened into ridges by the ice.

"This can't be the road," Graham insisted. "It probably leads to some deserted farm or something."

Graham kept complaining that they were going the wrong way but it did turn out to be the main road for, at last, they spotted buildings in the distance. The closer they got, the more disappointed they became. They had imagined a cosmopolitan metropolis but the capital city of Akmenuth was more like a rundown old backwater. The place was drab, the buildings a messy collection of rotting wood, the streets nothing more than that same chewed up mud. The humanoid-looking inhabitants appeared as downtrodden as the place, few bothering to glance up as they passed by. The crew stopped outside a ramshackle building that had a dirty sign hanging over it. Opening the door slightly, Brash peered inside.

Closing the door again, he turned to the crew. "I think this is the pub." The crew tried to hide their jubilation. "Now, our primary objective is to find weapons and a craft. So, we need to find a military base. We're going to enter this place and get as much information as we can. Fraza, do you think you can pick up the language?"

"I will try, Captain," Fraza replied, rubbing his ears vigorously. Stepping from side to side, he followed the rest of them in.

The scruffy-looking place was half-empty. The voices they heard had a harsh-sounding dialect. They sat down at a table and looked around warily. Fraza's big ears got to work straight away.

A humanoid with striking blonde hair stood behind the bar, glancing their way every so often. Finally, she came over and began speaking that uncouth-sounding language.

"Canta speaka linga," Newark said and the woman stared at him oddly.

Fraza attempted to have a go. "Kuthz. Zack alliz, henza."

The woman punched Fraza before storming off.

Newark, Skinner, Johnson, and Graham erupted in fits of laughter. "That makes a change," Johnson managed. "It's usually Skinner getting punched."

Fraza sat there, shocked, as if he had never been punched in his life. Newark couldn't figure it.

Jenna noticed a repulsive-looking thing, watching them from across the room. Its hideous face had bulging green eyes and its nose looked obscene. A row of blue drinks was lined up in front of it. As the green eyes connected with hers, a shiver ran through her. She watched in horror as it hefted its unseemly weight and waddled over to them. The crew all reached for non-existent weapons.

"You are humans," it said, its mouth not matching the sounds. Newark knew it was doing that strange language implanting thing. "What are you doing so far from home?"

"I'm surprised you've heard of humans here," Brash said, trying to avoid the question.

"Most haven't but I have travelled and studied extensively. Can I buy you all a drink?"

Newark would have snatched his arm off but this being was just far too ugly.

"That would be very good of you," Brash said.

As the creature moved off, Newark whispered, "Captain, I don't trust that thing at all."

"It can communicate with us. We need information. Let me do the talking."

The thing came back, carrying a tray of pink-coloured drinks. Settling its disgusting weight down, it placed the tray on the table. "You'd better keep to the pink drinks if you're not used to this place," it said lightly, his bulging green eyes flicking to Jenna.

"Thank you." Brash reached for a glass.

"My name is Olberax." The creature smiled grotesquely, its dark grey lips curling outward as if possessed with a life of their own. "I'm not from around these parts, either. It's just that the grog here is rather special. I wouldn't try the blue drink, if you're not used to it."

Jenna, Brash, Newark and Fraza sniffed their drinks. The others dove straight in. The stuff nearly blew their heads off.

"Holy shit!" Johnson whelped.

"What's in this stuff?" Graham asked.

"I need the recipe for this," Skinner remarked, studying his drink.

"Your Hellgathen needs a little refining," Olberax said to Fraza. "Although, you seem to have the structuring right. The word for drink is 'zeck'. 'Zack' means sex. So, instead of saying, 'drinks for all, please', you said, 'sex for all, please'. Still, very impressive. What are you, by the way?"

Fraza rubbed his ears vigorously. "I'm Kaledian."

"Kaledian? In all my years, I haven't heard of them. Something always slips through the net." He stared at Fraza oddly. "Is there something wrong with your ears?"

"They're just itchy," Jenna told him, providing the shortest explanation.

Captain Brash tried to be conversational. "So... this place is called Akmenuth?"

"Such as it is," the creature replied. "This planet, I'm afraid, is a god-forsaken hell-hole."

"Right, so... there wouldn't be any military installations here, would there?" Olberax looked at him suspiciously. "Our spacecraft crash-landed and we need to find parts."

"I see... and where were you travelling from?"

Brash wished he had studied the map. "Err... I can't remember the name of the place."

"Well, it must be a spectacular space-craft to get you here from the Milky Way."

"It is," Newark piped up, importantly. "It has the Super Mega HyperDrive."

Brash wanted to slap his hands over his face. Olberax stared at Newark, incredulously. "You work for the Thunder God?"

"Yes," Newark said, beginning to flounder.

Olberax eyes flicked to Jenna in alarm. "I see. Well, I'm sorry, I can't tell you where the military installations are. Enjoy your drinks." He got up and lumbered back to his table. He picked up a drink and threw it back, before chucking back another one.

Jenna watched him, intrigued. Whatever he was, the thing did not approve of SLOB.

"What did you say that for!" Brash shot.

"I was thinking on my feet, Captain," Newark answered, sitting up straighter.

The Captain drew in a long breath. The old Captain would have hit Newark over the head but the new 'team-building' Captain had to give the man credit for trying. "OK, but it is imperative that you let me do the talking from now on. That thing was the only thing we have to communicate with and now you've shut him down."

"But how else could we have got all this way? Should I have mentioned the magic door?"

"*You* don't mention anything." He drew in another breath. "He doesn't know that we don't have something *like* the Super Mega HyperDrive but not. You told him we work for the Thunder God. We need to remain impartial, play our cards close to our chest."

Newark scratched his head. "OK, I'll keep schtum from now on, Captain." *At last,* Brash thought. "But shouldn't that apply to Trot, too, sir?"

"What?" Brash turned around to see her sitting herself down before the vile-looking creature. Exasperated, he got up and went over.

"Excuse me," Jenna said.

The green eyes looked up. As repulsive as they were, she saw a kind of despondency in them. She decided to smile at the thing. "My... friend over there was misleading you. We do not work for the Thunder God."

"What are you doing?" Brash whispered in her ear.

"I'm following my instincts," she whispered back.

The creature's eyes flicked to Brash then back to her. "Then who are you? What are you doing here?"

"First, you need to answer my questions. You are not a huge fan of the Thunder God?"

He laughed bitterly. "The little tow-rag betrayed me."

"You know him?"

"Of course, I know him. I trained him."

Brash and Jenna both stared at the creature.

"His name was Venn. A humanoid being like that woman over there." Olberax pointed at the barmaid with his barely-there chin. He leant closer. "They might look human but their biology is a little different. Things are back to front if you know what I mean."

Brash and Jenna spared a moment to try to figure that out then Brash shook his head. "What d'you mean, he betrayed you?"

"I, like two of your friends, have the power. And so does Venn. I trained him to destroy the universe. End it. End the charade, once and for all." Jenna and Brash gawked at him. "But that is not what he is doing. He is using the universe as his playground for torture and cruelty. He has no intention of ending it. He wants only to rule and be the god I told him he was." Olberax stared at the blue drink before him. "I wanted an end to suffering. I didn't want to perpetuate it..."

Jenna shook her head. "Wait. You trained him to end the universe? Why would you *do* that?"

"Life is completely pointless, my dear."

Confusion gave way to anger. "Who gives you the right to decide what happens to this universe! Who gives you the right to decide to end it! Just because you're a miserable old git with severe problems, doesn't give you the right to decide for the rest of us! Others might want to live, you selfish, fat, ugly git!"

Brash glanced at her then turned to look behind him. Objects were flying all over the place, the patrons ducking and diving out of their way.

"Jenna, calm down," Brash said.

"I want to kill him!" she screamed. "This is all his fault!"

The crew were standing behind her. They weren't sure what was going on but they were ready to annihilate the fucker if needed.

"Calm down, Jenna," Brash repeated, glancing at the creature with disdain. "We have a mission. Calm down and think."

Jenna sucked in deep breaths, forcing herself to calm down. Objects dropped from the air. The bar room was now empty.

"I'm an Ingui," the creature said. "I've lived for nearly two hundred years. You get a different perspective after so many years. I can see there is no point to existence."

"Well," she said through gritted teeth, "it would have been so much better for everyone if you hadn't lived so long, wouldn't it? And just because you can't see any purpose doesn't mean there isn't one. Perhaps you're just too dumb to see it. You're nothing but a... a... a bloody fanatic, imposing your views on everyone else!"

"Well, perhaps you are right, perhaps not, but neither of us wants what is happening now. The thing is, there is no stopping him. I have never known any with such a strong command of the power." He looked at her. "You and your Kaledian friend are no match for the Thunder God."

"SLOB."

"Pardon?"

"That's what we call him."

"Oh."

"Why can't you sort out the mess you have made?"

"His power is stronger than mine."

"Then we could join together. The three of us."

"I'd love to be able to help but you see I was killing myself today. And I think I just reached my tipping point."

"What?"

Olberax huge eyes rolled back and his head fell down on the table.

Brash checked him over. "I think he's dead."

"What!" Jenna exclaimed.

Johnson checked him too. "Yeah, he looks dead, alright."

Jenna stood up and started punching the dead weight over and over.

Loud sounds drew their attention. The sounds of engines and voices and panic. The crew ran outside. Four black craft were descending on the city. One was coming down in the city itself, the other three taking positions on the perimeter.

"It's him," Jenna said, panic seizing her chest.

"How d'you know?" Brash asked.

"I can feel it. Something so overpowering... It's making me feel sick."

The crew stared at Jenna then stared back at the looming black craft.

# A Great Escape

"I'm not ready for this!" Jenna said hysterically. "You heard what he said! I'm no match for him!"

Brash thought fast. "We need to acquire one of those craft. Then we need to start drumming up some support, organise an effective resistance."

"From scratch?" Johnson asked.

"Maybe there is some resistance already. We don't know. We're operating blind here. So, we'll take it a step at a time. Come on, let's see what's going on. Pull your hoods up."

The crew followed the direction of the noise. The noise of the engines had stopped but an alien voice was blasting out over a speaker. Brash cursed that cretin for killing himself. He needed to know what was being said.

Assembled masses had gathered in a large square. The crew hovered behind a sea of blonde heads, struggling to make out what was going on. The black craft was clearly visible but they couldn't see who was speaking. Brash looked around then climbed up onto a wall. An ominous-looking figure caught his eye but it was a blonde-haired, scrawny-looking figure that was doing the talking. *That couldn't be the Thunder God, could it?* No. It had to be the other guy.

"Can you make out any of this?" Brash asked Fraza.

"No, Captain, but judging by the expressions on everyone's faces, it doesn't look good."

Brash glanced around to see terror on every face. He whipped his head back. The talking had stopped and the blonde-haired man was searching the crowd. Brash wondered what he was looking for. Whatever it was, he was distracted by an old man walking forward. The old man was pleading with him, grovelling at his feet but the blonde just gloated, seeming to enjoy the spectacle. Within moments, the pleading man was writhing in pain. *Holy fuck, that was the Thunder God!* When the writhing stopped, SLOB continued with his diatribe as if nothing had happened. Brash couldn't speak Hellgathen but he knew these people were being well and truly told off. This couldn't end well.

Jumping down, he gathered his crew. "Come on. We need to get to one of those craft."

Leaving the masses behind, they made their way to the outskirts of the city, searching around for the nearest craft. Finding one at last, they kept well out of sight. A small army of about fifty soldiers was standing at the ready. It was hopeless, Brash thought.

Noise erupted back in the city... shouting, screaming, pain-filled cries...

"What the hell's going on!" Jenna exclaimed.

The army before them sprang into action, pouring into the city like an avenging plague. Brash realised the sick bastard was cutting off the citizens means of escape. It was a massacre.

More sounds erupted from inside the craft. To their amazement, a soldier came flying down the gangway, falling lifeless on the ground. Brash's brain clicked into gear. Someone was rebelling, taking out the remaining crew. It was like a gift from the gods.

"Fraza, you'd better speak Hellgathen and quick! Whoever's in there is a rebel and we need to communicate with them before they take off."

Fraza rubbed his ears vigorously. "Kuthz, ger tret ki!" he shouted. "Ger tret!"

A voice came back. "Tret? Fribz tuk ki? Ki Hibsterna?"

"Hibsterna. Fa!"

A nervous-looking young man, with bright blonde hair and fearful eyes, came down the gangway, pointing his weapon as he peered out. "Hibsterna?" he asked, looking over the crew.

"Fa. Hibsterna."

"Launz," the man said, motioning with his weapon for them to come aboard.

"We're in," Fraza said.

Leaving the sick sounds of a dying city behind, the crew ran aboard to find two more dead bodies. The rebel, who didn't seem to know what he was doing, started pressing buttons in an attempt to raise the gangway. Skinner sprang into action straight away. The man was on fire. The Captain had never seen his brain work so fast and he realised just how much of it had been tied up in fear. This Skinner *was* a fucking genius. Before long the craft was moving, leaving the ground and the city behind. Jenna looked out on the scene of carnage below. It seemed unreal, like a slow-motion horror movie.

The rebel started shouting something at them. He began pointing his weapon at the floor.

"I think he wants us to attack," Fraza said.

"No," Brash said definitively. "The other craft will take us out."

"We're experiencing some drag, Captain," Skinner called.

"Drag?"

"Something's pulling us down."

Jenna looked out. A blonde-haired man in a black cloak stood out in bold relief. The carnage around him seemed to exist in a different time frame as his sights were fixed on them. Her insides turned to jelly for she knew, without a shadow of doubt, who that man was, knew that he was dragging this ship down.

"SLOB's doing this!" she yelled.

"Calm down, Jenna," Brash said, crouching before her. "Work against it. You've got the engines on your side."

Despite the panic and dread, she forced herself to calm down. She had to act. Now. Casting SLOB from her mind, she closed her eyes, opening herself up to the power. Allowing it to come through, she marshalled the power, directing it up to the roof of the ship. The ship hovered in a strange tug-of-war but she stayed focused.

"Fraza, can you help her?" Brash called.

Fraza came over and sat beside Jenna, focusing, marshalling the power as she was.

At last, the ship broke free, blasting out of the atmosphere.

"We're free, Captain," Skinner called. "But we have two craft on our tail."

Brash climbed into the cockpit. "Right, Skinner, how do we make this thing shift? Newark, Johnson, Graham, find some weapons, get them firing! Fraza, see if you can get any sense out of that man! Jenna, pull that crazy mind shit again! Help get these bastards off our tail!"

The team pulled together in a way they never had before. The weapons began firing. Jenna used the power to give their craft the edge. It bought them time to locate the controls for the hyperdrive. The last thing they saw before they jumped space was one gigantic, monstrous-looking mothership.

"Who were they!" SLOB raged.

"I don't know, Lord," Rotzch vented, coming out in sympathetic, tactical anger. "They must be from here! Opportunists maybe? Nobody could have known of our arrival!"

Walking around in circles, SLOB started kicking dead bodies, setting the odd one on fire. Nothing would relieve his ire. "One of them had the power," he spat out viciously. He thought of Olberax but it didn't feel like him. Whoever it was, they were putting a chink in his god-like status and he wouldn't stand for it! He would hunt them down and they would suffer! Clenching his fists, he screamed into the air. "Damn it! This was to be a good day! I haven't got to my home village yet!"

Drawing in a deep breath, he forced himself to calm down. "That'll have to wait for another day. Let's get back to the ship."

The blonde-haired rebel was sitting with his head in his hands.

"Did you get much out of him?" Brash asked Fraza.

"His name is Serza. I think that was his home planet. He wanted to save them."

Brash sat down heavily. "What did you say to him before, to get us on the ship?"

"'Ger tret ki' means 'we help you'. The people fleeing for their lives were shouting 'tret'. The other words, I picked up in the bar. 'Hibsterna', I didn't know. I deduced that it meant resistance or rebels. Luckily, I was correct."

"And do you think you can communicate with him now? We need his knowledge of this region. We're going to need to drum up some support, build an army of our own."

"I will try my best, sir."

Brash looked at the Hellgathen. "Tell him we are all sorry." He got up and went over to sit by Jenna. "How are you?" he whispered.

"I failed, didn't I? He was right there, within reach, and all I wanted to do was run."

He discreetly touched her hand. "You weren't ready. None of us expected to see SLOB today. You helped us get away. We need more preparation."

She rubbed her forehead. "He's insane... All those people he just murdered..."

Brash squeezed her hand. "We'll kick his arse somehow."

"But that creature... Olberax. He said I wasn't strong enough."

"That creature was as much a lunatic as SLOB. You're not a lunatic. That's got to count for something. Besides, SLOB's not seen you when you're angry."

She managed a smile.

"You're very sexy when you're angry, you know."

Her smile broadened.

He smiled back. Then he looked around the flight deck. Skinner, sitting in the cockpit area, was doing a more thorough examination of the controls. The rear part of the flight-deck was lined with black, cushioned seating. In the far corner, a table was screwed into the floor and Serza's head was now resting upon it. Fraza looked unsure how to comfort him. Beyond them, was a view of space. There was a view of space behind Brash and up front in the cockpit.

Brash squeezed Jenna's hand as he got up to inspect the rest of the craft. The long loading bay was blindingly white and lined with drop-down seats. To his left, ladder-like steps led up through a hatch. Climbing up, he walked along a narrow gangway, poking his head into small cabins, realising these were where the officers were accommodated. More steps and another hatch led up to a weapons deck.

Newark, Johnson, and Graham turned to him. "They've got some cool shit up here, Captain," Newark said.

"Surprisingly sophisticated for such a small craft," Skinner remarked.

Brash nodded. "Good work today, team," he said and they stared at him. "Fraza's working on the guy downstairs. Hopefully, we'll have a heading soon."

"Captain?" Johnson asked and Brash looked at her. "What sick fuck murders innocent civilians?"

"A twisted sick fuck. At least, now we know what we're dealing with." Brash looked at them seriously before making his way back down.

The others searched the ship, finding food, drink, weapons and, to Fraza's immense joy and surprise, a translator guide for all the systems in the region.

"This is a gift from the gods," Fraza said and Brash stared at him. Two gifts in one day? The crew watched Fraza rubbing his hands together vigorously and couldn't decide if it was an excited ritual or just excitement.

Newark's brow creased. "It won't have English or Kaledian in there, you know?"

"No, but once I learn Hellgathen, the others will be child's play."

"You're that clever?"

"I have a gift for languages."

Newark glanced at Skinner. Two geniuses on one ship? He wondered what he was good at. "Are you better than Flint?" he asked, unable to let the subject go.

"The Kaledian brain works faster than the human brain," Fraza said in a matter-of-fact way. "It has been scientifically proven to have way more connections."

Newark sniffed. "So, it's got more connections. That doesn't prove anything."

Fraza stared at Newark. "Actually, it does."

"This translator is going to help us, right?" Brash asked Fraza.

"We have a chance now," the Kaledian said, looking at him in earnest.

A chance is better than no chance, Brash thought.

"Captain," Jenna said and he turned to her. "I'll see if I can find blankets and places to bunk down." She gave him a meaningful look.

"OK. I'll help you with that." Yes, a chance was better than no chance at all.

# Venulas

Newark watched Serza and Fraza with a fascinated interest. In what seemed like no time at all, they had gone from short awkward sentences to an actual conversation. With their drinks and packet food in front of them on the table, they were huddled into a little unit, which Newark affectionately termed, Serfraza.

"Have we not got a heading yet?" Johnson complained. "I'm sick of eating this packet crap."

Graham and Skinner were in the cockpit, talking about architecture and the basics of good structural design. Graham was starting to go up in Skinner's estimation. Brash and Jenna were 'stretching their legs'. They came back, looking well exercised.

"We have a heading, Captain," Fraza said.

"Hit me."

"Excuse me?"

"I mean, tell me."

"Oh. Serza thinks we should start at Venulas. They are a peaceful, intelligent race but they have a strong force and might be open to persuasion. Serza knows a couple of Venulians. He thinks we might be able to stay with them for a while."

"What's Venulian food like?" Johnson asked.

Venulas was a beautiful place... lush green landscape, rolling hills. It was a moon and the ringed planet it orbited stood out in bold relief against a fading pink sky. Jenna stared at it, beguiled. "It's beautiful, isn't it?"

"Yes," Brash said, staring up at the planet and rubbing a painful ache in his chest.

"Why would anyone want to end this?"

"I don't know... Come on. They're going in."

Jenna turned and followed the others into the circular farmstead. The Venulians were not what she would have expected. The name suggested Venus, the beautiful goddess of love. Consequently, she had imagined beautiful beings. The actual beings were a little less beautiful. Think Shrek with yellow skin. Their eyes, too, were yellow. Still, they were extremely pleasant and welcoming. The large man and woman threw their arms around Serza and, as the crew were Serza's friends, they ushered them in with enthusiasm, pressing their hands together and bowing their heads to each one of them.

The rooms and corridors were circular too. It was like an over-ground burrow. The furniture was half a size too big and when the crew sat down, the chairs drowned them. An old Venulian woman, sitting in the corner, pressed her hands together and smiled. The crew nodded in acknowledgement and smiled back. She never looked away. Just stared and smiled. After a while, the crew looked anywhere but at her, Newark examining some photographs, Fraza rubbing his ears.

When Serza came through and spoke to Fraza, it was a welcome distraction.

"Serza says they are going to feed us," Fraza said. "He's explained our mission here. He has told them what happened in Hellgathen. Tomorrow, Gati, the man, is going to take us into the city to see the Council."

"Have they heard of the Thunder God here?" Brash asked.

"Oh, yes. They live in fear of him arriving here. They have been building up their forces."

"Will you be able to translate for me tomorrow?"

"I am starting to master Hellgathen," he said, at which Newark's eyes popped open, "and Serza has agreed to work on it with me tonight. So, if you could give me an idea of what you intend to say."

"Will do. Tell Serza to thank these people for their hospitality."

Their hospitality was overwhelming. They were taken to a round room with a huge round table heaped up with food, like a banquet. The crew looked like hobbits as they sat at the table. Whatever they were feeding them, it tasted good. Newark piled up his plate, giving Johnson a 'we've hit the jackpot here' look. Johnson, her mouth stuffed with heaven, gave him a reciprocal look. Then she turned to Graham with a look of sheer love.

Conversation between them and their hosts was limited and long, having to travel through Fraza and Serza. Any response went through the same tedious process. In the end, the crew talked amongst themselves and Serza chatted to his large friends.

They feasted like kings and as the table was cleared they all sat back, rubbing their distended bellies. Moments later, more heaped plates were brought in.

"Sartay," the woman said.

"Fetz," Serza said.

"Eat," Fraza said, less enthusiastically.

The Venulian woman was relentless. She kept shoving food at them.

Shaking your head and saying no, thank you, made no difference. Shaking your head and saying jir, tor unri, which meant no thank you in Venulian, made no difference. Looking like you were going to throw up made no difference. The woman was kind to the point of cruelty.

Breakfast was the same and the crew were glad to get out of there and get some fresh air. Climbing aboard Gati's circular craft, they took off for the capital city, which, confusingly, was called Venulas. Green fields sped by beneath them. It was so beautiful and peaceful here, Jenna thought. It reminded her of the place they had left behind. She saw what she would describe as fish throwing themselves up out of a river below.

"What are they doing?" she asked, pointing.

Fraza eventually translated. "There must be an arkai in the river. Apparently, it's a sort of water dragon that eats them by the bucket load."

"Oh." Not like the place they had left behind.

Graham sat up straight when the tall circular buildings of the city came into view. They were not the crystalline structures that the Erithians had but there was a lot of glass which shone brightly in the morning light.

Setting his craft down on a large concourse, Gati motioned for them to disembark. There were many craft parked there and Gati led them away from the concourse, through wide curving streets. Yellow-skinned ogres glanced at them as they walked by.

"Thank god they're friendly," Johnson whispered to Graham.

The building they entered had a huge, round lobby. Glass lifts ran up all the way around. Gati went to talk to a man sitting behind a desk. The crew hung around and waited, aware of many eyes looking down on them as the bodies travelled up.

Jenna had a sudden fearful thought. "Do you suppose our craft has some kind of tracking device?"

"Not now," Brash answered. "Skinner disabled it."

"Oh. Good. He's going to be looking for us, though, isn't he?"

"That's why we have to work fast. I just hope these people will work with us."

Gati returned and spoke to Serza. Fraza translated. "The Council will see us."

The man from the desk led them to a room beyond the lobby. There, they entered another lift. The Venulian pressed his hands together and bowed his head. Gati returned the gesture as the doors closed. The lift was very spacious. Newark wondered how many fat Venulians would fit inside it. Gati was taking up more than his fair share of space. Judging by the length of time they were in there, he surmised they were heading to the top.

The lift doors opened and they emerged into a spacious circular room.

The room was quite bare, apart from a seated section in the middle.

"Do these people have a problem with angles," Newark remarked.

Glass walls ran most of the way around and from there they had a spectacular view of the city. Jenna saw some cute chubby Venulian children playing in a nearby park.

They turned on hearing a door open. Five Venulians, three men and two women, walked in. They wore long red robes, which clashed horrifically with their yellow skin. One of them motioned to the seating area. The crew sat down, dwarfed by Venulian furniture, which left them feeling at a distinct disadvantage.

Gati said a few words of introduction.

Brash sat forward and asked Fraza to ask Serza to translate. "Tell them we are starting off a resistance. Tell them we intend to drum up as much support as we can and that all the peoples of this region must unite and stand as one. If they do not, they will eventually fall to the Thunder God. Tell them he has no mercy, tell them what we've seen, tell them their cute little children playing in that park will be torn to shreds in a barbaric display of cruelty." Brash felt the crew staring at him. "Maybe leave out that last part. For now."

Serza relayed the message and one of the Venulian men began to speak. Brash looked to Fraza expectantly.

Fraza turned to him. "He says, 'are you all partial to fish?' They rarely eat meat here but as you are their guests, they could have a yola sacrificed in honour of your arrival."

"What...? Has he heard what I've just said?"

"Yes, Captain. But, from what I can gather, the Venulians seem to be a very hospitable race who feel the need to feed us first. I think we might offend them if we don't eat."

"But we're not hungry. We've already eaten a mountain. Anyone hungry?" Brash asked, looking around.

The crew shook their heads.

"OK," Brash said. "Tell them we'll have fish but only a little."

"What's the yola?" Newark asked.

"Forget the yola."

Fraza translated and the Venulian faces lit up. What was it with these people and food? The food was brought very quickly as if it had been lying in wait. Brash ordered the crew to eat. So, in the name of saving the universe, they steeled themselves to eat another mountain of food. Fraza managed quite well and Brash looked at his large pot belly with envy. The Venulians watched with delight as every mouthful went down and the crew steadfastly turned their grimaces into smiles.

"Will they reply to me now?" Brash asked Fraza.

"Yes," Fraza said. "After the next course."

"There's another course...?"

One course later, Jenna stood up abruptly. "Do they have toilets here?" Johnson, Graham, and Skinner stood up too.

Fraza pointed the way and they rushed off to puke up Venulian hospitality. Brash kept it down, waiting for his moment. At long last, it came. One of the food-voyeuristic Venulians began to speak. Serza and Fraza translated: "We, here, Captain Brash, believe in signs. We have been more and more aware of this growing scourge. Reports come to us from those who visit. Terrible tales... We have debated it in the Chamber every week. And yet, to stand against this Thunder God would be to bring about our certain demise. So, we wait."

"Wait? For what?"

"For a sign."

"A sign?"

"A sign to tell us what to do. Until that time, Captain, we cannot act."

The Captain held back his impatience. "Right, well, the sign is here and we are it."

The Venulian looked at him dubiously.

Brash upped the ante. "Me and my crew are humans from a galaxy on the other side of the universe. We travelled here through a magic door because a race from another dimension told us we were chosen to stand against the Thunder God. Two of our crew have the power, like the Thunder God. The magic door took us to Hellgathen where we met Serza who brought us here. Is that enough of a sign for you?"

The Venulians stared at Brash. "We'll arrange a meeting of the Chamber," one of them said.

The crew stayed with Serza's friends for another two days while the Chamber met. The Chamber agreed to join the resistance and the city could be used as a meeting place for delegates from other planets. Following the decision, the crew and the Council poured over maps, the Venulians advising Brash on which planets to visit to enlist help, giving them as much background information as possible.

So, they had a plan and provisions as they set off on their quest. Serza thanked his friends for their hospitality and the crew boarded their craft a few pounds heavier.

"Right," Brash said, "set a heading for Quenbrar. Fraza, get learning Quenbrarian."

As Fraza brought out his translator, Johnson stared back at the tiny moon shrinking behind them. "Sorta feels like we're doing the work for them, doesn't it," she remarked, turning to Jenna.

"They were waiting for a sign," Jenna said with disgust. "I wonder what the rest of them have been waiting for."

"Balls maybe?" Johnson offered.

Jenna smiled. "Well, they're going to have to get some balls," she asserted. "And quick."

Jenna's gaze followed Captain Brash as he walked past. Feeling Johnson's eyes on her, she looked at her nails and started biting them.

For the next hour, she looked anywhere but at the Captain. Brash started to wonder if he'd done something wrong. Jenna wouldn't make eye-contact with him. He racked his brains for what it might be. Newark was watching Fraza reading the translator, wondering if *he* had any undiscovered talents. He racked his brains but couldn't think of any. Graham thought Johnson's birthday was coming up soon. He racked his brains but couldn't remember the date. Serza was watching Johnson, thinking that, for a human, she was a pretty fine specimen. He needed to learn their language. He wanted to communicate with her. The other one, Trot, looked helpful. Maybe she could help him. Lost in their own thoughts, they sat bolt upright when Skinner shouted, "We've got company!"

# The Wrong Impression

Johnson, Newark, and Graham scrambled to their stations.

"They've got a lock on us, Captain," Skinner said. "They've got a traction beam. They're pulling us in."

"Is it him?" Jenna asked in alarm.

Brash pressed a coms button. "Newark, what can you see? Is it SLOB?"

Newark was too busy letting off fire. Brash cursed. "Hold on. I'm going up to take a look."

Rushing to the weapons deck, Brash yelled at Newark to stop firing. Peering through Newark's viewfinder, he saw a round silver ship. It didn't look like one of SLOB's but whoever they were, he doubted they were friendly.

"Continue firing," Brash ordered.

"It's no good, sir. The fire is being deflected."

"Then why did you carry on?"

"It's the only thing I'm good at, Captain."

"Christ sakes." Brash raked a hand through his hair. "Right, leave your stations and grab a weapon."

Weapons at the ready, the crew waited near the gangway. Hollow sounds of metal told them they were entering the other ship. The crew stumbled as the ship touched down. Then it was eerily silent. "Wait for my command," Brash said.

An alien voice rose out of the silence. Everyone looked to Fraza. Fraza shook his head. Everyone looked to Serza. Serza shook his head. Another alien voice came through. Fraza and Serza both shook their heads. The next voice was Hellgathen. Fraza translated. "Come out peaceably and you will not be harmed."

"They must think we were born yesterday," Johnson said.

Brash formulated a reply, which Fraza relayed. "Go shove your alien head where the sun don't shine!"

There was a long pause. The Hellgathen spoke again. "If you do not come out, we will be forced to perform a controlled explosion which will rip open your craft. You will almost certainly die."

The crew looked at each other. They were like rats in a cage. "Right,"

Brash said decisively. "We're going to go out there but keep your weapons poised. No firing unless you're fired at. You hear me, Newark?"

"Yes, Captain."

Skinner lowered the gangway. The Captain went first, keeping his weapon aimed. As they walked down, they came face to face with a shabby collection of disparate beings, about thirty. Most of them were humanoid, though a few defied description. They were standing about twenty feet away, their weapons trained on them. Brash didn't like the way the Hellgathen was looking at Jenna and Johnson. Jenna didn't like it, either. In fact, it was starting to piss her off.

"Ask him who they are and what they want," Brash said to Fraza.

The answer was not encouraging. "They're pirates, Captain. They want our ship and our compliance. If they get our compliance, they'll spare our lives."

"Yeah, right," Newark spat, his finger teasing the trigger.

Jenna was getting more and more pumped. The look she was getting from the Hellgathen was making her blood boil. They were on a mission to save the universe and this group of rapist, murdering bastards was holding them up! Objects started to shift in the cargo hold and heads turned but she made herself calm down. She was going to use this power of hers in a targeted way and she allowed it to come up in her as she walked forward.

"What are you doing," Brash hissed, grabbing her arm.

"Trust me," she whispered. "Fraza, tell that creep I am giving myself to him as a gift."

Jenna yanked her arm away from Brash and walked toward the Hellgathen. The Hellgathen looked at her oddly but she smiled seductively as Fraza relayed her message. The Hellgathen's eyes widened but she detected a look of excitement there. Brash prepared to fire, watching in horror as Jenna took the Hellgathen's hand and led him through the alien group. Newark thought he was seeing things. The rest of the crew looked to Brash.

Jenna stopped and performed a Total Body Shot.

The crew watched on, amazed, as bodies flew all over the place. It was like an explosion.

"Kill them!" Jenna yelled and the crew sprang into action, firing on the enemy before they could stagger to their feet. The pirates didn't stand a chance, Brash performing overkill on the leering Hellgathen.

From a gangway, high above, another Hellgathen stood watching. "She's amazing..." he murmured, watching rapt. They were not at all what he expected to step off that ship.

"Shall we fire, Leader?"

Hendraz turned to his second, Paikra. His men were positioned all along the gangway, right around the loading bay, their weapons pointing down. "No. For now, I want her to live." Raising his voice, he spoke into the hold. "You are surrounded." The newcomers searched for the voice, craning their heads upward. "We mean you no harm. You have my word that we will not hurt you."

Hendraz watched a pot-bellied alien translate. The girl's face turned angry. She shouted something which the creature relayed. "The word of murderers and rapists!"

"I will come down there alone, unarmed. Perhaps we could get past this... unpleasantness."

"This doesn't look good, Captain," Graham said. "D'you see how many are up there?"

"Keep calm," Brash said. "If they wanted us dead, we'd be dead already."

The crew watched as a lone figure came walking out toward them. Blonde-haired, with a scar on his face, the Hellgathen was tall and muscular. He showed no fear as he approached them. His eyes were fixed on Jenna and it was her to whom he spoke. "I didn't realise we had such... interesting company."

Fraza translated and she glared at the Hellgathen. "I'm pleased to have provided such an entertaining show," she shot.

Hendraz scratched his neck. "Yes. Life does become a little... dull."

"So, you want to end it?" Hendraz' brow creased. "Coming down here alone?"

"Without me, you'll never get that craft out of here."

"Maybe we'll take your craft."

The crew stared at her, aghast. What was she doing? Talking him out of his amenable mood? Brash started to speak and, though Fraza translated, the Hellgathen ignored him.

"As remarkable as you are," the Hellgathen said to Jenna, "my men would kill you before you got the chance. What is your name?"

"What's yours?"

"Hendraz. What race are you?"

"Human."

"I haven't heard of them. What are you doing in this region?"

Her instincts were telling her to be honest. "We are here to kill the Thunder God."

His eyes widened. "Kill the Thunder God...? But you are on his ship?"

"We *stole* his ship."

Hendraz stared at her. They were rebels? "And you think you can just kill him? The man is unstoppable."

"How would you know? I bet you've never stood up for anything in your life. Is that why you're a murdering bully?"

"A murdering bully? You are the ones that have killed my men."

Serza suddenly spoke and their eyes flicked to him.

"Serza recognises him," Fraza said. "He was a Hellgathen first minister."

"Government?" Jenna asked, turning to the man. "And now you're a pirate?"

"That's just a cover," Hendraz explained. "You have stumbled across the only pocket of resistance in this god's forsaken universe."

Jenna and the crew stared at Hendraz. Then they looked at the dead men on the floor.

They sat in Hendraz' private quarters, eating reasonable-sized portions of food. The rickety, dirty, dust-bucket of a craft was tiny compared to Osiris but Hendraz seemed proud of it, boasting that it had everything it needed.

"I'm very sorry about your men," Jenna said through Fraza. "I thought... That other Hellgathen was leering at me."

Hendraz smiled. "Remind me never to leer at you."

She rubbed her forehead, feeling guilty and foolish. "Your men told us you were pirates."

"Yes, well, at that point we didn't know who *you* were."

"So, you were in government?"

"Yes. I tried, persistently, to get them to act. It fell on deaf ears. After that, I went off on my own trying to engage other planets to act. That fell on deaf ears too."

"But that's what we're intending to do." She turned to Brash, feeling hope siphon from her. Brash rubbed his forehead. "Why won't they do anything?" she asked, turning back to Hendraz.

"They're scared. They don't want to bring about their own damnation. They hope that if they lay low, they'll be overlooked. The universe is such a big place, they think they can hide in it."

"But he'll get to them eventually. He's already attacked Hellgathen."

Hendraz stared at her. "Hellgathen?"

Serza filled him in on the details.

"So, it's hopeless," Jenna said to Brash. "Nobody's going to do anything."

Hendraz turned to her. "Perhaps you can persuade them. If they see what you're capable of, maybe they'll rally around you. Where were you heading first?"

"Quenbrar."

Hendraz nodded thoughtfully. "That's a good choice but I suggest *you* do the talking."

"Me? Why?"

"Trust me."

Jenna looked to Brash. Brash nodded.

"Maybe ask questions first this time," Skinner remarked around a mouthful of food. "Blasting them and shouting, 'kill them', might not be so diplomatic."

"I thought they were pirates!"

"I thought she was great," Johnson said proudly.

"Yep, she kicked ass!" Newark said, just as proudly.

"Next time, wait for my command," Brash said. "You misjudged the situation. That cannot happen again."

"From now on," Hendraz said, "you should travel with us. It won't go down well if you arrive on these planets in a Thunder God craft. We'll advise you on the planets to head for. Some are disparate, a collection of countries warring with each other. Others are global entities. Those are the ones we need. Oh, and one more thing," Hendraz said, standing up. "The men need to exact punishment for those you have killed."

The crew looked up. "What?" Brash asked.

"They've voted for water bobbing."

"Water what?"

"You'll all be dunked in water until you almost drown. You killed twenty-eight men, so you'll each be dunked twenty-eight times."

"Nice one, Trot," Newark spat.

"Yeah, nice one," Johnson said sourly.

# Clear Intentions

Drowned almost senseless, the crew took a couple of days to recover. None of them spoke to Jenna, apart from Brash, who loved her, and Skinner, who seemed unaffected by the experience. Jenna lay on her bunk, feeling guilty and ashamed, deserving of the black looks she got. In one fell swoop, the past few months had been eradicated. She was the dumb girl she had always been.

Lost in her drowning thoughts, she wasn't aware of Brash until his hand stroked her forehead. "Don't give yourself such a hard time," he said. "You could have been right. This time you weren't."

"I misjudged the situation, like you said. I was angry. I shouldn't have got angry."

"What you did was very impressive, though."

"Impressive? Because of me, all those... men are dead."

"Don't feel too bad. One word from Hendraz, and they'd have killed us without question."

She grabbed his hand and turned to him. "I wish this was all over."

"It's barely begun," he said, smiling at her sadly.

As the craft descended through Quenbrarian airspace, a flotilla of smaller craft came up to meet them. One of the alien craft made contact. Hendraz identified himself and his purpose. After being instructed to circle for a time, they were finally allowed down.

The crew disembarked to find themselves two hundred feet up on top of an enormous landing platform. Fields of colourful plants stretched off into the distance. Multi-hued clouds hung in an intense blue sky. Behind them, there were other platforms, with craft descending. Below, smaller craft were heading off toward a sprawling metropolis far over to the left.

Hendraz strode to a lift and they followed, looking around. The temperature was warm, the air oppressively humid. Wiping sweat from their brows, they entered a lift, holding onto the sides as the lift shot down at breakneck speed.

The doors opened onto a busy hive of activity. Various beings were loading themselves into smaller craft. Purple uniforms dotted the place.

Five of those uniforms were making their way over to them. The crew stared at them. They were tall and thin with pale pink skin, violet eyes and violet hair that was arranged into buns on their heads. Newark had to supress a giggle. *"I mean, look at them,"* he whispered to Johnson.

After talking to Hendraz, the men escorted them to a nearby craft.

The vehicle did not head for the city. Instead, it veered right, flying over water. On the other side of an enormous waterway, they could see a mini-city of fine stone buildings.

"That is where the government is located," Hendraz informed them through Fraza. "I've been here before... with little success, I'm afraid."

"And you think they'll listen to me?" Jenna asked.

"They might respect you more." Jenna looked at him, unconvinced. "The government here is comprised solely of women. On this planet, women are thought to be the superior sex."

Newark and Graham snorted. Johnson punched Graham's arm. The punch was particularly hard because today was her birthday and, as yet, he'd made no mention of it. She kept pressing the calendar display on her watch, looking at it forlornly. Each minute that ticked by was storing up a whole heap of trouble.

The nearer they got, the finer the buildings appeared. Round marble pillars edged doorways. Colourful plants interspersed the buildings.

The craft set down on another landing platform. The crew descended another lift, this time walking out onto a square concourse that was edged with those same colourful plants. Two lines of uniformed men formed a purple passage in front of them. One of the men led them forward.

"I don't think they trust us," Newark whispered to Johnson.

Johnson looked around at the crew. "I don't blame them. I wouldn't trust us, either."

"Are they men or women?" he whispered, staring at their up-dos.

Johnson frowned. She wasn't sure.

Passing through marble pillars, they entered a grand stone building, walking over a marble-floored hallway into a huge oval-shaped room. The domed ceiling was a mile off and decorated with strange designs. The marble floor, too, held elaborate designs. There was no furniture in the room, apart from a row of ornate, high-backed chairs sitting on a dais ahead.

A group of women emerged from a doorway and went to occupy the seats. Their violet hair was braided and they wore long purple gowns. Newark could see now that the uniforms lined up to either side of them were men. They couldn't carry their colour as well. Indeed, the women's faces were softer and had a strange beauty. Faces aside, their arms looked strong, like they could throw a mean punch. They all looked remarkably cool. Newark was feverishly trying to wipe sweat from his forehead. Did Quenbrarians not have sweat glands? He stood a little straighter, unaware of the fact that the women's gaze barely touched him.

Hendraz spoke by way of introduction. The women's faces were serious to the point of arrogance.

Hendraz turned to Jenna. Fraza relayed the message. "He says you must talk to them now. Tell them why you're here."

Hendraz and Fraza translated:

Jenna coughed. "Hello," she said. "I'm here to gather support to stand against the Thunder God. You cannot sit by idly any longer. You cannot hide. He is hell bent on destruction-"

One of the women held up a hand. "You are boring me."

Jenna stared at the woman. "Err... Why, exactly, am I boring you?"

"You speak mechanically. Speak from the heart and get to the heart of your message."

Jenna looked at her oddly. She drew in a breath and started again. "The Thunder God, or SLOB, as we like to call him, is a sick, twisted, psychopath, rampaging and bullying his way through the universe, inflicting horror, cruelty, and suffering. It's what he gets off on and we've seen it first-hand. I've felt his power first-hand. I don't want to be here, zillions of miles from home. I don't want to have to face him but I've been saddled with this because, like SLOB, I have the power too. So, me and this crew are making the ultimate sacrifice and it's really pissing me off that we're doing this when all you pussy, chicken-shit cowards are hiding in your holes. I intend to see this through but in the meantime, a bit of unity and support from the rest of you, whose hides we intend to save, wouldn't go amiss."

The crew stared at Jenna, thinking she'd fucked up again. Brash was mentally shaking his head.

Astonishingly, a smile possessed the radiant pink face. "You make an excellent case. Demonstrate this power of yours and we will become part of your alliance."

Hendraz couldn't help himself. He had to ask why she had succeeded when he had failed. Was it because he was a man? The woman's violet eyes descended on him. "She speaks with intention. You referred to the Thunder God as unstoppable. I wonder that you came here at all."

Jenna couldn't help herself, either. "Err... I hope you don't mind me asking-"

"Jenna," Brash said in an undertone.

She carried on, looking to Fraza and Hendraz to translate. "I've never come across a race where women ruled. Do you find it hard being the physically weaker gender?"

The women looked at her, incredulous. Brash thought they'd lost their new alliance.

Finally, one of the women smiled at Jenna, as if she felt sorry for her. "We are not physically weaker than men. On our planet, evolution has made it so the wisest and most compassionate are also the strongest, be they women or men. The alternative would be a hell-hole of a planet, would it not? Those without compassion or wisdom ruling? Of course, today our system of government is more in place so physical strength is less important."

"So, this isn't reverse sexism then?"

The women looked at her oddly, as if they weren't sure what she meant. Jenna didn't think the women looked particularly strong but then she glanced at the soldiers who, on closer inspection, appeared quite weedy. She finally discerned there were men *and* women standing there.

"So, the strongest form the government?" Jenna pressed on.

"No, the government is elected."

"But you're all women?"

"Your point?"

"I think you're the one being sexist," Johnson whispered in her ear.

"But Hendraz said women are considered the superior sex," Jenna said, confused.

Hendraz didn't translate that.

After Jenna had levitated, freaking out the rest of her crew, not to mention the Quenbrarian soldiers, Brash, through Jenna, through Fraza, through Hendraz, invited delegates to Venulas where precise plans could be formed. The crew were then offered a luxury hotel in the city and they looked at Brash expectantly. Brash, however, declined. They were on a tight schedule. They didn't have time for sight-seeing.

In fact, Brash dragged them around the next few systems. Hendraz had to remind him that they were on *his* ship but Brash reminded Hendraz that they were on the same side and time was short. Some of the peoples they visited confirmed this with tales of the Thunder God's latest exploits.

The planets they visited were as diverse as the peoples. Some planets had breathable air, some didn't. The crew hated donning suits and it made communication difficult. Some places were like Quenbrar, others had pink, green, even multi-hued skies. The stranger the planet, the stranger its inhabitants. Ixier was strangest of all, Newark refusing to communicate with beings that looked like overgrown octopi. Skinner reminded him that he couldn't communicate anyway. Yet, even Fraza struggled, despite his translator, and Brash cursed that final frontier – language.

Though some places had refused to join the good fight, many were now part of the alliance. Hendraz had been right. Jenna's power had proved to be a rallying point. Even Fraza joined in with little displays of his own. Some cultures wanted to revere them as gods but Jenna told them they didn't have time for that. Newark saw a missed opportunity, imagining himself surrounded by a bevy of beauties feeding him grapes. If the inhabitants had been a little more attractive he may have pressed the point.

On a couple of occasions, they'd had to fight for their lives. Hendraz' information had been inaccurate and, instead of civilised races, the Brachians and the Ghios were a blood-thirsty lot of barbarians. If it were not for their advanced technology, the crew's heads might well be sitting on spikes. Brash had harsh words with Hendraz after those two disasters.

All in all, though, it was going well. With their mission, at least. Privately, some cracks were starting to appear. Johnson had not forgiven Graham for forgetting her birthday. It had been weeks now and he still hadn't mentioned it. Jenna had been teaching Serza English, picking up various objects and identifying them. Hendraz had wanted to learn the language too and had joined in with their sessions. Brash wasn't too happy about this. He was sure the Hellgathen was flirting with his woman. Newark had wanted to learn Hellgathen but gave up after two lessons with Fraza. It was a bloody stupid language, he told anyone who would listen, which was basically no-one. Graham and Skinner were having more involved conservations now. Newark didn't like this, either. Graham used to have fun conversations with him about all manner of stuff. Now he wanted to learn technical shit? Skinner was the one that did all that stuff. Apart from Skinner and Flint, they'd all lied on their application forms. He, Graham and Johnson were a band of brothers. They were the ones that kicked butt.

Graham, whilst wondering about technical stuff, did not wonder how he'd managed to get off with forgetting Johnson's birthday. He wasn't sure if he had missed it or not, but if he had she obviously wasn't bothered. She'd said nothing about it. He made no connection with the subtle knockbacks. Of course, she was tired. They had been doing so much lately. Of course, he should fuck off and leave her alone. He didn't notice the resentful looks, either. Nor did he notice Serza trying out his English on her. Johnson laughed at the man's funny accent. Serza adored that laugh. It inspired him to learn more. Hendraz, too, was inspired to learn more. He would come to the sessions showing off his muscular, tattooed arms. Jenna hated tattoos but was far too polite to let it show. In fact, she overcompensated, taking far too keen an interest in them. Brash kept an eye on the situation, waiting for the time when Hendraz might need putting in his place.

That time was to come on the next planet they visited.

# The Dynamics of Change

*Success!* Brash thought, mentally punching the air with his fist. This time, he'd taken the three-eyed President up on his kind offer of an all-expenses-paid stay in a top establishment. The crew deserved it. Indeed, the crew were ecstatic. Even more so, when they found the place laden with bars, fine food, clubs… Newark dragged Skinner into a strip joint but they came out quickly, gagging and looking pale.

"What the fuck were those things!" Newark shrieked.

Skinner rubbed his eyes as if he could rub the haunting images away.

They caught up with the others, finding more soothing sights to take away the pain. In the corner of the large bar room were a group of unimaginably beautiful beings. They were humanoid but on an angelic scale.

"Fuck me," Newark said. "Who are they?"

The crew looked around, the men gawking, their eyes on stalks.

"It's such a diverse city, isn't it?" Jenna said to Brash but he didn't seem to hear her. She looked to the women then back to Brash, feeling increasingly irritated and insignificant.

Johnson was experiencing similar feelings. Her hand tightened into a fist beneath the table. Serza was watching her and she gave him a tight smile. He came to sit beside her, giving his English a work-out. Graham was still staring, so she turned to Serza and started flirting with him.

Jenna was trying her best to read Lucas' thoughts. She'd been practising for a while now but with no success. She tried to clear her mind but it wasn't easy. Her mind was spewing out all sorts of vitriol. *Of course, he prefers them to you. Why wouldn't he? Who'd want second-rate Jenna Trot?* Putting her head in her hands, she fought against it, trying for all she was worth to hear what he was thinking.

"You, me, dance?" someone asked her. She looked up to see Hendraz' outstretched arm.

"Dance?" she asked, looking around. Jenna saw a room over to the right where strange shapes were moving around. *Ah, that's what they're doing.* Glancing at Brash, she accepted the offer.

"You know the word for dance?" she asked as they walked into the other room. Hendraz couldn't quite grasp what she was saying, so he just smiled at her, flirtatiously.

Brash was thinking the women were too perfect. There was something staid and boring about such perfection. Newark was wondering aloud how they'd react if he asked one to dance. Graham told him they were way out of his league. Skinner got up to give it a try. The others watched in amazement as Skinner used some strange sign language to communicate. When one of the women got up and walked off to dance with him, they stared in wonder. Newark got up and steamed in.

"Wanta danca?" he asked, pointing to the other room and mimicking some dance moves.

The women laughed but one of them got up to dance with him. He stood there in shock for a moment then led her away, making some obscene gesture to Graham.

Fraza was coming back from the bar with a tray of drinks, stepping forward then back as he made his way over.

"Come on, Fraza!" Graham called. "I'm dying of thirst here! At this rate, we're never going to get a drink." He turned to Johnson to find her talking to Serza. "You speaking English, Serza?"

Serza looked up. "Yes, I is. You understanding I?"

Graham nodded, impressed. Brash elbowed him and he looked up. One of the goddesses was standing by the table, offering Graham her hand.

"I think she wants to dance," Brash said.

Johnson watched in horror as Graham took the hand and got up. Brash looked at him, surprised, then glanced at Johnson.

Johnson turned to Serza. "D'you want to go back to the hotel?"

Serza nodded and they left the bar together. Brash watched them go, wondering whether to get involved. No. This was personal business, he decided, looking around for Jenna. His eyes widened on seeing her dancing with Hendraz.

When Fraza finally arrived, Brash threw back a drink. His eyes kept straying to the dancing pair, focusing on the Hellgathen hand on her waist. After drinking two more redundant drinks, he got up and strode into the other room. Dragging the tattooed bastard off her, he punched him squarely in the face. Hendraz recovered quickly and fought back but the pair were unceremoniously carted out by a pair of enormous hands. Thrown into the street, the fight began in earnest.

Jenna went to sit with Fraza and helped herself to a drink.

"Should we try to break that up?" Fraza asked, rubbing his ear.

"Nope," she said, staring at the table.

"Daria... That nice name," Serza said, stroking her arm.

Johnson threw back her drink. "My mother never got me birthday presents, either," she said miserably.

Serza looked at her sadly. "What is presents?"

"Tokens of love."

"What is tokens?"

"Never mind..." Turning to him, she grabbed his head and kissed him.

One of the beautiful beings ran past, holding its jaw. Newark ran in after it. "It's a bloody man!" he shrieked at Jenna. "A bloody man!"

"A man?" she asked.

"Shit. Graham and Skinner are still in there!" Newark charged in to save his buddies.

Brash came back with a bruised and bloody face. Striding over, he thrust his hand out to Jenna. "Come on, we're going," he said stiffly.

"Like hell I'm going," she shot.

"What's wrong with you?"

"What's wrong with you! I was only dancing. If you'd been paying attention instead of gawking at those women, who are *men*, by the way, I might have been dancing with you!"

Something suddenly occurred to Fraza. The revelation was quite shocking. He looked from one to the other as they continued their slanging match. Noise erupted in the other room. Moments later, Graham, Skinner and Newark were dragged out by enormous hands.

A bloodied Hendraz came back into the bar, demanding more action. Brash was only too happy to oblige and the pair were unceremoniously chucked out again. Jenna was crying into her beer. Fraza's ears were getting sore. He thought being human was complex. He didn't think he was strong enough to be human. He had enough trouble being him. His little rituals took up a lot of energy. The Erithians had helped him and it was far more manageable than it had been, but the roots were still there, always growing more shoots. He decided to get drunk.

Johnson went into the bathroom to get out of her clothes. Serza did the same in the bedroom. The sense of anticipation mounted. She opened the door and turned to face her errant lover.

She screamed insanely. He screamed back. Things were in the hideously wrong place.

\*

Breakfast was strained and quiet. Johnson and Serza wouldn't look at each other. Graham kept fawning over Johnson but Johnson had reached her tipping point and decided she was done with men. Brash and Hendraz looked a mess. They wouldn't look at each other, either. Jenna wouldn't look at Brash. The others just stared at the table, Fraza because his head was aching in a way it never had before.

Nobody was very hungry, apart from Newark, and no-one spoke as they made their way back to the craft. Once aboard, they set off on their new heading, remaining firmly in their own worlds. It would be a while before they opted for a night out again. The rest of the resistance were in better spirits. They had been out on the town too. They looked at their leader's face but Hendraz gave them hard stares. They knew better than to go there.

Serza and Hendraz spent more time away from the crew. Jenna and Johnson spent more time away from Brash and Graham, more time with each other. The dynamics were changing. Fraza kept watching Jenna and Brash but their interactions were short and concise. Jenna finally confessed her doomed relationship to Johnson.

"I knew it," Johnson said. "I knew there was something going on between you two."

"Well, I'm not sure there is anymore. He completely over-reacted and I'm not having him order me around."

"Yeah, well, technically he *is* the Captain."

"You know what I mean. At this moment, if I had to pick, I'd pick Hendraz."

"You do *not* want to go there," Johnson said, staring at her meaningfully. "Trust me on that one."

"He's nice and very attentive."

"Yeah, but he's got balls and shit where they ain't oughta be."

Jenna's eyes widened. "What?"

The meaningful look intensified.

"Wait a minute. How d'you know that?"

"I've seen Serza." A haunted look came in Johnson's eye. "Everything's round the back."

Jenna stared at her. "They sit on them...?"

"They're situated in the small of the back. You never notice how they wear those baggy trousers with the leather codpieces at the back?"

"I thought that was some kind of Hellgathen fashion." Staring at the floor, she looked back up to Johnson. "So, what's at the front?"

"Zilch."

"Nothing?"

"Zero, zilch, nil, nada..."

Jenna scratched her head. "What about the women?"

"By the way he reacted to me, I'd say theirs are in the same place."

"Well... how do they...?"

"They must do it without facing each other. Don't ask me how. Maybe they've got eyes in their bollocks. Maybe they've got some weird alien homing device."

Jenna scratched her head again. "Don't their... arses get in the way?"

"They're practically none existent."

Jenna shivered. "Well, none of *that* make sense."

Johnson thought about it and came up with a theory. "Maybe they evolved in a very dangerous environment. Maybe they evolved that way so they could keep look-out while they were doing it. Who knows? Sometimes cock-ups survive."

"Wait a minute. SLOB's a cock-up!"

Johnson nodded thoughtfully. "That might be good to know if you're ever at close quarters with him."

"Yeah. Knee him in the arse..."

"What are you two whispering about?" Newark interrupted.

"We're not whispering, arsehole," Johnson snapped.

"Alright. Shit. What's got into you?" Newark was feeling particularly left out. Skinner and Graham seemed tight. Brash didn't want to talk to anyone. Trot and Johnson were all cosy. Fraza's best mate was his translator. He felt things were different but he didn't know why.

He dumped himself down and Jenna felt sorry for him. "D'you want to know a secret?" she asked.

Newark perked up like a puppy waiting for a stick. Jenna fed him the juicy gossip.

"That's fucked up..." Newark mouthed, staring into space. "How d'you know that?"

Jenna glanced at Johnson. "Olberax told me," she suddenly remembered.

"That's fucked up..." he repeated.

Johnson sniffed. "Yeah, well, keep that under your hat."

"Why?"

"Because if you piss Hendraz off, you could get us thrown off this ship. He's only just tolerating us as it is."

"Yeah, what *was* all that shit between him and the Captain?"

Johnson shrugged, glancing at Jenna. Jenna shrugged too.

Newark gave up wondering what had happened between the Captain and Hendraz. He devoted more brain power to the mechanics of Hellgathen procreation. Over the next few days, he couldn't stop staring at

Hellgathen arses.

Brash, blissfully unaware of Hellgathen arses, attempted to make amends with Hendraz. The success of their mission could well depend on it. Hendraz, after being informed of certain things by Serza, assured Brash that he would keep away from Jenna. He told Brash that he wasn't even aware they were having a relationship and he would never have danced with her had he known. This was a lie, of course, but it certainly smoothed things over. Brash, however, wasn't even sure he and Jenna *were* having a relationship anymore. Jenna had no desire to build bridges. Though he regretted his rash behaviour, he realised that, as Captain, he had to put any relationship on hold. It was interfering with the mission. For the sake of the universe, he had to be a more responsible captain. Tregailia was under their belt now. The next stop was Rengar. He had to focus on that.

"I want them found!" SLOB raged.

"We're looking everywhere," Rotzch said. "It's like they've disappeared."

"How am I expected to carry on with my mission when I have to attend to details!" He paced around, fury seeping out of every pore. "Kill someone! That'll provide some focus!"

"Anyone in particular, Lord?"

"*I* don't know! Must I think of everything? Pick someone!"

"Very well, Lord."

SLOB stared at Rotzch's back as he walked out. He wondered who this thorn in his side was. It was clear now that he couldn't trust his men to find them. He would have to put his plans on hold and seek them out himself. He sat down on his throne, closing his eyes, imagining what he would do to them when he found them. This brightened his spirits slightly.

Rotzch returned sometime later, informing him that the job had been done. The job had not been done. Rotzch was getting tired of killing their own men.

SLOB suddenly sat up. "I need a disguise. Get a craft ready. I'm going planet hopping."

"Planet hopping? What does that mean, exactly, Lord? We're going on sporadic killing sprees?"

"No. Well, maybe but our primary objective is information gathering."

"Right. Gathering information on what, Lord?"

"On the fugitives! It'll be an interesting detour," SLOB decided. The Thunder God undercover. It had a certain wickedness about it.

# Keeping the Faith

SLOB sat in a crowded bar, wearing a long dark wig, tied back in a ponytail, and sporting a spray tan. He felt the disguise gave him an edgier appearance and was considering keeping it full time. As usual, everyone ignored him, focusing their attention on Rotzch, but as he was officially in disguise, he decided to overlook it.

This was their first port of call. Rotzch had been asking pedestrians if they had spotted a Thunder God craft in this region. The inhabitants went pale and it gave SLOB a certain amount of satisfaction. Their answers, however, were not encouraging. Still, he was keeping the faith. The one thing he was banking on was being led to the right place by this power of his. As a child, he knew well in advance if his father would come home in a bad mood. He knew when to keep out of his way. He hadn't used his power to track someone before but he was relying on the same principle.

He looked around. This bar was the same as every other in this city, a noisy collection of misfits. He noticed a group of more beautiful-looking beings sitting over in the corner. Their perfect looks were marred by bruises, which seemed almost like a travesty. If it were not for the ugly marks, he would have considered collecting them to adorn his ship. He had never collected specimens before but it was an interesting idea.

As Rotzch went to find the toilets, SLOB waved his menu in the air. He didn't need Rotzch to translate. He could speak Tregailian. A male server came over. Like all Tregailians, he had three eyes, which made eye contact difficult. SLOB's gaze flitted between the three of them.

"Yeah, what d'you want?" the server asked gruffly.

*Your head on a platter!* SLOB thought, incensed. He managed to hold himself in check. "What's this?" He pointed at the menu. "Sniffil?"

"Sea worm."

"You're offering me sea worm!"

"Err... *no*," the man said, talking to him as if he were a moron. "I'm not offering you anything. I'm waiting for you to *tell* me what you want."

The Tregailian started to feel his collar. His throat felt tight. SLOB retracted the power. He had a part to play and up to now, he had prided himself on how well he had been playing it.

"I'll have the frenji," SLOB said, chucking the menu at him.

The man scowled. "What about your friend?"

"What friend?"

"The large man you came in with."

"He'll have the same. I want it well done but don't burn it. And bring me your best beverage."

"Anything else, your highness?"

Now the man was taking the piss. SLOB used every grain of willpower to restrain himself. "Watch yourself, Tregailian scum."

The man's face turned red and he stepped forward. Fortunately for him, his boss walked past at that precise moment. "I'll get that straight away, sir."

"Just a minute," SLOB said. "Who is that group over there? What happened to them?"

The server turned to the beautiful beings. "Had some ruffians in here a couple of days ago. Three of them got assaulted." The server's eyes lit up. He turned back to SLOB. "They're extremely beautiful, aren't they? I've heard that when they pleasure a man, they take him to the heights of heaven."

"They're prostitutes?"

"They prefer to call themselves escorts. If you feel like some company whilst you're here, I know they won't disappoint."

"Heaven, you say?"

The man nodded.

\*

"Tregailia's out?" Brash asked, confused. "But we've just visited there."

The scaly-skinned Rengiard shook his head heavily. "So has the Thunder God."

"What...?"

The crew stared at Brash, alarmed.

"News has just reached us," the Rengiard continued through Fraza. The Kaledian was feverishly flicking through his translator guide. "He obliterated the capital city. There were no craft, no weapons... He used his... god-like powers. How can we stand against a god?"

"He's not a god," Jenna asserted. "And you have no choice but to stand against him because if he's been there, the chances are he'll be coming here next."

"But what shall we do? Our forces are no match for him. All we can do is throw ourselves on his mercy."

"He has no mercy."

"You have to act quick," Brash said. "Gather your forces and head for Venulas."

"But what about our people?"

"Evacuate them, if you can. If you can't, I'm afraid there's little you can do."

The Rengiard looked devastated. Jenna's heart felt heavy. She wished there was something she could do. "Did you say his fleet was not with him?" she asked.

"That is correct."

She turned to Brash. "Why would he go there alone?"

Brash shrugged. "Maybe he was taking a holiday."

She rubbed her forehead, a fearful feeling taking hold of her chest. "Then if he's alone, perhaps it's time to make a stand." She looked up at Brash. "It could be the best chance we get."

Brash looked at her, concerned. "You're not ready for this."

"If I'm not, I never will be. I can't keep putting it off. If there's a chance he'll come here alone, we've got to take it."

Brash looked around his crew.

"I say we annihilate the fucker," Newark said.

"We've got to take the shot," Johnson said.

The rest of the crew agreed.

"We have an advantage over him," Brash said, rubbing his chin thoughtfully. "We know what he looks like. He doesn't know what we look like. We have to use the element of surprise. Fraza, tell Hendraz his men must have the ship ready should we need to make a quick escape. Jenna and Fraza, get practising."

This was it. If SLOB came here, they would face him. Brash reminded himself that they had been picked for this mission. He had to have faith in that. He had to keep the faith.

# Time to Pray

"We're not drinking, Newark," Brash said, looking around.
"I know, Captain. I was going to get *non-alcoholic* drinks."
"OK."
This was the twentieth bar they'd entered. They had been informed of an unidentified craft having entered Rengar airspace. They'd been combing the city for hours, their weapons concealed under their jackets, their attention on full alert. Well, all except Newark's. His attention had been straying, his head craning, his eyes following the towering buildings that pointed up like tapering fingers. Walk-ways connected them. Tiny craft flew around up there. To Newark, they looked like swarming insects. Brash kept having to remind the man to focus.

They took their drinks and walked around, their eyes peeling the room. Draining their glasses, they left to try out another bar.

Days went by and still, he did not materialise.

"Maybe he's not coming here," Johnson said.

Brash considered this. He looked at Jenna. She seemed tired and strained. "Johnson, take Jenna back to the hotel. She needs to rest."

"I'm fine, Captain," Jenna insisted.

"That's an order," he said.

"May I take her, Captain?" Fraza asked. "I could do with some fresh air." He was sick of traipsing through bars.

Brash nodded and Jenna glared at him as she walked out. The Captain sat down, heavily. The distance between him and Jenna was painful.

Graham wished they could have a real drink. His relationship with Johnson was over and he didn't know how to bring it back. When he'd asked her what he'd done, she told him to go and drown himself in a bucket of piss. He shouldn't have danced with that... man. He had no idea she was so touchy. Newark, who had become closer to Johnson of late, told Graham he was a jerk.

"You see, the problem is," Newark had said, "you've got to be more sensitive. Chicks love that kind of shit."

Graham stared at him. This, coming from Newark? "What do you suggest I do?"

Newark sniffed. "Pay less attention to Skinner, for one."

"The guy knows shit."

"I know shit."

"What shit do you know?"

"Tons of shit."

"You talk tons of shit."

Newark stood and squared up to him. "You questioning my shit?"

"Yes, I'm questioning your shit!"

So, trying to help Graham had turned into trying to beat him up. It was a low point for both of them and though Brash had ordered them to make up, the rift was not entirely mended. Neither Newark nor Johnson made eye contact with Graham now as they sat at the table.

Hendraz spoke but nobody understood him. Serza attempted to translate. "He can be on any... err... panet. We shall to go."

The crew didn't understand him. Newark got up to go to the gents. He hoped they had proper urinals in this place. He was sick of pissing in holes.

He entered the gents to find a dark-haired man staring back at him. Newark nodded with his chin then went to stand beside him. As he relieved himself, Newark wondered what the guy was doing, just standing there. Was he a perv or something? Glancing to his right, his breath caught. What he saw was unholy in how fucked-up it was. A penis projecting from a back...?

Zipping himself up, he made it out the door. Bending over, he drew in a large gulp of air. He gagged but managed to hold onto it. After a moment, his brain began to work. The man was a Hellgathen. Weren't they all supposed to be blonde? Unless there was another travesty of nature out there.

He needed to tell someone – knowing something and seeing it were two entirely different things. The Captain, aware of Hellgathen anatomy because Newark couldn't keep a secret, considered it thoughtfully.

"He had dark hair, you say?" Brash asked.

"Look, he's coming out now."

Brash watched the man. He didn't look Hellgathen. The man sat down at a table with another, more imposing man. Brash's eyes suddenly widened. He recognised that man. And now he recognised SLOB.

"Shit. It's him. He's in disguise."

"How d'you know?" Graham asked.

"It's a shit disguise. We've got to act fast."

"What the plan?" Newark asked.

"Stay here. Keep an eye on him. Do *not* engage him. I'm going to get the others."

Brash rushed out. Newark, Graham, Johnson, Hendraz and Skinner tried not to look at the mark or draw any attention to themselves. Serza was glaring at the mark with hatred. Hendraz had a word with him and he looked away, his hands pressed into fists beneath the table.

"He keeps looking over at us," Johnson said.

"You're imagining it," Graham told her.

"I'm not imagining shit!"

"He's coming over," Skinner said.

They turned to see the mark coming up behind them. He started speaking Hellgathen. Only Serza and Hendraz understood what he was saying.

"You are Hellgathen," SLOB stated. "What are you doing here?" His eyes brushed over the others.

"Excuse me, I didn't catch your name?" Hendraz asked.

SLOB's eyes narrowed. Then he remembered he was undercover. "Venn," he said. "My name's Venn."

"You are interested in Hellgathen?"

SLOB, for the first time ever, was stumped. Why would someone who was ostensibly not Hellgathen be interested in Hellgathen? Anger rose in him. Why was he even allowing himself to be questioned?

"I have a friend there," SLOB replied rather cleverly. "So, what are you doing here?"

"We have friends in Rengar," Hendraz countered.

"I see."

Newark's hand gripped his weapon. It would be so easy to take him out now. He battled with himself for all of two seconds before deciding to go for it.

As he pulled his weapon, it flew out of his hand. The others, having no choice now but to engage SLOB, drew their weapons too. Weapons went flying all over the place, smashing into the screaming clientele, who were desperate to escape. Weaponless, the crew rushed SLOB but were blown back by a soundless explosion, sent crashing into walls and tables.

Staggering to their feet, they went for him again but SLOB swept out his hands, conducting an orchestra of pain. Hendraz and Serza smashed into a mirror, falling bloodied on the floor; Newark and Graham crashed headlong into the bar; Skinner went careering through a pocket of terrified customers who hadn't yet made it out the door; and Johnson's head thumped into a table. Her dazed body rose up. Graham tried to get to her but was flung back.

"Who are you?" SLOB asked her. "Why did you attack me?"

She couldn't understand what he was saying but she could guess. She smiled at him, sourly. "Because you're one ugly mother fucker."

SLOB turned to Rotzch. The man just shrugged.

SLOB's face turned twisted. Johnson's throat constricted and she struggled to breathe. Graham and Newark were slung back again and again as they desperately tried to reach her.

"Let her down, you evil fuck!" Newark screamed.

Seeing how desperate the two of them were, SLOB decided to put on a show. Johnson's body spun around in the air above his head. The crew stared at the speed she was going.

"The cycle of life!" SLOB called out crazily. "Birth," he announced, slamming her legs and arms into her chest then stretching them out as he pressed her body on all sides. "Childhood," he announced, slapping her face repeatedly with imaginary hands. "Life," he announced, slamming her from wall to wall. "And dea-"

Johnson was dropped like a sack of discarded rubbish. SLOB stared at the doorway. *"You..."*

Jenna stared back at him, her muscles going weak. What the hell did she do now? SLOB's whole attention was fixed on her, like he could feel it in her, as she could feel it in him. Aware of the bleeding carnage around her, her one thought was to lead SLOB away from there. Forcing her legs to work, she turned and ran.

She ran from the bar, ran down the street, ran as fast as she could. Scaly-skinned Rengiards looked at her oddly. Rengiard concrete had a bouncy feel and her arms were going everywhere as she struggled to stay upright. Dodging bodies, she turned to see him coming after her with a large man in tow. She caught sight of Fraza and Brash running behind them.

"Stop!" SLOB yelled, having the same problem Jenna was. Bodies flew out of his way as he cleared a path to get to her. "I want to talk to you, dammit!"

She wouldn't stop until she'd led him away from the populated areas. Soon, she was running through desolate streets. Up ahead, the streets gave way to black emptiness. Her objective was achieved and she wished she knew what she was going to do now.

"Wait, damn you!" SLOB shrieked. "Do you know what restraint I'm showing here!"

Something clicked. He hadn't, yet, been trying to kill her. He was talking. Maybe that gave her something to work with. This was it. It was time to stop and face SLOB.

Out of breath, she turned around fearfully. SLOB surveyed her with curious arrogance as he came ever closer.

"Who are you?" he asked, scrutinizing her.

Her eyes flitted to Brash and Fraza, who were watching on, helplessly. She took a deep calming breath. She couldn't fall to pieces. The universe was depending on her. Summoning the power, she levitated in the air. "You have displeased the gods," she said in a deep voice.

"What is she saying?" SLOB asked Rotzch.

Rotzch shrugged but Fraza translated. SLOB glanced around at Fraza then turned back to Jenna. "What gods? *I'm* the only god!"

"No. There are many of us. We exist on a different plane. You must repent your sins or face the wrath of all the gods."

"I'm the only god!" he insisted petulantly.

"Come, kneel before me and I will absolve you."

She saw confusion, hesitation in his eyes. If he would buy this and kneel before her, she could get a clear shot. Maybe a few shots. But his eyes turned hard. He swept out a hand and she fell back to earth. "You're no god," he spat. "Whoever you are, you're going to die."

He thrust out his arm and power shot out of him. She managed to block it but it knocked her back. She threw out power of her own and he deflected it easily. Brash started firing and Fraza started doing what Jenna was doing. SLOB deflected it all as he blasted Jenna again and again. Rotzch started shooting at Brash. Brash ducked for cover as he returned fire. Fraza and Jenna continued on at SLOB but they were getting nowhere. If anything, SLOB's power seemed to be increasing whilst theirs was wearing thin. The next hit took Jenna back twenty feet. Dazed for a moment, she looked up horrified to see a ball of lightning whizzing her way, the air cracking with thunder. She only just managed to knock it away. Her throat began to constrict and she had to use all her focus to push off invisible hands. He was tireless, so much stronger than she was.

Finally, he laughed insanely, punching his hands out to either side. The walls of the buildings crumbled.

"You call yourself a god!" he taunted. "You are no match for me!"

He was right. She couldn't hold out against this.

"Use the power, Jenna!" Brash shouted.

"I *am* using the power!"

Her face was being punched over and over by a sick fuck that was now just playing with her. Any minute he would go in for the kill and she was powerless to stop him. Why did she ever agree to this…!

"Time to pray to your gods," SLOB goaded with a sickening grin.

# Cold Realisation

Light flooded the street. Noise erupted. For a few moments, SLOB and Rotzch considered that she had been telling the truth. Those moments were all Brash needed to grab Jenna up and pull her toward the ship, Fraza racing beside them.

"Come on!" Hendraz yelled from the gangway.

The resistance was already firing on SLOB. SLOB, now busy deflecting fire, had little chance to focus on Jenna. As the gangway raised and the craft pulled away, SLOB screamed into the air. To make matters worse, it was one of his own craft. He used every ounce of focus to drag that ship down.

"We're banking, sir!" Paikra shouted.

"Keep it steady!" Hendraz ordered, jumping into the seat beside him.

"Jenna, do what you did last time," Brash said. "Fraza, help her. Remember, the engines are on your side."

With the help of Fraza, Jenna focused the power on lifting the craft and, at last, it broke free. Before long, they were being pulled in by Hendraz' ship.

Jenna stared at the floor as they left Rengar behind. Brash sat down heavily. "Fraza, tell Hendraz we need to head to Venulas, work with the alliance, form a strategy."

Fraza translated and Hendraz nodded.

The rest of the crew were sitting there, bloodied, bruised and subdued.

"I'm sorry," Jenna mumbled.

"You tried," Graham said.

"I failed."

"That's because the bastard *is* unstoppable."

"He was just playing with me," she murmured. "I was seconds from death. I couldn't do anything…" She looked up at Brash. "I couldn't do anything."

Brash would have given her a pep talk but he had been there. She was right. The hope they'd pinned on her seemed now to be in vain. It was a cold realisation.

# Friendship

SLOB's planet hopping was over. He was back on the mother ship, incensed that she had slipped through his fingers again.

"Who were they?" he demanded of Rotzch.

"A band of rebels, Lord."

"I know they were a band of rebels! But who? What race were they?"

"I couldn't say, Lord. Whoever they were, they would fight to the death to protect each other."

"My men would fight to the death to protect me!"

"Of course, Lord." *Only not as vigorously.* "They just seemed like... friends."

"So?" SLOB asked, regarding him curiously.

Rotzch shrugged. "Just commenting, Lord."

"Well, don't." He paced around. "I'm not used to failure, Rotzch. I don't like it." He turned to him, suddenly. "Word of this cannot get out."

"Of course, Lord."

"Get out, Rotzch."

"Of course, Lord." He bowed and left.

SLOB stared after him. He was feeling very unsettled. He moped around for a while then he went for a walk about the ship. Wherever he wandered, his men looked efficient, none of them wanting to make eye contact with him. He had always considered this a mark of respect. They feared him, as they should, yet it wasn't satisfying him enough.

He made his way up to the recreation sector. He could hear banter and laughter as he approached. Peering in, he saw his men having fun. Some of them were playing hologun, shooting at each other without fear of injury. Some were sitting around drinking, others flirting with the female members of his crew. He watched them with a fascinated interest as he considered the concept of friendship. Were they friends? Would they die for each other? Would they die for each other before they would die for him? The thought enraged him but beneath the anger was a rebellious question. Why, in all his life, had *he* never had a friend? Why, as a child, did other children laugh at him? Why did they treat him like a second-class citizen? He was a god, he told himself, reviled by his people... but... nobody knew he was a god then. Even he didn't know. So, the niggling question, obscured for years, remained unanswered.

The laughter and talking stopped as he was spotted. He turned and walked away.

The crew were hanging out in their quarters. Graham was staring hopelessly at Johnson, who was lying on her bunk, listening to some weird tunes. Brash was staring hopelessly at Jenna, who was lying on her bunk, staring hopelessly at the ceiling. Fraza kept standing up and down, the shock of recent events now hitting him with full force. Skinner was tossing a plastic cup in the air whilst simultaneously trying the calculate the volume of the entire universe. Newark was idly watching the cup as he tried again to work out the mechanics of Hellgathen procreation. Bored with that, he became increasingly restless. He would have got up and walked around the ship but he couldn't communicate with anyone and when he tried, they just stared at him as if he was a freak. *Him a freak? His* nose and *his* junk were in the right place, thank you very much, and he certainly didn't have a fucking tail!

A Jolting bump brought them alertly to the room.

"What was that?" Graham asked.

Piling out after Brash, they rushed toward the flight deck, another jolt rocking the ship. Some of Hendraz' men ran past them.

The flight deck was a hive of activity. "What's going on?" Brash shouted. "Are we being attacked?"

Fraza asked the question and Hendraz blurted a flustered reply.

"We're not being attacked, Captain," Fraza answered. "He thinks they've got a short in one of the drive circuits. We're being sucked in by the gravity of that enormous planet. He wants us to get the hell off his flight deck and strap ourselves in."

"We're going to crash!"

Hendraz hit a red button and an alarm sounded.

"Right," Brash said. "Let's get strapped in."

The crew ran as fast as they could to the first landing room to find the seats all taken. They ran all around the ship to find somewhere to strap in but they were too late. The ship banked and started to plunge. They rolled around, grabbing onto whatever they could find, feeling sick and terrified. Graham, surmising they were going to die, shouted, "I love you, Daria!" Through the nausea-inducing pressure, Johnson stared back at him. He'd never said that before. Newark, feeling closer to Graham and Johnson than he had to anyone in his life, shouted, "I love you guys!" Fraza was chanting some strange words. Brash locked eyes with Jenna. "I love you, Jenna," he called over the din. Skinner yelled, "Bring it on!"

The pressure intensified, the seconds long drawn-out minutes that brought everything into sharp focus. For Jenna and Brash, they had failed in their mission. The universe was lost. For Johnson and Graham, they had just turned a corner to come up against a dead end. For Newark, he would never know what a real relationship was like. Fraza gained a few moments of acceptant peace. Skinner was acceptant too. He had done this too many times before.

Impact was brutal. They were slammed against the walls, the wind knocked out of them, bracing themselves for an explosion that didn't come. Objects flew all over the place as the craft careered along, slinging them around like billiard balls, Johnson's broken arm taking a painful battering.

At last, it all came to a stop and an eerie calm pervaded the ship.

Stunned for a moment, Brash sprang into action. "Is everyone alright?"

The crew lay dazed and bleeding.

"Is everyone alright?" he pressed.

One by one, they replied. Newark did not reply.

"Is he alright?" Johnson asked, scrambling to get to him. Newark wasn't moving.

Brash checked him over. "I don't think he's breathing."

Graham came over and started shaking Newark. "Wake up, buddy! Wake up!"

Newark wouldn't wake up. Brash began pumping his chest and giving him mouth to mouth. The others watched on in dismay as the Captain tirelessly tried to revive him. At last, Brash sat back, staring at Newark, lost. Graham took over, pumping Newark's chest relentlessly.

Finally, Brash laid a hand on Graham's shoulder. "He's gone…"

Graham made a strangled sound and fell back. Johnson stared at the floor. Jenna watched on, horrified, her throat constricting. At that moment, she realised just how much she cared for Newark, how much he had grown on her.

"Move aside," she said, crawling to get to him. Placing her hands on his chest, she tried to do what she had done once before. Of course, last time he wasn't technically dead but she had to try. She closed her eyes and focused, emptying herself, letting the power well up in her, letting it flow into Newark. She suffused his whole body with this power, power she didn't even understand. She couldn't allow herself to lose focus; she couldn't allow herself to give up.

"I think it's too late," Brash said sombrely.

She carried on regardless. She wasn't stopping until this oafish, yet strangely endearing man, opened his eyes. All at once, she felt something, like a tank being filled up, the power spilling back into her. She could do no more. She opened her eyes and waited. The crew waited with her. Newark's eyes did not open and she dropped her head, defeated.

A deadly silence wrapped around her like a shroud. Tears stung her eyes. She looked up to see the shell-shocked faces of the crew. She wanted to say sorry but the words wouldn't come.

"You want a piece of this, Trot?"

Jenna looked down to see Newark's brown eyes staring back at her. Tears gushed down her cheeks and she hugged him. Graham and Johnson, ecstatic now, mauled him too. Newark didn't know what to make of it. He couldn't remember ever being hugged. It was totally surreal.

Jenna turned to Brash. The shock and relief were palpable on his face. He crouched beside Newark. "How are you feeling? You had us worried there."

"She saved your life," Skinner remarked distantly. He stared at Jenna oddly. He was coming to accept there were things outside of current science but his brain still struggled to fit them into new scientific constructs.

Newark drew himself up, staring at Jenna too. The girl had cried for him. Nobody had cried for him before. Jenna wiped the tears away, feeling a little embarrassed now. "How many times do I have to save your hide," she complained lightly.

"D'you think you can do anything for a broken arm?" Johnson asked. Graham touched Johnson's arm and she yelped.

"Sorry." He turned to Jenna.

Jenna began to work her magic.

"How are you doing that...?" Skinner asked, observing her closely.

"I'm not doing anything," Jenna replied, thoughtfully. "Whatever this power is, that's what's doing it. I'm just... directing it."

"Is it that thing called chi?" Graham asked.

"No idea."

"Is it some kind of electromagnetic force?" Skinner asked.

"I don't know."

"Is it magic?" Newark asked.

Jenna glanced at him and smiled. Newark had a simplistic way of looking at things. "Yes, it's magic," she said, taking in his look of wonder and satisfaction, and feeling satisfied herself.

Johnson stretched her arm. It seemed to be in one piece again.

"The impact should have destroyed the ship," Brash said, puzzled. "This doesn't make sense... I'm going to see what's going on. Fraza, come with me. The rest of you, head back to our quarters."

As the crew made their way back to their quarters, some things were starting to become clear. Graham had told Johnson he loved her. As she hadn't thumped him when he'd touched her arm, he took this as a positive sign. The crew now knew that their Captain loved Trot. Since, with the exception of Johnson and Fraza, they'd had no build up to this, they were struggling to make sense of it. Newark had blurted, 'I love you guys.' Unfortunately, the near-death experience had not obliterated the memory and he felt embarrassed by the declaration. Sometimes, expressions of undying love should only be made if you actually die.

Brash got to the flight deck to discover they had crashed into a sea. Some of Hendraz' men were out there surveying the damage. Others were examining the drives.

"How far off land are we?" Brash asked through Fraza.

"One hundred queyans, at a guess," Hendraz replied.

Brash raised his eyebrows. "Queyans?"

"It's..." There was no basis for comparison. "It's a very long way."

Brash raked a hand through his hair. "Right, well, we'll have to take our craft, maybe tow the ship."

"How? Can your craft travel under water? The doors are submerged."

"So, we're stuck here, in the middle of a goddam sea?"

"Maybe Jenna and Fraza could try to move the ship."

"They could try but it's... a very long way in choppy water with no engines to help them."

"Well, they might as well try because otherwise we're screwed."

"I'll go get them."

When Brash walked into their quarters, he felt many sets of eyes on him. Those eyes seemed to be assessing him in a new light. He knew why, of course, but there was little he could do about that.

Jenna and Fraza did try to move the ship but their progress kept being knocked back by big waves. It was a losing battle and they finally had to admit it.

"Well, we're screwed then," Hendraz said, punching the control panel.

Fraza attempted to translate but Brash held up a hand. The sentiment was clear.

At that moment, something peculiar happened. The craft began to move.

"Are you doing that?" Brash asked Jenna.

She shook her head. He looked to Fraza. He shook his head too.

"The ship's dead," Hendraz said. "If they're not doing it, what is?"

Jenna looked up at Brash. "Could it be SLOB?"

They all looked at each other. Whoever was doing it, they were powerless to stop it. Someone or something was reeling them in.

# Old Crone

The whole of the resistance was ready with their weapons as the craft neared land. Brash and Hendraz surveyed the shoreline, expecting an army to be waiting there. What they saw was a single solitary figure. The figure was rowing toward them.

"Is it SLOB?" Jenna asked.

"I don't think so," Brash replied. As the tiny boat came ever closer, Brash saw what looked like a withered old being struggling with the oars. "He... looks pretty harmless. Still, we can't take any chances."

Hendraz unlocked the hatch manually and several weapons covered the circle of amber sky. The amber sky was eventually replaced by an ugly, withered, leathery blue face. The hunch-backed body it belonged to climbed down the metal ladder. It wore a woolly jacket and loose trousers. When it reached their level, it turned, its piercing blue eyes roaming over the unfriendly-looking welcoming committee. The eyes settled on Brash, who had assumed an air of authority.

"Good day to you, sir," it said, its lips not matching the words.

"Who are you?" Brash asked, looking at it suspiciously.

"Tynia. I pulled you in."

"*You?* You pulled us over thirty miles...?"

The old being smiled, which had a hideous effect on its wrinkles. "I did."

"But you're an old man?"

"Actually, I'm an old woman."

"Oh. Sorry."

"Don't mention it. I might have mistaken you for a woman. I didn't, though," she said, smiling steadily.

He eyed her oddly. "You used the power?"

She smiled again. "I have more boats ashore. I'm afraid you will have to go back and forth to get everyone off. Could someone row *me* back? My arms are aching terribly, and it was quite a struggle climbing over your craft. I *had* thought you might have come out to meet me."

"Err..."

Jenna stepped out from behind the circle of weapons. "I'll come back with you."

Brash, Hendraz, and Serza went with them. When they reached the shore, the three of them took a boat back each.

"It's going to take forever to get everyone off," Jenna remarked, watching them go.

"Yes. My home is just over this rise. Walk with me." The old woman shuffled on. Jenna couldn't believe she'd pulled their ship all that way.

They walked up between sand dunes and when they got to the top, Jenna saw a squalid little dwelling with smoke rising from a chimney. It sat in a copse of trees. The land around looked wild and over in the distance she could see purple hills. The amber sky gave everything a muted feel.

"I'm sorry about crashing your ship, dear," the old woman said, "but otherwise you would have gone straight past."

"What?" Jenna said, stopping. "You crashed our ship…?"

The woman turned to her. "Yes, dear."

"You crashed our ship…?"

"Yes, dear."

"You crashed our ship…?"

"We could go on with this for days."

"How the hell did you crash our ship…? *Why* did you crash our ship? Do you know what you put us through! You could have killed us!"

"I provided a cushion where you landed. I do hope nobody was harmed."

"You killed my friend!" The woman's eyes widened. "He's alive now but he *was* dead!"

She smiled sweetly. "Well, as long as he's alive now."

Jenna stared at the woman.

"I crashed your ship because I needed to meet you. The way you are going, you're going to fail."

"Just a minute, back up. How do you know about me and how do you know what I'm trying to do?"

"I have dreamt about you. I have seen you. Those with the power are like a magnet. You guided that ship here as much as I pulled you. The difference is, you are not consciously aware of it."

"Hendraz brought that ship here, not me."

"You chose the flightpath and influenced him, neither of you knowing."

"That's crazy! Are you insane?"

"No, dear. I don't think so."

"Look, there is only one flightpath from A to B," Jenna insisted.

"Yes, and he veered off it. He'll be cross with himself when he realises." The old woman looked at her, thoughtfully. "Think of it this way. The whole of life could be compared to a dream. Those with the power have more influence over the dream but it all works at a deeper level."

"I have no idea what you're talking about…"

"I know. Just remember, for now, that we're working on the level of wholeness. Hold that thought while we go and get some tea."

The old woman tottered off over the scrubby grass, Jenna staring after her.

"Come on, dear," she called. "It's a little chilly out here."

Jenna followed in a daze.

The basic wooden shack had only two rooms. A huge metal pot was hanging over a fire in the middle of the living area.

"I hope I've made enough," Tynia said, fussing over a stew. "I wasn't sure how many of you they'd be."

"You made us a stew…?" Jenna peered into the pot. It was green in colour but it smelled good.

"Well, you are my guests."

Jenna scowled. Plummeting down at an alarming rate didn't feel like an invitation.

The old woman glanced at her. "I made the landing as comfortable as I could… the air cushion gradually increasing in density. It could have been much worse."

"Don't, for god's sake, mention that you crashed our ship to the others. They'll lynch you."

"Mum's the word."

Jenna eyed her oddly then looked at the wrinkly blue hand as it stirred the pot. "Do all the people on this planet look like you?"

"Yes, though few reach my age. I'm over two hundred years old, you know."

Jenna was coming to the firm conclusion that two hundred-year-old beings were a hazard to everyone.

The woman turned to her with a toothless smile. "This planet is called, Cyntros, by the way. The inhabitants are generally friendly and tolerant of other species. Give it a stir for me, would you, while I dig out some bowls."

Jenna started to feel a little dizzy. She had to sit down.

"Oh, yes, I knew I'd forgotten something." Tynia rummaged in some cupboards. "Where is that blasted stuff. I collected a whole bag of it yesterday." Reaching under a chair, she retrieved a tattered sack. "Here it is." She brought out a handful of broken up purple leaves. "Now, eat these, dear."

"What's this?"

"Bata leaf. The air on this planet is a little thin for many species. Eat this and you get oxygen into your bloodstream. They do a roaring trade with this over in the cities."

"Really? It gives you oxygen? That's-"

"Very handy, I know, and so much better than wearing cumbersome masks. Things like that make me claustrophobic." She shuddered. "It took every grain of willpower to enter your spaceship, and that's no lie."

"You're claustrophobic?"

"Oh, yes, dear. They taste nice, don't they? Are you feeling better now?"

"Yes."

The sounds of voices and Brash shouting 'hello!' drew their attention.

"Hand this around, dear," Tynia said, giving Jenna the sack. "If anyone is from Aerthia, don't give it them. Tends to boil their blood for some reason."

"What do they look like?"

"Stubby noses and tails. On second thought, you carry on stirring the stew. I'll hand this around." She walked out with the sack.

A few moments later, Brash entered. He came straight over and took Jenna's arm. "What you did for Newark was incredible. I just want to-"

He cut off as the door opened and the rest of the crew ambled in. The hand removed from Jenna's arm but not quickly enough. Graham and Skinner were staring at it.

"D'you think she's a witch?" Newark asked, looking around. "Magic powers, cauldron, wooden shack in forest. Maybe that stuff she's given us is poison."

The crew looked at each other then shook their heads. Skinner wandered around, looking in nooks and crannies. Newark covertly studied Brash and Jenna, looking for tell-tale signs. Fraza started to laugh.

"Are you alright, Fraza?" Brash asked.

Fraza couldn't seem to answer for laughing. They'd never heard him laugh before. It bordered on a squeal.

"I think he's lost it," Newark said, patting Fraza's back as if this was a cure for losing it but it only made Fraza laugh more, then cough and splutter, then laugh again.

"Newark, that's not working," Brash said.

The old woman came rushing back in. "There's always one. Come on, now," she said, taking Fraza's hand. "Let's sit you down." She started rummaging through cupboards and brought out a green concoction. "Have a little slip of this." She guided a spoonful into Fraza's mouth.

"What's wrong with him?" Brash asked.

"Just a side-effect," the woman told him.

Fraza's laughter turned to hiccupping. Finally, he was back to himself.

Tynia got up and stirred the stew before handing a bowlful to Jenna. "Now, if the rest of you would help me dish up," she said, pointing to a stack of bowls, large mugs, small mugs and whatever other vessels she could find.

Through the ensuing chaos, Brash came over to Jenna. "Maybe the old crone can help us," he whispered.

"Don't call her an old crone," she whispered back.

"Sorry. It's just, if she can pull us all that way, maybe she could help us defeat SLOB."

"I know. I'll have a word with her."

Newark watched them whispering, recognising this as a sign. He glanced at Johnson and Graham, who seemed much cosier now. He felt oddly glum. He diverted his attention to Skinner and Fraza, who, he was sure, didn't stand a chance of getting a girlfriend. Skinner was skinny and far too nerdy. Fraza was a Kaledian. Sure, he could get a Kaledian girlfriend, maybe, but who wanted one of them. Newark decided he was not the saddest member of the group.

As they sat down to eat, Graham raised his chin to Newark. "You go dying on us again, I'll bloody kill you."

"You scared the shit out of us," Johnson said.

Newark was choked up. He concentrated hard on eating his stew.

Hendraz walked in and said something that Fraza relayed. "He sees we've grabbed the sheltered accommodation."

Brash replied. "Tell him, that's because *his* crew nabbed all the seatbelts."

Fraza translated and Hendraz smiled. The Hellgathen said something else.

"The circuits in all the drives are fried," Fraza told them.

Jenna glanced at Tynia. The old woman was staring at the wall.

Brash looked at her too. "We need parts for our ship. Do you know where we might get them?"

"The city of Cankar is approximately five of your miles away," she told him. "If you have a translator guide, you should be able to communicate. You will need currency. I'll get you some." The woman walked to a large cupboard in the corner and retrieved a sack of coins. Jenna noted there were many sacks in there.

As she hauled the sack over, she registered the crew looking at her. "I'm rich, you know," she said to their stares.

The crew stared at the sack then stared around the cabin.

Half an hour later, all the crew, apart from Jenna, were fast asleep.

"What have you done to them?" Jenna asked, running to the door to discover more sleeping bodies outside.

"Oh, please, dear, don't worry about them. A good rest will do them good. It's a natural sleeping potion. No harmful effects, whatsoever. They'll wake up feeling ready to conquer the world."

Jenna turned, viewing Tynia with suspicion.

"We need a little chat," the old woman told her, "and a bit of peace and quiet. There are too many bodies, too much noise. I can't hear myself think. And just between you and me, some of the language out there was absolutely appalling."

"I can't understand any of them," Jenna remarked, her eyes still fixed on Tynia.

"Yes. You haven't developed the mind-reading skill, have you?"

"So, what do we need to chat about?"

"If you are going to defeat the Thunder God, you can't think like him."

"I don't think like him!"

"You're working on the same level he is, digging a little well into the infinite. His well is larger than yours but, as I said, you are approaching it from the level of the finite. Once you change your perception from the finite to the infinite, you will achieve so much more."

"I don't understand," Jenna said, shaking her head. "I'm doing the best I can."

"You need to work on changing your whole perspective. The only barriers you have are self-imposed. Shed the barriers and the power of the entire universe will be at your disposal."

"How...? Wait a minute. If you can do all this, why don't *you* conquer the Thunder God?"

The woman's eyes widened. "I can't come with you. There is a certain element in the air here that my body requires. Besides, I'm claustrophobic. I can't wear a spacesuit and I refuse to get on a spacecraft."

Jenna stared at her, incredulous. "So, it's left to me, yet again!" Up to now they'd met two beings who could really have helped them. One killed himself and the other had claustrophobia. It was like the universe was playing a sick joke.

"I'm sorry. I know it's disappointing, but I am trying to help you."

"So," Jenna said, folding her arms, "you're saying I'm thinking small?"

"In a sense. Remember, a well is a trickle to an ocean around you. The barrier is one of perception. See, when I towed your spacecraft in, I wasn't drawing from a well. I was using the immense power of the whole universe... the entire whole." Tynia rubbed her blue lips with her knobbly blue fingers. "Let's go back to the dream. In a dream, nothing is real, so, if you wanted to fly, you could. You could do anything because you are only limited by the power of the dreaming mind. There isn't really any time and space. Well, in terms of the power, there is no time and space either. You could have a well or the entirety, and you are only limited by your mind. Get rid of the concepts, from and to. They really do get in the way."

"What…? I draw on the power and it comes up. I don't know what else I can do," Jenna said, frustrated.

"Don't give yourself a hard time, dear. When you've lived in a mass delusion all your life, it is very difficult to cut loose from it."

"Mass delusion…?"

"Time and space. They don't really exist." `

"Of course, they exist!"

"Well," she said, moving her head from side to side, "OK. But not from the level of the power. Come on. Let's go out and practice."

Tynia took her to the shore. "Now, watch. First, I'm going to draw from a well, like you do." Jenna watched a column of water rise out of the sea. The column fell back again. "Now watch again." This time, a mountain of water rose up. "I could go higher but you get the point." The mountain gently returned to the sea. "The second time, I used the wholeness, the height only limited by my intention. Now, you try."

Jenna tried. She managed two columns by pushing the water up but the second was no bigger than the first. "See, I can't do it!"

"Well, no. If you do the same thing twice, you get the same result. You're drawing the power up through yourself. There's nowhere to draw from and to, just the power and your intent."

Jenna tried again but to no avail. "I can't do this!"

"Well, throwing a tantrum won't help you."

"I'm not throwing a tantrum!"

"Yes, you are."

"No, I'm not!"

"Young girls…" Tynia complained, shaking her head.

Jenna glared at the woman then stomped off.

Tynia watched her go. *Why couldn't she be an old crone like me?*

# Reading minds

The resistance had woken up feeling mildly invigorated. Hendraz and Brash put their tiredness down to the stress of the landing. Jenna did not put them straight. Brash and Hendraz assembled a party to head into Cankar. For his part, Brash took Skinner, Fraza and a bag of bata leaves.

They were gone for two days, in which time Tynia persevered with Jenna. Jenna still couldn't grasp what she had to do. She'd taken in so much these past months, but this was one giant leap too far.

The remaining members of the resistance spent their time lounging or wandering around the area. Graham and Johnson took the time to reconnect. Newark had come across them reconnecting behind a bush and was completely weirded out by it. Seeing your buddies buddying up was not something you should ever have to face. Backing away quietly, he wandered around aimlessly, deciding, at last, to go and find Trot.

Walking down between the dunes, he stared ahead at a towering wall of water. *Holy Fuck!* The water fell away and a smaller column appeared. His attention turned to the old woman and Trot, who were standing on the shoreline. Newark watched the old woman shaking her head and wondered what her problem was. He wished he could do shit like that. The woman walked away and Trot fell down on the sand. Newark went over, sitting himself down beside her. "What ya doing?"

Jenna glanced at him. "Failing miserably."

"Really? That looked pretty impressive to me."

"Did you see the little column of water?" Newark nodded. "That was mine. Did you see the towering wall?" He nodded. "That was Tynia's. I have to make my column into a wall and it's just not happening."

Newark scratched his head. She was obviously fed up about that and he wondered what to say. "Inner peace?" he offered with a shrug.

"Inner peace?"

"I heard that shit somewhere."

Jenna smiled. "What I wouldn't give for some of that."

He shuffled a little. "Err… listen… I just want to… thank you for saving my life."

"Don't mention it."

He scratched his cheek. He was feeling something odd. Something like guilt. He wanted to apologise for trying to kill her all those months ago. Of course, he couldn't admit to that, so he apologised for grabbing her arse instead.

She smiled at him. "Don't do it again."

"Don't worry. I'm not touching your arse again. If you don't kill me, the Cap will." Newark spied a chance to get more information. "So, you and the Cap then?"

"Yeah…"

He kept his eyes trained on her but that was all he was going to get. She looked distant and glum. He thought of something that might cheer her up. "D'you want to know what I've just seen?"

Captain Brash returned the next day. The party had acquired a cart to put their supplies on. As they approached, Newark thought the Captain looked subdued. Must be all that walking, he considered.

"What was Cankar like?" Newark asked.

"Very blue," Brash replied, looking rather blue himself.

Newark looked to Skinner for more. "It was surprisingly sophisticated," Skinner told him, glancing at the old woman's shack. "Fraza had another fit. We looked everywhere to get the antidote, which was grossly overpriced."

"Where's Je- Trot?" Brash asked.

"She said she was going for a lie down," Newark replied. "Between you and me, she doesn't seem too happy. She's not learning the stuff the old crone's teaching her."

Brash pursed his lips, nodding thoughtfully. "Where are Johnson and Graham?"

*Screwing in the trees.* "No idea, Captain."

The cart was taken down to the shore and parts loaded onto the boats. Brash found Jenna lying on Tynia's bed. She seemed to be asleep. Closing the door behind him, he went to sit on the bedside chair. He stared at her for a moment then rubbed his brow. Something awful had happened last night, something he wished he could erase. The place they stayed had a bar on the top floor. There, he had met a shape-shifter. Of course, he didn't know it was a shape-shifter at the time. He didn't even know shape-shifters existed. The beings were prostitutes that could change their appearance to match your deepest desire. As Jenna was his deepest desire, that's what he saw. He'd been completely duped. The thing didn't tell him what it was. Surprised to see Jenna, he'd asked her what she was doing there. When she told him she would very much like to sleep with him, it completely blindsided him. When she kissed him enthusiastically and begged him to take her to his room, he was swept away. It was only after, when the being switched to its original form and he ran to the bathroom to throw up, that he realised what he'd done. He had committed the ultimate betrayal. Fraza helped him make sense of it and told him how much he owed. Fraza promised not to breathe a word but Brash couldn't hide the truth from himself. The sense of guilt and revulsion was overwhelming.

He put his head in his hands, racking his brains, trying to figure out if there was any way he could have told them apart, any clue he had missed. But, like Jenna, that woman looked just too perfect...

Jenna's dream was fading. Strange words invaded her mind. *"That woman looked just too perfect..."* Becoming more awake, she kept her eyes closed, relaxing in an empty state of mind. *"I couldn't be blamed, surely...?"*

She opened her eyes to see Lucas. He looked tired, desolate even.

"Did you not get your parts?" she asked.

He whipped his head to her and put on a smile. "Yes, we got them. They're fixing the ship now. I'm going to see how they're getting on." He got up and left the room without looking back at her.

Jenna stared at the door.

She didn't see him for the rest of the day. The old woman tried to give her another lesson, but it seemed to be in vain. By the following morning, their ship was up and running and Tynia, at last, accepted defeat. She had done all she could. The girl seemed determined to fail.

Despite everything, Jenna hugged her. "Thank you for trying to help me."

"Good luck to you, dear." *You're going to need it.*

Tynia even helped with their take off, giving the craft a shove as it blasted out of their atmosphere. She stared after it for a few moments. Then she breathed out. "At last, I can die."

"Straight to Venulas now," Brash said to Hendraz through Fraza.

Hendraz looked at his bearings and frowned. They had veered off course. How had that happened? He was an excellent pilot. He decided not to share this information with anyone.

Fraza looked at the Captain. The Captain's secret was safe with him but Fraza could see how it pained him. The little Kaledian wondered if it *was* a betrayal if you thought you were sleeping with the one you loved. Still, he doubted Jenna would see it that way. Good job she couldn't read thoughts. Fraza had tried to spare the Captain yet more pain by neglecting to mention that the creature never actually changed shape. It was all a mind trick. The thought of himself rolling around with that hideous ungainly form might prove a little too much for him.

Brash avoided Jenna as much as he could. The guilt and shame made it impossible to face her. Jenna, picking up on his avoidance, started to wonder if his feelings for her had changed. She lay in her bunk, considering this and the pain of that possibility sapped her energy. The cabin was quiet, the crew lost in their own thoughts. Casting her own painful thoughts aside, she allowed herself to doze.

*"It's better than it's ever been. Who'd have thought three little words could make such a big difference."*

*"Blue men and blue women doing it. Yuck!"*

*"A force directed by will… It throws everything into question…"*

Jenna sat up, staring at Graham, Newark, and Skinner. "Did any of you say anything?"

They turned to look at her. "Nope," Graham said.

"You hearing things, Trot?" Newark asked.

Jenna lay back down and stared at the ceiling, her eyes growing wide. Had she just read their thoughts? She tried to get into that relaxed state again but the excitement was making it hard. At last, she gave up.

*"Nobody's saved my life before… Pity she's with the Cap. She's a cute little thing, really."*

*"Three children and a house by a lake. Would she want children?"*

*"Well done, Jenna."* Wait. What? *"It's Cornelius. I always knew you'd get there."*

"How?"

*"Minds can bridge distance. I've been reaching out to you ever since you left. How are-"*

The link broke. She couldn't maintain the right state of mind. But wow… This was mind-blowing stuff. Had she really just heard Cornelius from all that distance away…? That wasn't her voice in her head. Feeling immensely proud of herself, she smiled from ear to ear. She was on a euphoric high but the high crashed and her smile dropped. *That woman looked just too perfect… I couldn't be blamed, surely…?* The words repeated in her head like a death knell. They definitely weren't her thoughts. They were Lucas'.

Pain seared her chest. He had betrayed her. He had been with someone else. Everything she thought she knew crumbled around her. Was he in love with this perfect woman?

She rolled onto her side, clutching herself tightly. She had never known such pain. She hated him. Hated him with every fibre of her being.

Objects smashed against walls.

"Shit, Trot!" Newark yelled but she could do little about it. The pain was too excruciating.

"What's wrong with her?" Graham shouted, dodging a metal chair. "Trot?"

In the end, Graham, Skinner, and Newark ran out to fetch the Captain. When they returned with Brash and Fraza, everything was calm.

"Jenna, what's going on?" Brash asked.

Holding onto her hurt and anger, she sat up. "What d'you mean?"

"Graham said objects were flying everywhere."

She shook her head, confused. "I don't know, Captain. I just had a nightmare," she said, staring him hard in the eye. "Did I make things move?"

"I say we opt for different sleeping arrangements," Newark remarked under his breath.

"Right, well, I suppose we'll have to monitor the situation," Brash said. "If it happens again, we'll have to consider getting you your own quarters."

"Of course, Captain," she said. "That would be the obvious solution. Sleeping arrangements are so important, aren't they?"

Brash looked at her oddly. She was acting weird.

Johnson came in with wet hair. "Do you know there's a fucking spyhole in the wall of the female showers! I've just poked someone's eye out and when I find the fucker I'm going to mutilate him!"

"Typical low-life male," Jenna said, her eyes fixed on Brash.

Brash felt his collar. "I'll have a word with Hendraz about this," he said, walking out.

"D'you know who it was?" Graham asked, incensed. No-one looked at his woman but him.

Johnson threw her stuff on her bunk. "Come on, let's see if we can find the creep."

Fraza looked concerned. "This is going to cause trouble."

"So what?" Jenna said, jumping down from her bunk. "Sometimes you have to stand up for things. I bet the little creep's been ogling me too!"

She strode out after Graham and Johnson. Now she had somewhere to direct her anger.

They scoured the ship, looking for the culprit. All types of weird eyes stared back at them but none of those eyes looked damaged in any way. Jenna and Johnson wondered how many of those eyes had seen them naked. Someone needed to pay for this!

They found him in the medibay. The room was empty apart from a humanoid being with grey skin and slanting eyes. One of those eyes had a compress over it.

"Scumbag!" Johnson yelled, launching in, dragging it off its seat and kicking the crap out of it. Graham joined in, leaving little room for Jenna but when the creep landed near her feet, she kicked it hard in the stomach.

Paikra, hearing the commotion, stormed in. Jenna gawped at him. His eye was red and swollen. Her gaze slowly transferred to the beaten alien. "Wait!" she screamed. "We've got the wrong guy!"

Johnson let go of the grey and stared at Paikra. A moment later, she was laying into him. Jenna knelt beside the grey on the floor. He was a broken mess. Immediately, she laid her hands on him and worked her magic.

Hendraz and Brash arrived with Fraza and the fight was split up. Paikra pleaded his case to Hendraz, and Fraza translated. "He says all the men do it, even this one," he said, pointing to the grey.

"Eww!" Jenna removed her hands, stood up and kicked the grey in the chest.

"Jenna!" Brash scolded.

"I want them punished!" she shouted.

"Right on, sister!" Johnson called out. "An eye for an eye!"

Brash scratched his neck. "Tell Hendraz they're right. This cannot go unpunished."

Hendraz insisted that *he* had not been perving and he was sure this did not apply to all his crew. Most of them would not find the humans attractive, though he was sure quite a few were a little freakish. The trouble was: how to know who the culprits were? At last, he decided that all male kind would have to suffer for the sake of the few.

"Not our crew," Johnson said.

"How do you know any of them aren't guilty?" Hendraz asked.

The thought was horrifying. It was almost like incest.

"It's all or nothing," Hendraz said.

Johnson looked at Graham. "I'll take it," he told her and she looked at him with pride.

"OK," she said to Hendraz.

Hendraz asked Jenna and Johnson to choose their punishment. The punishment had to fit the crime, they considered, so it had to be humiliating.

"How about twenty minutes in a freezing cold shower with us watching them?" Jenna suggested.

"Are you serious?" Johnson asked. "They'll get off on that."

"Oh. Yeah. OK, how about the freezing cold shower but three of them to each one?"

"I like your thinking. But no loopholes," Johnson said, looking at Hendraz. "They have to be butt naked."

Fraza translated and Hendraz agreed.

The rest of the crew had mixed feelings about the punishment. Fraza was horrified. Skinner wasn't fussed. Brash wasn't too happy but Jenna reasoned that he needed punishing anyway. It was Newark who surprised Jenna, telling her he'd take one for the team.

So, Newark took one for the team but he looked a little dazed when he came back to their quarters. "There was all kind of shit in there..." he told them.

As Fraza entered, he did various intense stepping rituals. He went over to his bunk and curled up into a rocking ball. Jenna felt bad. Fraza shouldn't have had to suffer for this. Brash came in and walked over to him. "Are you alright, Fraza?"

Fraza made a strangled sound and Brash patted his shoulder. "Sleep it off, Fraza."

Brash glanced at Jenna. "Happy now?"

Jenna shot to her feet. "Happy? No, I'm not! Not only have I had a load of scumbags ogling me, but I have to watch Fraza suffer for it! But I suppose I should just put up and shut up, is that it?"

Newark, Graham, Johnson, and Skinner sat up. Life was getting interesting.

Brash was taken aback. "No, but-"

"But? There are no buts! I'm not going to put up with any old crap! Not from you, not from anyone!"

If it wasn't the Captain, Johnson would have yelled, go girl!

"I'm still your Captain, Trot," Brash growled in a low voice.

"I know what you are," she said harshly, staring him hard in the eye.

Something in that stare made him shiver. "Graham, for fuck's sake, plug up the hole in the shower."

"Already done, Captain," Johnson said.

Brash walked out and Jenna was even more disappointed in him than she had been before.

"Wow..." Newark said. "Was that a lovers' spat?"

"There are no lovers," Jenna threw out. "It's over. As far as I'm concerned, he's just the Captain."

"Err... does he know that?" Johnson asked.

"I shouldn't think he cares."

Newark thought relationships were very unstable creatures. One minute they're on; then they're off. Maybe they were overrated. And he certainly wouldn't want his head chewed off like that. Still, he had to hand it to her. She did chew him out.

Brash wandered around the ship, feeling at odds with himself. Jenna was acting strangely. If he didn't know better, he would say she could smell guilt on him. He shouldn't have said what he did. It wasn't her fault. He'd just spent an uncomfortable time in the shower room then walked in on Fraza looking like that. He was trying to be the captain the crew deserved but things kept getting in the way. He pulled himself up short. A good captain would deal with those things. He turned his focus to the mission. They would be arriving in Venulas soon. He prayed all the delegates would be there.

# The Dark Side

To Brash's immense relief, the delegates were there. The huge oval chamber was awash with colour, packed-out with yellow-faced Venulians, pink-faced Quenbrarians and various other colours of the rainbow. There must have been three hundred bodies and they all wore headpieces – translators programmed with over fifty languages. Unfortunately, English wasn't in there so Fraza picked Hellgathen and had to translate to the crew. The assembly spoke and debated and, at last, the leaders headed off to formulate a detailed plan. Brash, Hendraz, Fraza and Serza went with them.

The crew and the rest of the resistance were put up in a hotel. Indeed, the hotels would have done a roaring trade were it not for Venulian hospitality. The delegations were treated as guests. The Venulian staff were equally hospitable. As the crew lounged in enormous red chairs, stuff kept being brought to them. But it kept coming and coming and the staff hung around like bugs they couldn't shake off.

The oval-shaped lounge had a round bar in the centre but, with their translators away, the crew struggled to make use of it. The room was bright as there was lots of glass, which afforded an excellent view of the garden. Symbolic pictures hung on the walls and Jenna stared at a picture of chubby yellow fingers clasping hands. She wondered what it was trying to say. Newark stared in horror at a picture of a naked Venulian woman. He couldn't contemplate how awful that sight would be in the flesh.

Their bedrooms, surprisingly, were square, the owner, no doubt, compromising here for the sake of space, which they definitely needed as the beds and baths were gigantic. Jenna waited an age for her bath to fill up.

Brash and the others came back for the evening meal. Hendraz and Serza sat with the crew, the big circular table dwarfing them all. The Captain tried to relay the plans as the waiters kept appearing with different dishes and the manager kept asking Serza how things were. Serza relayed the message to Fraza, who relayed it to the rest of them, and the message had to travel all the way back again.

"Could you ask them to leave us alone?" Brash asked.

"That would be the height of bad manners," Fraza told him.

Brash had to work around it. "Spies are going to be sent out to gather information on SLOB, find out his exact location and heading. Once this is known, the forces are going to converge and surround his fleet. SLOB believes there is no resistance, so hopefully, we'll have the element of surprise."

"Do we know how big his fleet is?" Graham asked.

"Hendraz says the mothership is the main threat. It's well equipped and has numerous fighters but there are ten other ships too. We don't know how many fighters there are altogether. Hopefully, the spies will relay this information to us, together with any weaknesses they might find. It will have to be a quick and stealthy attack. The element of surprise is vital. We have sixteen planets working together now, so let's just hope it's enough."

"So, now we just wait for information?" Johnson asked.

"No. When the attack happens we'll be on a Quenbrarian craft. Its technology is advanced. Each craft has thirty fighters. Newark, Graham, Johnson, you will spend some time mastering the weapons systems of the main craft."

"Cool," Newark said.

Brash looked to Jenna. "Hopefully, we'll have enough strength to defeat SLOB but it's important, Jenna, that you continue to practice what the old woman has been teaching you."

Jenna's eyes lifted to him. "Of course, Captain," she said with a sour smile. "I'll be *devoted* to it."

Brash looked at her oddly. Johnson looked at her too.

After the meal, Johnson took Jenna aside. "OK, what's he done? This isn't just about the shower incident, is it?"

Jenna felt conflicted. As angry as she was with Brash, he was still the Captain and she didn't want to undermine him in any way. "Nothing. It's just not working out."

Johnson viewed her critically. "He's done something, hasn't he?"

Jenna let out a reluctant sigh. "OK, but you can't tell anyone."

"Sure. Hit me."

"When he was in Cankar, he slept with someone else."

"What? He told you that?"

She shook her head. "No. Err..." She'd shot herself in the foot for she didn't really want any of them to know about the mind reading. That could lead to problems. She had to back-track. "I just know... I can sense it."

Johnson looked at her oddly. "Have you asked him about this?"

"No." It hadn't occurred to her to ask him. He would just deny it anyway.

"Listen, Trot, you need to get your shit together. If you think something's off, you've got to come out with it."

"Maybe you're right…" Of course, she was right. She had to confront him. "I'll do it."

"Do it now."

Nodding, she sought out Brash. "Can I speak to you?" she asked.

His deep brown eyes fixed on her as he got up. "Of course."

"Not here." She led him out into the garden, staring up at the beautiful ringed planet. Turning to him reluctantly, she asked, "Did you sleep with someone in Cankar?"

Brash's eyes widened. "Fraza told you…?"

Jenna stared at him, her heart splitting in two. Somewhere inside, she'd been hoping there was some other explanation for what she'd heard. An involuntary cry escaped her and she clamped a hand over her mouth as she ran off.

Brash stared after her, his heart breaking too. The pain turned to anger. He went to find Fraza. He found him sitting alone, reading his translator. "Why did you tell her!" Brash demanded.

Fraza looked up at him, puzzled. "Tell her?"

"Did you or did you not tell Jenna about what happened in Cankar?"

Fraza looked offended. "No. I did not."

"What happened in Cankar?" Newark asked from behind.

Brash turned to him, fuming. "This is private." Newark nodded and moseyed away slowly. Brash watched him until he finally disappeared from view.

He turned back to Fraza. "Then how does she know?"

"It didn't come from me." Fraza turned away and resumed what he was doing.

As Brash went to look for Jenna, Newark returned and sat down next to Fraza. Unfortunately, Fraza wasn't talking. He was rubbing his ears vigorously, muttering something about humans.

Brash couldn't find Jenna anywhere.

"She went out," Skinner told him.

"Did you see which way she went?"

Skinner shook his head. "She looked upset, though."

Raking a hand through his hair, Brash knocked open the door and went outside.

"What's going on?" Newark asked Skinner.

"Woman troubles. Don't ask me. I haven't been near a woman in ages."

Newark had a bright idea. "Shall we go out and find some then?"

Skinner considered this. "OK, but if we end up in a strip joint like the last one, I will kill you."

"Strip joint? You think I want to see a naked Venulian? No, but a few of those Jaleans look alright. Let's find out where they're staying."

Jenna walked past various eating establishments, not taking much note of any of them as she trudged down the broad curving street. Venulians kept pressing their hands together and bowing their heads but she ignored them. Over to the right, she could see towering glass but these buildings were stone, the fronts arching out onto the pavement with huge bow windows. She imagined the curves wanted to go all the way around the buildings but that would take up too much space. Newark was right. These people did have a problem with angles.

Hearing familiar sounds, she glanced through a window to see Hendraz and his men having a good time. She watched them for a while then she stood back. Was this a bar? It was amazing that most planets they'd visited had places like this. It was an almost universal feature. Serza spotted her and waved. She waved back but as she turned to leave, he came out, encouraging her to join them. She shook her head. After the shower incident, she had no desire to mix with the resistance. She didn't know who she could trust anymore. Giving up, Serza went back inside. She just stood there for a while.

"Are you lost?" a voice asked behind her.

She turned to face a big Venulian in a cloak. "No," she said, shaking her head. "Wait, you speak English?"

The man frowned. "You mean, human?" She noticed the strange mismatch with his lips.

"You read minds?" she asked, startled.

The Venulian smiled. "It is a gift I have developed. It comes in handy in my line of work."

"Do you have the power too?"

He stared at her, confused. Obviously not.

"I'm just learning to mind-read," she said.

"I see... Well, why don't you come with me? I could help you."

"Come where?"

"My home is just down the street." He hit his head. "What am I thinking? You don't know me. I am a stranger to you. How thoughtless."

A Venulian boy ran over and threw his arms around the man, jabbering happily in their language. "My son," the man explained. "It's time for his tea. Well, I'll bid you good evening then."

"Wait," Jenna said. "If the invitation is still open, I'll come."

The man smiled. "This way then."

The walk was longer than expected, the street curving this way then that, the man chatting to her pleasantly all the while. Soon, they were leaving the main part of the city behind, passing residential homes that looked like stone roundhouses. Turning into a narrower street, she saw larger roundhouses. The man stopped at the second door on the left. Unlocking the door, he led her inside, switching lights on as he went. As Jenna looked around the main circular room, the man reached into his pocket and brought out a purse, handing a few coins to the boy. They said some words in Venulian then the man escorted the boy through the front door before locking it behind him. Things were starting to become clear.

"What do you want?" Jenna demanded angrily.

"You really are too trusting, aren't you?"

"I asked you what you want?"

"Quite feisty, too. What do you think I want?" There was no mistaking the lewd look in his yellow eyes. "I intend to have some fun with you before I hand you over."

"Hand me over to whom?"

"You would think of me as a game catcher. I collect specimens for my client. And you, my dear, are a wonderful specimen. You know, I hadn't even heard of humans before. But after your last visit, you were the buzz of the town. I've been waiting for your return."

"Who is your client?"

"I'm afraid I'm done answering questions. You're a captivating specimen," he said, stepping forward.

She stepped back. "Your mind-reading's not very good. And you've picked the worst night to piss me off."

"My mind-reading's excellent," he said, confused.

"But you're missing something huge." His confusion deepened. "You've messed with the wrong chick on the wrong night. And you're going to pay for all the wrong you've done."

Brash looked around him. There were beings everywhere but no sign of Jenna. Spotting Hendraz in one of the bars, he went inside and tried to communicate with sign language, pointing at his eyes and saying Jenna and Trot, over and over.

Serza got the point and nodded his head. Brash pointed to his watch and Serza stuck up five fingers. Either that was Hellgathen swearing or she'd been here five minutes ago. That was as much as Brash could get out of him. Brash left the bar and carried on down the street.

As the street got quieter, he suspected he'd gone too far. She wouldn't come out here on her own. He was just about to turn back when he spotted her coming around a corner.

"Jenna!" he called and she looked up. "It's not what you think! I need to explain!"

As she came closer, he saw a strange look in her eyes. "Jenna, are you alright?"

"Yes. I've just killed someone," she said matter-of-factly.

"What...?"

"He was a species trafficking arsehole who was going to rape me." She wiped the back of her hand over her mouth. "But he won't be doing that to anyone else."

Brash stared at her then looked down the street. "Wh... Where is he?"

"Second door on the left."

"Come with me. I'm not leaving you here."

Brash took her back down the street and looked in the house to see a dead Venulian splayed out on the floor. There was stuff everywhere and the body looked like it had taken a severe beating. Realising they needed to remove themselves from the scene of the crime, Brash led her quickly away.

"How are you feeling?" he asked, studying her.

"He got what he deserved."

"But... don't you feel anything?"

She turned her head to him, her eyes looking empty. "Glad."

The streets became busier. The two of them were quiet as they walked through them, Brash not quite sure how to handle her.

Graham, Johnson, and Fraza were hanging around in the lounge when they got back to the hotel.

"I'll get you a drink," Brash said, pointing for her to sit down with the others.

"You alright?" Johnson asked her.

"Fine."

Brash came back with a drink and handed it to Jenna. She knocked it back in one. He decided to tell the crew what had happened.

The three of them stared at Jenna. "Good one, Trot," Johnson said.

Jenna smiled, in a rather twisted way, Brash thought. This wasn't Jenna. The Jenna he knew might have killed the man but she would have been shaken up after. Brash rubbed his forehead. It was like something had gotten hold of her and he didn't know what. Maybe she would feel better after a good night's sleep. Maybe then he could finally explain what had happened in Cankar.

In the morning, his hopes were dashed. She was the same different person.

At breakfast, Newark and Skinner strolled in with smiles on their faces. Graham and Johnson hung on every word of their recounted tales. Apparently, the Jaleans were as close to humans as you could get in these parts and they were extremely promiscuous and adventurous. Skinner and Newark were snapped up straight away.

After breakfast, Brash pulled Newark and Skinner aside and filled them in on last night's events. They glanced around at Trot. "Not a word of this to anyone," Brash told them.

Jenna watched them looking over at her. It annoyed her immensely. She had listened to their euphoric accounts of the previous night, knowing Brash's account would be something similar. Well, she didn't care. He could go screw himself. Maybe it was time for *her* to have some fun. Jaleans, they had said. Pity Johnson was tied up with Graham. They could have had a girls' night out.

Brash and Fraza were going back to the Council today but Brash told the crew not to let Jenna out of their sight. She wasn't herself.

As Jenna walked to the door, Johnson stepped into her path. "Where you going?"

"Somewhere," Jenna said.

Johnson sniffed. "We'll all come with you."

"Suit yourselves."

Johnson thought the Captain was right. Trot wasn't herself. As Jenna walked out, Johnson yelled for the others to get off their arses.

"Where are we going?" Newark asked as they followed Trot down the street.

"Well, Trot?" Johnson asked.

"We're going to a bar," Jenna told her, "to pick up some Jaleans." The crew, even Skinner, stared at her. "Where do they hang out?" She turned to Newark.

Newark's mouth hung wide.

"What?" she asked. "It's alright for you but not for me?"

"But the Cap?"

"I'm not with the Cap anymore."

"OK," he said, scratching his head.

They hung around the bars, drinking. As yet, they hadn't seen any Jaleans but Newark asked if she'd like to try her luck with a Venulian.

"Am I a joke to you?" she shot.

Newark held up his hands. "Shit, man. I was just messing with you."

"So, what's this about, Trot?" Johnson asked her.

Jenna turned to her. "I want to have sex. Captain Brash is the only person I've had and that's over now so-"

"You were a virgin...?" Johnson asked, incredulous.

Newark lent across the table. "You know, if you want-"

"Don't even go there," Jenna said in a hard voice.

He held up his hands again. The knock-back was easier to handle after the incredible night he'd just had.

Graham whispered in Johnson's ear. "D'you think we should let her go through with this? The Cap said she wasn't herself."

Johnson whispered back. "Give the girl a break. She was a fucking virgin!"

Two Venulians walked into the bar with the boy Jenna recognised from the previous night. The boy whispered to one of them and the man looked over at her. Jenna stood up, a menacing expression on her face. The crew looked up at her then turned to look at the two approaching Venulians.

"Is she going for one, after all?" Newark asked, astounded.

One of the Venulians smiled at her sourly. "Let's take this outside," he said, his lips not matching the words.

She nodded slowly, a mean look in her eye. As she followed the men out, Newark stared on, dumbfounded.

"We shouldn't let her do this," Graham insisted.

Johnson got up and moved to the door. The others followed. Trot was standing outside, facing the men.

"The man you killed last night was my brother," one of the Venulians said, bringing out a weapon.

The crew rushed out but Jenna shouted at them. "Stay back! They're mine!"

"Are you insane, Trot!" Johnson yelled.

"I mean it," she said, glaring at the woman.

"What are you going to do, little girl?" the Venulian asked. "Dodge a laser beam?"

"No."

The man stared at her oddly. "You're a very foolish little girl. You could, at least, plead for your life."

"Don't call me foolish and don't call me a little girl. You really are going to pay for that."

He stared at her, surprised. Then his face turned hard and he began to fire.

As the lasers shot out, so did her hands, deflecting the fire into the sky. The crew backed up; pedestrians ran for cover, some of them screaming. The Venulian men fired frantically but all to no avail. Never had they encountered anything like this. Hopelessly out of their depth, they dropped their weapons and ran but an invisible force tripped them up, slinging them to the ground. One of them looked on horrified as the other rose into the air, hovering there, his arms and legs flailing wildly.

"Let me down!" he yelled but Jenna threw out an arm and the man smashed against the wall with bone-crushing force.

The other one scrambled to get away but he was picked up too and the wall took another battering.

The first one was on his feet again, desperate to get away. A metal sign above broke free and slammed down, slicing into his head. He didn't get up a third time. The other one turned, pleading for his life.

Jenna walked over to him, standing above him, staring down with cold disdain. "No mercy today," she said, lifting him high in the air and letting go. The force smashed his skull. "Still think I'm a foolish little girl?" she said before walking away.

"Fuck me..." Newark mouthed.

The crew stared after her as she walked past them.

"She's turned to the freaking dark side..." Johnson murmured.

# Reaching Out

"That was some serious shit, Captain," Johnson said.

"Where is she now?" Brash asked.

"I don't know."

"She was magnificent…" Skinner murmured, finding himself in love for the first time.

"This is going to cause a whole heap of trouble," Brash said, though he was more concerned about Jenna. What the hell was going on with her? Was this all to do with him?

"No mercy today…" Skinner recounted in admiration.

"Right, well, we need to find her," Brash said.

At that exact moment, Jenna walked in, looking at the band of them collected together. "Talking about me?" she asked, walking over to the bar. There was something different about her walk. It was… sexier.

Skinner couldn't keep his eyes off her. None of them could.

She came over with a drink and sat down.

"Jenna, we need to talk," Brash said.

"Shouldn't you have said that before you screwed the other woman?"

Brash gawked at her. The crew stared at Brash.

"You've got the wrong end of the stick, Jenna."

She brought her eyes up to him. "You mean, you didn't screw somebody else after admitting that you had?"

There was no way he was going to explain that whole damn debacle in front of his crew. "We need to talk about your behaviour."

"Oh, *my* behaviour."

"Do you realise what you've done today? This will necessitate an inquiry."

"Let them inquire away."

It was time for Brash to be frank. "It isn't just that you killed three men in the space of two days, two of them in a public place or that there will be an inquiry, it's… it's the way you're doing it."

"Oh," she said, putting her hand to her mouth dramatically. "Should I have killed them in a touchy-feely way?"

"Don't be ridiculous! You're… What was that phrase Johnson used?" He moved his hands, searching for the words. "You're going over to the dark side."

Jenna burst out laughing. "Seriously?"

"I am serious," Brash said, staring her full in the eye. "This is how it starts. You need to rein yourself in."

"I thought she was fantastic..." Skinner murmured.

"Skinner!"

"She was pretty amazing," Newark agreed.

"Newark!"

"Sorry, Cap. Yes, it's a slippery slope. I think."

"I need to speak to you in private, Jenna," Brash said.

"Sorry. Got plans."

"What plans?"

She tapped her nose with her finger, before getting up and slinking over to the lifts.

"I don't know what I'm going to do with her," Brash said.

Newark sniffed. "You could try saying sorry."

Brash had the awful feeling it was too late for that.

The inquiry was conducted straight away. It was short and sweet. Following the death of those three men, the lid was blown off a whole species trafficking racket. Indeed, the Council wanted to honour Jenna. Not only that, they were extremely pleased that in these dark times they had her on their side. The crew were too. They wouldn't want to be on the other side of what they had witnessed. Brash seemed to be the only one concerned.

He made it a priority to tell Jenna the truth about what happened in Cankar. He relayed the whole painful saga and she listened rapt. Then she burst out laughing.

"You're laughing at me...?"

"Well, I mean, you've got to admit, it is quite funny."

Brash held onto his anger. "The point is, I thought it was you."

She nodded.

"Do you forgive me?"

"Yes."

"Can we start again?"

"You and me?"

He nodded.

"I'm not sure I can. Something's sweeping me along and I'm not sure I can go back." She brushed his cheek with her hand. "I don't know who I am anymore."

She left him staring after her. Whatever they had, he knew it was over.

Newark was right. The Jaleans were promiscuous and adventurous. Jenna found herself opening to a whole new world of possibilities. She felt liberated for the first time. She couldn't speak a word of their language but she didn't need to. Still, she knew she had to perfect her mind-reading technique. So, after getting a few things out of her system, she settled down to it.

She stayed in her room, learning to get into that relaxed state. Thoughts came to her but they were random. She wasn't always sure whose they were, though some were pretty obvious.

*"Seventeen nights of mind-blowing sex. I'm a fucking god!"*

*"The Captain wants to sort his shit out. If he was my boyfriend, I'd had chopped his bollocks off!"*

*"She's amazing... Why does she keep hiding away in her room?"*

Jenna opened her eyes, wondering who had thought that last thought. She realised she needed to be able to know whose mind she was reading. This was hit and miss. Somehow, she needed to be able to plug in to a specific target. Tapping her chin with her fingers, she decided to try to tune into Brash. He was back with the Council today, so it was some distance away. But it was worth a shot.

Closing her eyes, she focused on him for a few minutes. Then she emptied herself completely...

*"I don't want any more fucking food! I want to know if you've heard anything yet!"*

Jenna sat up. Those were definitely his thoughts. Amazed by what she had done, she wanted to go further. Cornelius? Could she connect to him again?

Excitement was pulsing through her. It was ruining everything. It took quite some time before she could quell it and settle down once more. Just as she was getting into that relaxed state of mind, there was a loud knock on the door.

"D'you want to come out with us?" Newark called.

She sat up, annoyed. "No!"

"OK. Jeez."

Jenna lay down again.

"Are you sure you don't want to come?" Skinner asked.

"No! Fuck off!"

Jenna lay down again, glancing at the door. Was that Skinner...?

"She told you to fuck off," Newark said.

"Yes..." Skinner murmured, starry-eyed.

Newark eyed him oddly. "What the fuck's wrong with you? You look weird. Everybody's having personality transplants."

They met up with Graham and Johnson downstairs.

"So, what's this thing we're going to then?" Newark asked Johnson.

"Venulian culture. Some sort of concert. Hendraz said it'd be great."

"Is he coming?"

"He's with the Captain. Is Trot coming?"

"She told us to fuck off."

Johnson's eyes widened.

The crew trekked through the streets, wondering what a Venulian concert would be like. They'd only agreed to go because they wanted something different to do. They'd already mastered the weapons systems - weapons were their thing – and they were getting a little restless.

The grand glass building was packed out with Venulians, who kept pressing their hands together and bowing their heads. Newark nodded his head occasionally but soon became bored.

A large well-dressed Venulian man came over to them, pressing his hands together and bowing before ushering them through a door. Johnson held up the tickets Hendraz had bought for them but he kept ushering them away.

"Maybe they don't like foreigners at these things," Newark said, noting they were the only other species he had seen.

When they got through the door, the man led them to a lift. Realising they weren't being thrown out, they got in to find that the lift led up to impressive balcony seats. Cottoning on to what was happening, Newark pressed his hands together and bowed his head.

"The best seats in the house," Newark said pleased, gazing around the huge theatre. They must have been a hundred feet up. The place was packed out with Venulians... down below and all around on other balconies. "D'you think we got these seats because we're guests or because Trot's a hero?"

"Probably both," Graham replied.

The large seats meant that they could lounge, so they lounged as the theatre filled up.

At last, everyone was seated. The lights dimmed and the red curtain went up. A large plump Venulian woman was standing on the stage. Her flimsy dress afforded a shockingly clear impression of what lay beneath.

"Get the sick bags out," Newark remarked, turning to see the man that had brought them up. He was sitting in a chair behind them. Newark thought Venulian hospitality was a little creepy. He smiled and nodded then turned back around. "Good job they can't speak English."

Music began to play. Well, they assumed it was music. Discordant notes shot off in all directions. The woman, at last, opened her mouth and what came out was stunning... in its awfulness. The sounds grated, jarred and screeched. Together with the music, it created a riotous, horrific, brain-assaulting cacophony.

The four of them looked at each other, their eyes drawn back to the stage. The assault went on and on... until Newark wanted to kill someone and Skinner wanted to die.

As the torture, at last, came to an end, the crowd clapped and cheered enthusiastically. For the benefit of the man behind, they clapped too, only far less enthusiastically.

"What universe are they in...?" Graham murmured.

"It's definitely not ours," Johnson replied, dazed.

Discordant notes started up again and the crew didn't think they could take much more. What followed was infinitely worse. A troop of naked Venulians came prancing out, dancing around the stage with gusto. The yellow folds of skin wobbled grotesquely.

"Holy fuck..." Newark mouthed.

"Jesus..." Skinner uttered.

As the monstrous sights cavorted around, the singer returned, throwing out more knuckle-clenching noise. The combination was intolerable.

"Can we go," Skinner pleaded.

"I'm going to get us out of here," Johnson said decisively. "Follow my lead."

Johnson stood and flopped over dramatically, pretending to faint. The crew fussed around her. Graham picked her up and eventually they escaped.

Outside, Johnson stood up straight. "I'm going to fucking kill Hendraz!"

*"You finally found me. Keep the link as long as you can."*

*"We're on a moon called Venulas. Sixteen planets are joining us. They are formulating plans."*

*"That's excellent. How are you, Jenna?"*

*"Weirded out that I'm speaking to you. Other than that, still in one piece."*

*"I'm so proud of you. It takes most years to master this. Please use it wisely."*

*"How's Flint?"*

*"He's doing great. Remember, Jenna, you are a powerful channel."*

Jenna didn't want to tell him that SLOB was more powerful. The worrisome feeling broke the link and she cursed herself. But then a thought occurred to her. If she could reach out to Cornelius, could she and should she attempt to probe SLOB's mind?

# Winners and Losers

SLOB sat attending his own devotional ceremony. The ceremony was held in the loading bay. It was the only place big enough to accommodate all his men. He was sitting on a platform that had been erected especially as one of his generals extolled his virtues. He wasn't listening to the general; he was viewing his men with disdain, wondering how many of them wanted to be there. Many of them were mercenaries, paid from the plunder SLOB had accumulated. Some were ex-cons. The rest, he wasn't sure about – his generals sorted out recruitment. As he cast his eyes over the assembled flock, he noticed some drooping lids. He started to get angrier and angrier.

Finally, he lurched to his feet. The drooping lids shot open. The general stiffened. SLOB pointed to a man at the front. "You. Why are you in my forces?"

The man saw his life flash before his eyes. "To serve you, Lord."

"Why?"

Not sure how to answer, he began to stutter. "B-Because you are g-great, Lord."

SLOB's lips twisted. He wasn't sure the man was telling the truth. He looked around the assembly. "I'm going to ask the question again. I'll know if you are lying and if you're lying you will experience my extreme displeasure." He gave that a moment to sink in then he pointed at another man. "You. Why are you here?"

Looking extremely conflicted and sweating profusely, the man answered, "The p-pay's excellent, Lord."

He pointed at another. "You?"

"T-To be on the w-winning team, Lord."

"You?"

"I like murdering, pillage and plunder, Lord." An ex-con.

"You?"

"The pay... and the violence, Lord." Another ex-con.

"You?"

"The pay, Lord." A new recruit, who was a spy and nervously waiting to see if SLOB was telling the truth.

"You?"

"Death, destruction, torture, screaming..." A psychopath.

The answers were the same. Not one of these men worshipped him. With the exception, perhaps, of the last guy, there was plenty of fear in this room but no love.

"You?" SLOB said, pointing. He hesitated for a moment. The green-skinned, knobbly-headed creature was of a race unknown to him. "What are you?"

The creature couldn't seem to speak Hellgathen. This enraged SLOB. Everyone on the ship had been instructed to the learn the language. SLOB turned to his general.

"The Uriath currently has a throat infection, Lord," the general lied, bracing himself. "His vocal chords have seized up. Apparently, they're very fragile, Lord."

SLOB turned back to the creature, viewing him with curious disdain. Dismissing him, he pointed to another unfortunate victim. "Do you love your god?" he asked.

If the man told the truth, he was in trouble. If he lied, he was in trouble. His mind battled with itself until it was on the verge of blowing a fuse.

"Answer me!" SLOB shouted.

"No, Lord."

"All of you, answer me!"

Since they risked death either way, they opted for the truth. "No, Lord!"

SLOB stared at them. The assembly held its breath, a few at the back slipping surreptitiously away.

"Then fear me," SLOB spat as he walked off.

Back in his quarters, SLOB lay on his silken sheets, staring at the wall. *Why had nobody ever loved him...?* The emptiness threatened to consume him. Years evaporated before his eyes...

*"The boy's useless! A complete loser! He's not strong enough for manual work and his school work is atrocious! He's an embarrassment! Other fathers have sons to be proud of! What are you looking at, boy? Look at him, standing there, sulking. Ah, gods! He's bloody crying now!"*

"He's only eight."

"He's nine, isn't he?"

"Eight, nine... Stop crying, Venn. Hellgathen boys don't cry!"

"And he's always coming home with bruises. The other kids don't like him, either."

"You listening, Venn? Hellgathen boys don't get bullied. You're embarrassing us!"

"What have you got to say for yourself?"

"Sorry, daddy..."

"You're too old to use that word! What kind of man is he going to grow into? Some soft sissy?"

"Gods, that would be embarrassing..."

"Stop crying, boy, or you'll feel the back of my hand!"

Jenna opened her eyes and began to cry.

There was a knock on the door. "It is Serza. Can I to come in?"

Wiping her eyes, she got up and opened the door. Serza and Hendraz barged in, closing the door and pressing their ears up against it. Jenna watched on, intrigued. Serza turned to her. "Hendraz waiting them stop angry."

Jenna heard Johnson shouting Hendraz' name out in the corridor. The noise moved past. Hendraz turned to her and smiled. Then he opened the door and the two of them went out.

Well, that was weird, she thought.

She wandered across the room, feeling incredibly sad. The sadness threatened to swallow her, so she got dressed up and went out to find a Jalean.

Brash watched her leave the hotel. Turning around desolately, he went to the bar to get a drink. Despite the onslaught of Venulian hospitality all day, he had an empty feeling in his gut. Skinner came to the bar and sat beside him. The two of them drowned their lovelorn sorrows. The more drinks that went down, the more Brash blamed Fraza for his troubles. When the Kaledian approached the bar, Brash glared at him harshly. "You like causing trouble, is that it?"

Fraza rubbed his ears. "She didn't find out from me," he said, hurt.

"Then how?"

Fraza didn't have the answer to that. He walked off and went up to bed with his translator.

"Maybe he's telling the truth," Skinner remarked, tossing back a stiff one.

"He was the only one that knew."

The rest of the crew appeared, ordering free drinks. "You wouldn't believe the day we've had," Newark said but Brash wasn't interested. "I have to hand it to Hendraz. That was a good one. You alright, Cap?"

"Could you please leave me alone," Brash said through gritted teeth.

Johnson, Graham, and Newark exchanged glances. They got their drinks and moved away.

As far as his love-life was concerned, Brash was at rock bottom. He got wasted that night and, in the morning, came to a firm decision. Him and Jenna were over. He wouldn't waste any more time moping. Jenna got wasted and laid that night and, in the morning, came to a firm decision. She was going to find some water and continue to practice what Tynia had been teaching her.

The lake was half a mile out of the city. Serza, knowing the area well, had told her about it and given her directions. He'd offered to come with her but she wanted to be alone.

It was a calm, peaceful day, the surface of the water appearing like a mirror in the light, the ringed planet slightly visible in the sky. There were hills over to her left, a few trees on the other side of the lake, green meadows all around...

Jenna drew in a breath. It was beautiful here...

Standing beside the lake, she brought up the power in the way she was used to, watching the column of water rise. Letting it go again, she stared at the surface of the lake. *No from, no to... Just the power and intent...*

She stared at the lake for quite some time. Then she closed her eyes. She started to imagine her body disappearing... disappearing until there was no her... just her consciousness floating in the vastness... she and the vastness becoming one...

Thoughts came up, unbidden, but she let them pass away, returning to emptiness. She started to view her mind as something separate, as a little toddler begging for attention. She ignored it, rising above it, lingering in the vastness...

As her physical boundaries slipped away, she started to imagine the vastness disappearing too... disappearing into nowhere, no time... There was just the power and her intent. The towering wall of water was all there was. Nothing else existed.

As she opened her eyes, she gazed at the wall of water collapsing back on itself. After a few moments of dazed delirium, she jumped up and down, punching her fists in the air, feeling like a winner. Unable to contain herself, she rolled around in the grass, making grass angels with her arms and legs.

At last, she sat up. She had made the wall. She now needed to practice keeping it there.

She practiced every day over the next two weeks and, as her proficiency increased, she thought about the lightning ball SLOB had chucked at her. How had he done that?

*This power is an all-purpose entity*, Cornelius had said.

Lightening, she thought, tapping her chin. What caused lightening? Polarized charges, if she remembered correctly. So... she needed to create an electrical imbalance. She wasn't sure how thunderclouds did it, nor did she know how SLOB did it, but she realised she didn't need to know. All she needed was the power and her intent.

Closing her eyes, she focused, beginning the process of removing herself, removing time and space itself. There was just the power and her intent...

On hearing a lame crack of thunder, she opened her eyes to see a ball of lightning hovering in the air just as she had intended. *Holy cow...! So, this was why he was called the Thunder God.* She thrust the ball away and it shot over the lake, crashing into a tree and setting it ablaze.

"Crap!" The fire was burning out of control. Focusing on the water, she produced a giant wave to put it out.

Crisis averted, she threw herself into the lake, splashing around exuberantly. She felt like an alchemist, a wizard even. *This was so cool!* She had never had so much fun in her life.

The crew stared at her wet clothes when she returned to the hotel.

"Went for a swim," she explained.

"In your clothes?" Johnson asked, staring at her oddly.

"You should try it," she said, smiling to herself as she walked to the lift.

"Hey, Trot," Newark called. "D'you want to go skinny dipping tomorrow?"

"In your dreams, Newark," she called back.

Newark smiled. "I love that girl."

Jenna got dried and changed then came back down to join them for the evening meal. Her next objective was to achieve a relaxed state of mind in company.

Skinner pulled out a chair for her as she approached the table.

"Err, thanks," she said, looking at him oddly.

"So, you're joining us tonight?" Newark asked her.

"Yep."

Almost immediately, a dish was brought for her. They were having fish, which was no surprise as they served fish every night. Starting on her meal, she tried to detach herself as the conversation flowed around her. Graham and Newark were recounting some funny story that had happened that day, but she didn't listen to the details.

"You're quiet, Trot?" Johnson said.

"Just chilling. Been busy practicing," she qualified, her eyes glancing to

Brash.

The Captain nodded without looking at her. "That's great, Trot," he said.

She sunk into the background again.

"Want to go to a Venulian concert, Trot?" Newark asked. "I'll get you a ticket."

Sighing inwardly, she turned to Newark. "Nice try. Skinner told me all about it." Indeed, Skinner went on to talk about all manner of stuff. She'd never known him so communicative, especially with her.

Drawing in a breath, she tuned out again.

"Why don't you come out with us tonight, Captain?" Newark asked, realising now that the relationship with Trot was over.

The Captain thought about it. "Maybe I will. OK. Yes."

"Are you coming, Jenna?" Skinner asked.

Holding onto her annoyance, she forced a calm reply. "No. Thank you."

As the conversation drifted onto other things, Jenna continued to soften her hearing and relax her mind. She chose Skinner as her focus of interest. He was different and she wanted to know why. Sights and sounds became irrelevant as her mind opened a channel to Skinner.

*"Jenna Trot, I want to screw you so bad."*

Jenna's focus shot back into the room and she stared at Skinner. Skinner was gazing at her and he took her sudden interest as a good sign. The joy she felt at her success was dampened by her sudden creeped-outness. She glared at him harshly but he just smiled back at her.

Turning away, she realised that Fraza wasn't with them.

"Where's Fraza?" she asked.

"Sulking in his room," Newark told her.

"Why?"

Newark's eyes flicked to Brash. "He's been sulking for the last few weeks."

"Why?"

"Because I chewed him out for squealing on me," Brash said, without looking up.

Jenna stared at Brash. "Then apologise," she insisted.

"What?" he asked, looking up at her.

"Apologise to him. Fraza didn't tell me. You volunteered the information yourself. I asked you what happened in Cankar based on... a feeling. You filled in the rest."

Brash stared at her. He was a much bigger idiot than he'd given himself credit for.

Brash did apologise but the damage had been done. Fraza's trust that his Captain trusted him had been broken and he held onto his hurt. He refused, point blank, to go out with them.

Jenna had a quiet night in the hotel lounge, practicing her new-found skill. She had discovered that language was not a barrier in thought. Thoughts were like waves of vibrations that converted into familiar vibrations that matched her own language. And she was fascinated to discover that aliens had similar thoughts to humans. The aliens she was looking at now were a few straggling members of the resistance. Though they were all humanoid, they did not look like humans.

*"I wish he would get to the bloody punch-line, so I can tell my joke!"*

*"This story is taking forever. And it's not even funny."*

Jenna noticed Fraza walk in. He was a solitary-looking figure. The little Kaledian took an age to get to the bar with all his to-ing and fro-ing."

*"What is that guy's deal? Do his species walk like that?"*

Jenna whipped her head to the resistance, realising she had a problem. She had to learn to switch this off now. Her brain was still in relaxed mode and she sat up straight in a bid to shake it off.

Fraza got his drink and came over. "Are you not going out tonight?" he asked.

"No, not tonight." She studied the Kaledian, realising she knew relatively little about him. "We've never really talked, have we, Fraza? How did you end up with the Erithians?"

He scratched his ears, looking a little embarrassed. "My parents died with a mountain of debt. In Kaledia, it is considered the height of dishonour not to settle debts. I sold my house but it wasn't enough, so rather than face jail, I left Jakensk."

"But it wasn't your debt?"

"It makes no difference."

She blew out a breath. "That's harsh. So, how did you get all that way? The Erithians were a long way from Jakensk."

"The same way you did. I stole a Yact."

"Ah, that's what they're called."

"It didn't get me all the way. It ran out of fuel in the wasteland but I saw the mountains in the distance."

"So, it was the wasteland or jail?"

"Yes. A rather stark choice."

"What were your parents like, Fraza?"

He tilted his head, thoughtfully. "They were upstanding citizens but made a few poor financial decisions." He smiled fondly. "They fussed about me when I was young." He scratched his neck. "Worried about me to the point of…"

"Distraction?"

He smiled and nodded. "As an adolescent, I didn't go out very much. They saw danger around every corner. They didn't believe I could look after myself."

"I can relate to that," Jenna said. "My father was over-protective."

Fraza smiled sadly. Jenna didn't know if he looked sad because he missed his parents or because of his misspent youth. Perhaps both. She wondered if he'd ever had a girlfriend.

She leaned forward. "Do you want to know a secret?"

Fraza shook his head vigorously and rubbed his ears. "I'm not keeping any more secrets."

She chewed her lip, assessing him. "OK. D'you want to come out with me tomorrow?"

"Out? Where?"

"Just for a walk to a nice scenic lake."

Fraza stared astounded at the towering wall of water. "You've done it..."

Jenna opened her eyes. "Why don't you try. Cornelius said your power is weak but it could be stronger."

"How? I've been practicing."

"Yes, but you've been practicing within a confined set of limits. When Cornelius said, your power is weak, that's just how it is now. I think you feel that's all it can ever be. But I don't believe that."

Fraza looked unconvinced.

"I don't know why the power comes through us and not others but for some reason it does. It can be an ocean or a well. The mind enables it or stands in the way. So, you have to let go of preconceptions about what you're capable of, preconceptions about the universe itself. I believe one hundred percent that you can do what I just did. And *you* have the incredible fortune and privilege to be half-way there."

Fraza stared at Jenna. "You have changed so much."

She smiled at him. "Shall we start then?"

Three weeks later, Fraza produced a wall of water.

"I did it!" he squealed. He turned to Jenna. "Thank you for believing in me," he said, overcome.

She smiled. "Tonight, we're going out to celebrate. The Jaleans will love you."

# Fighting Evil

"D'you notice anything different about Fraza lately?" Johnson asked.

"Nope," Newark said, watching the Captain making out with a Jalean. Thank God for Jaleans, he thought.

"These past few days, Fraza hasn't been doing any of his strange shit."

"Or his ear rubbing," Graham suddenly realised.

"What d'you think that means?" Newark asked.

"Fucked if I know," Johnson said.

"Has he gone out with Trot again?" Graham asked.

"Yeah."

"Those two are pretty chummy, lately."

"I can't keep up," Newark said. "Trot's different, Skinner's different, Fraza's different, the Captain's changing…"

Graham leaned forward. "For the past week, he hasn't even asked if the spies have returned."

Johnson glanced around. "Well, he's sure as hell over Trot now."

Jenna and Fraza had bumped into Hendraz and Serza. Having Fraza around made things so much easier. Though she was getting more proficient at reading thoughts, she couldn't communicate. The two Hellgathens were having a drinking competition. Jenna and Fraza had bets on which one was going to throw up first. Jenna's man was Serza, who was now starting to sway. After downing another glass, he staggered back, hitting a firm green body. A green fist flew at his head but it swerved wildly of course, smashing into a large chest. Jenna laughed.

Serza staggered to the door as the fight broke out. Jenna and Fraza followed him, watching as he puked up on the sidewalk, pedestrians dodging out of his way.

"Pay out," Jenna said, turning to Fraza.

Fraza smiled. "The bet's void. You interfered. Serza would have been knocked out before he was sick and it would have been a draw."

Jenna smiled. "I like you, Fraza."

Serza muttered something then staggered back into the bar. Jenna turned to see the fight still in progress. "Should we try somewhere else or should we place another bet?"

Fraza looked into the bar. "My money's on the green man."

Jenna smiled mischievously. "I'll take the Venulian then."

They went back into the bar, walking around the patrons who had formed a circle to watch. Jenna pointed to a low balcony and they went up to get a better view.

"You're the green then?" Jenna asked and Fraza nodded. "Let the games begin."

The fighting pair soon lost control of their limbs. The green man found himself orchestrating a kick he had not intended.

"Nice one, Fraza!" Jenna called out. "I didn't see that coming."

"This is like having an avatar!" Fraza exclaimed before his man took a blow to the chin.

The crowd watched rapt as the green man and the Venulian pulled off some crazy moves, no-one more surprised than the fighting pair themselves, who were now struggling to control their limbs. Some moves earned cheers from the crowd. Fraza's kick to the groin earned a chorus of boos.

"That was a miscalculation," Fraza insisted.

"OK but you've got to give me a minute to recover."

"Minute over!" Fraza announced.

The Venulian jumped up onto the bar, the crowd wondering how he'd managed to lift all that weight. From there, he threw himself down on the green but the green dodged quickly and the Venulian landed face-first on the stone floor. Jenna spun the dazed Venulian around, driving his booted foot up into a delicate green scrotum. As the green buckled, the crowd booed again.

"Sorry, I was aiming for the chest," Jenna said.

"Ok, but I get a free shot."

Fraza took his shot and the fight continued, the senseless pair mere passengers on a ride their bodies shouldn't have been able to make. Jenna noticed Serza staggering senselessly close to the action. "We'll have to abort, Fraza," she said.

"Damn," Fraza muttered.

"We'll call it a draw."

The fight suddenly stopped. The green man and the Venulian dropped to the floor, breathless and bewildered. The audience watched them, confused.

"Shall we go somewhere else then?" Jenna asked.

"OK."

As they walked down, they saw the bewildered pair still sitting there.

The crowd were now dispersing.

Stepping outside, Jenna drew in a deep breath of air. Fraza glanced at her. "Do you think that was morally wrong?"

She tilted her head. "Probably. But I won't tell if you don't."

Fraza smiled.

"Let's try that place over there," she said, leading him over the street.

Walking into a long oval room, Jenna noticed Brash kissing a beautiful Jalean. As if sensing someone watching him, Brash looked up, his eyes fixing her. He nodded and she nodded back. Brash turned away and Fraza glanced at Jenna. Jenna went to sit next to Johnson, the crew watching her closely. Johnson studied her. Trot seemed unaffected and she couldn't fathom it.

"Alright, Trot?" Newark asked.

"Yep."

Jenna was becoming bored. She tapped her fingers on her knees, feeling restless. Newark's attention moved away from her and, as she watched him looking around the room, she wondered if she could transfer a thought to him. Allowing her mind to slip into that relaxed state, she tuned in to Newark, transmitting a thought along the airwaves: *Could you get me a drink, Newark?*

Newark turned to her. "Did you say something?"

*Yes!* She did a mental fist pump. *How easy was* that*!* "I said, could you get me a drink."

Fraza placed a drink down in front of her and Newark looked at it. She smiled. "Cancel that order."

Brash walked out with the Jalean. Newark got up and went to find one. Graham and Johnson began whispering to each other and Jenna went to sit beside Fraza. "I just transmitted a thought to Newark."

"You did...? How did you do that?"

"I don't know. It's like the more I do, the easier it seems to get."

"Accelerated action..." he said, staring at her thoughtfully.

"Accelerated action? Oh, shit!"

"What?"

"Skinner's just walked in. I'm off. The bloke thinks he's in love with me."

"What?"

"*I* don't know what's got into him."

Skinner came over. Jenna got up, smiled at Skinner briefly then walked out. Fraza followed her.

As the two of them walked down the busy street, Fraza turned to her. "You're really not bothered about Captain Brash?" he asked, confused.

Jenna considered this. "No. It's like... all the feelings I had have been...

frozen. Perhaps what happened in Cankar was a blessing in disguise."

"What do you mean?"

"In some ways, he reminds me of my father... a little over-protective... and I didn't like the way he spoke to me after I'd been dancing with Hendraz. I went straight from my father's umbrella to his. And I don't like the way I was so... needy, dependent on him... emotionally." She turned to Fraza. "The thing is, I've never known who I really was. I'm not the person I thought I was. I'm still finding out and I'm enjoying it. Does that explain it?"

"Yes... I think it does..."

"Good. Now let's go and get laid."

The news came the following morning. The spies had returned. Brash, Hendraz, Fraza and a tired-looking Serza made their way over to the Council. As they walked down the street, Brash turned to Fraza. "You're pretty paly with Jenna these days," he remarked.

"Jenna has helped me a lot," Fraza asserted. The Captain studied him. "She's changed a lot. If you want her back, maybe you should too."

Brash sniffed. "Who says I want her back?" He glanced at Fraza. "What do you mean, I should change?"

"You're thirty-three and I know you're the Captain but sometimes you seem so much older than your years."

"Do you know what it means to be in command?" he said harshly. "There are certain standards of behaviour, certain requirements."

"I understand that. But to Jenna, you remind her of her father."

"Did she say that?"

"Yes. All I'm saying is, who were you before you became the Captain? Who was that man? Do you remember? Maybe you could incorporate a little of him."

Brash's brow creased as he considered Fraza's words. His ambition had driven him for many years. He was a captain at an early age. Before that... He thought back to his teenage years, remembering how popular he had been with the girls; how wayward he could sometimes be. He used to laugh more then. Sometimes he got into scrapes. From his current vantage point, it was like staring back at a different person. He realised he'd been towing his own invisible line for many years and recognised that deep down he was getting a little tired of it. Perhaps he, like Jenna, had been rebelling of late.

The leaders were assembled when they got there. There were about fifty beings in the Chamber, all wearing their headpieces. Brash and the others sat down to hear what the spies had to say. The head of the Venulian

Council introduced them. None of the spies were Venulian. It had been decided that Venulians would stand out too much. The spies had been hand-picked from the various delegations and one of the requirements was an ability to speak Hellgathen.

A Rengiard from amongst their number stepped forward to speak. He relayed the information they had acquired; location and heading of the fleet; the fact that the mothership would be docked for weeks as its weapon systems were being upgraded; numbers of current weapons arsenals; number of fighter craft; even weaknesses in the mothership. All in all, the information was invaluable.

One of the Quenbrarian leaders stood up. "There are only five of you. Were there not six?"

The Rengiard bowed his head. "One of our number was killed."

"How?"

"The Thunder God is a vicious man. Kelab was... unfortunate."

"Explain," she said.

The man looked up, visibly distraught. "The Thunder God is insane. He has devotional ceremonies to himself. We attended one where he demanded to know if he was loved. At the next ceremony, he decreed that, since he was not worshipped enough, a sacrifice would be made to him." The man's voice faltered. "Kelab was chosen."

Brash stared on astounded. The man was struggling to hold it together.

"Did you see this sacrifice?" the Quenbrarian asked more softly.

"No. It was to happen at the following ceremony. He was to be imprisoned until then." Tears flowed from the Rengiard's eyes. "We wanted to attempt to free him but if we did we would have jeopardised the whole mission. Kelab will be dead now," he choked out. "There was little we could do..."

The assembly was silent.

The head of the Council stood up. "We are fighting evil and we must win."

# Taking Stock

The crew stood on a hill, staring up at the ringed planet. Darkness was closing around them. A breeze ruffled their hair and clothes and they felt like they were standing on a precipice. The last year had all been leading to this. Tomorrow, the ships would head out. Tomorrow, they would face death. Tonight could be their last. It was a sobering thought and one that required processing.

As Jenna reflected on the past year, she knew that she wouldn't change any of it. Crashing Captain Brash's craft was the best thing she ever did.

For Brash, getting involved with Jenna Trot was the best thing he ever did. He could see now that his obsessive drive to discover new life was just an addiction to distract him from himself. Success at living wasn't all about succeeding. He finally had the courage to face himself.

Skinner, now having the courage to live, was starting to have the courage to accept the unexplainable. His mind would always try to rationalise and explain but he was learning to live with the dichotomy. He thought about the Erithians and beings from other dimensions. Maybe they had a broader perspective than it was possible to have here. Maybe, in this dimension, we were like ants. An ant can't understand the whole planet in the way a human can. But just because it can't understand, doesn't mean it isn't understandable. He found some rationality in this.

Graham and Johnson were holding hands, each hoping that if the other died tomorrow, they would go too. Johnson thought that if they did both get through this, she'd try being a little more communicative with Graham. She was coming to the firm conclusion that he didn't know how to take hints. Graham thought he'd take Newark's advice and try to be more sensitive. He was starting to suspect there was a whole world of stuff that went on in Daria's mind that up to now, he'd been blissfully unaware of. He might have to do some digging to find out was it was.

Fraza was thinking about the crazy ride this crazy group of humans had taken him on. Humans were unstable creatures, he knew that now, but rather than think them weak, he thought they must be strong to deal with themselves all the time. They were volatile and passionate but fun too. He wanted to hang out with them some more.

Newark was thinking that if he survived, he wanted to learn shit. He was starting to have the sneaking suspicion that he was dumb. It was a niggling feeling but growing like a pearl in a shell. He consoled himself that at least he had the intelligence to realise this. Perhaps he wasn't that dumb, after all. That's the thing with thinking too much, it twists you in knots. Perhaps thinking is a dumb thing to do.

"Shall we sit down for a while?" Brash asked. They sat down in a circle. "I brought you out here because I want us to spend some time as a group before tomorrow. We're a team. We've come a long way together and I want you to know that, whatever happens tomorrow, I am immensely proud of you all."

The crew swelled with pride.

"We've had our differences," Brash said, glancing at Jenna, "but I couldn't have picked a better team, and that includes you, Fraza. If we die tomorrow, we die fighting for something worthwhile. This is the struggle of good over evil, of freedom over slavery. If we succeed, the universe owes you all a debt of gratitude. Do any of you want to say anything?"

"Yes," Newark said. "Tomorrow we kick SLOB's butt or we die trying."

"And some," Johnson affirmed.

Brash smiled at his brave and loyal crew. He glanced at Jenna. He knew that if she died tomorrow he would be devastated. He had come full circle from the Captain who had wanted to kill her. The irony was, if he hadn't wanted her dead, he wouldn't be here, worrying about her now. Life was full of contradictions, he thought. Nothing was a straight predictable line.

# No Surrender

The crew and the resistance were on a Quenbrarian battleship. It was huge compared to Hendraz' craft and far more advanced. Silver metal gleamed like a shining new pin. The ship was bright, airy and doors slid open effortlessly.

Men and women got into their positions straight away, climbing into the fighters, manning the weapons, because once they made the jump to hyperspace, it would all be on.

The Quenbrarians programmed the co-ordinates, checked their systems then waited. All the forces would make the jump together.

Brash, Skinner, Jenna, Fraza, and Hendraz were on the flight deck, strapped in. Johnson, Graham, and Newark were at their weapons stations. There were other members of the resistance up there too.

Brash was feeling apprehensive. They would only get one shot at this.

As they waited, Skinner's eyes roamed around, soaking in Quenbrarian technology. Jenna was glad to have his eyes somewhere else. She was tired of turning around to find him staring at her.

"They're firing up," Fraza said.

They felt a mild vibration at their feet. Brash glanced at Jenna. She glanced at him, feeling apprehensive too. Everything rested on what happened now. Their own lives and the lives of millions would be determined very soon. She thought about her father and what he would think if he knew where she was, what she was facing. If he did know, he'd be trying to get her off this ship, trying to tuck her up somewhere safe. She could clearly see that his efforts to protect her were completely at odds with his desire for her to do well. He just couldn't have it both ways.

The craft began to move forward, heading out into the blackness of space. The rising hum of the engines turned to a high-pitched shriek. They were knocked back in their seats, glued in place. Fighting the pressure, Brash reached out to touch Jenna's hand, possibly for the last time. The pressure became nauseatingly acute. Sights and sounds morphed into a disorientating blur...

Then it all stopped. Everything returned to normal.

The flight-deck sprang into action, voices shouting commands, fingers tapping screens, eyes checking instruments...

Those eyes suddenly lifted, all staring ahead.

Brash unstrapped himself and moved forward, staring out into empty space. The ships, way over in the distance, were resistance ships.

"He's not here..." Jenna murmured, her voice swallowed by the deafening silence.

A sudden jolt rocked the ship. Then another. They were being attacked.

SLOB stared at the sitting ducks huddled in a circle beneath him. His ships were taking them off-guard and the rebels struggled to launch a counter-attack. They may have more ships, he thought, but infinitely inferior firepower. He breathed in satisfied as the first startling explosion lit up space.

"Beautiful, isn't it?" he remarked, glancing at the spy he had dragged in to watch. "And it's all because of you."

The spy cried. The Jalean had folded at the thought of the grisly fate this monster had explained to him. He had bartered for his life, pleading with SLOB that he was more useful alive than dead. He didn't want to betray the resistance and he would have accepted death but the sick bastard's sacrifice was too gruesome to bear. As he watched the second ship go up in an orange blaze, he reeled around, yanking a weapon from one of the guards and firing at the devil. The fire was deflected easily. Another guard took him down and, as he fell to the floor, SLOB screamed. "What did you do that for! I wasn't finished with him!"

"Sorry, Lord."

The guard waited nervously but SLOB turned back around. "Get rid of that," he said, picking up on the action.

Another explosion lit the darkness in a glorious display of his superiority. The first resistance he had ever encountered was crumbling before him.

Brash stared in dazed disbelief as another resistance ship went up. Their fighters, too, were floundering, taking far more hits than they were giving. More of their fighters were heading out but Brash stared at the numbers pouring off the mother ship. A vast, deadly swarm of them. Far more than the spies had reported. Brash looked around the flight deck. The Quenbrarian Commander was barking orders, the Quenbrarian crew hard at work, calm under pressure. If they were his crew, he would have been proud but he wasn't sure it would be enough. Another explosion turned his head.

"Another one of ours," Jenna murmured desolately.

Brash raked a hand through his hair. He felt impotent; felt like a spare part. He was used to getting stuck in but all the weapons were manned, all the fighters taken. There was little for him to do but stand and watch. At last, he could stand and watch no longer. "I'm going up to the weapons deck to bolster the crew," he said, striding out.

Jenna watched him go, feeling as useless as he did.

Up above, Newark, Johnson, and Graham were firing like maniacs. They took out many fighters but the sheer number was overwhelming.

"We need more guns!" Johnson called out.

"They just keep coming!" Graham shouted. "There weren't supposed to *be* this many!"

Newark had never been more focused in his life. His aim was perfect, as always, his reflexes swift. "Take out as many of the fuckers as you can!"

Down below, the big guns were firing too but the mother ship was impenetrable.

"Their shields are too strong," the Quenbrarian Commander shouted. "We can't penetrate them! Weren't there supposed to be weak spots?"

"There are no weak spots," his second shouted. "We can't break through, sir!"

"How is our own shield holding?"

A sudden impact knocked them off their feet. "Not too well, sir!"

SLOB was annihilating them. Jenna knew this could only go one way. The element of surprise had been turned against them. SLOB's firepower was far superior. Their fighters were going down all over the place.

She grabbed hold of Fraza. "It's up to us," she said, dragging him off the flight deck and pulling him along as Quenbrarian personnel raced all over the place.

Searching frantically, she found an empty room and bundled Fraza inside. "We can do this," she said.

"Do what?"

"How are we doing?" Brash asked.

"We can't take out all these fighters, Cap!" Johnson called. "They're obliterating us!"

Brash stared at the sea of SLOB's fighters. Their own forces didn't stand a chance. It was looking hopeless. He racked his brains to think of something. Anything. Then an idea hit him.

"Just keep on at them," he called out, getting back into the lift.

Charging through the passageways, he ran back onto the flight-deck, shouting out for Skinner. The man turned to him.

"Skinner, I need a bomb. Can you build one?"

"A bomb? You want me to build a bomb?"

"Can you do it?"

Skinner shrugged. "I'll have a go. How are you going to deploy it?"

"We're going to use one of the shuttles and programme it to plough into those fighters. Make it a big one."

"What about our own fighters?"

"We'll call them away. We just need a small window of opportunity. Get on it now. I need Fraza," he said, looking around. Where the hell was Fraza?

Running out to find him, he banged into Serza. "You'll have to do." Brash dragged him back to the flight deck. "Right, Serza, I need you to translate for me."

As Brash went over the plan, Serza tilted his head. "What is bomb?"

"Kaboom!" Brash said, making an explosion with his hands.

Serza's eyes lit up. "Yes. Bomb. And... what is shuttle?"

Brash stared at him. It was like talking to a bloody three-year-old. Taking a steadying breath, he used every ounce of inventiveness to get the message through. "D'you understand now?" he asked.

"Yes."

"Good. Get Hendraz to tell the Commander."

Hendraz explained, telling the Commander they needed to withdraw the fighters at the right moment. Brash saw the Commander agree just as an impact knocked them to the floor. Alarms sounded all over the place. The deck struggled to get back in position as another hit rocked the ship. Brash looked up to see Hendraz dragging a slumped figure from its station. Another Quenbrarian took its place, the Commander furiously barking orders.

Brash's gaze transferred to the patchwork of explosions lighting up space. At this rate, there wouldn't be fighters left to save. How long would it take Skinner? Would he be able to do it? Had he ever done this before? What was he going to build a bomb out of? Brash raked a hand through his hair. Skinner wasn't going to make a bomb! What the hell had he been thinking?

Brash's sights locked on SLOB's mothership, drawing inexorably closer. It was coming under repeated fire but nothing was getting through to it. His gaze widened out. The whole of the resistance was taking a battering and Brash wondered if they'd done the right thing, dragging these people into a fight they couldn't win. They should call back the fighters. They should get out now.

"We'll have to abort!" Brash shouted but nobody could understand him. He looked around for Fraza. Where the hell was Fraza!

"What is abort?" Serza asked.

"Escape. Flee. Run away!"

"Ah. No."

"No?"

"The... err... Tractenz... not work."

"What?"

Another hit sent Brash to the floor. He looked up at Serza. "Tractenz?"

Serza explained with his hands, making his finger move slowly then very fast.

Understanding flashed through Brash and his eyes widened. "The hyperdrive's shot...?"

"Hyperdrive. Yes. Kaboom," Serza said, making an explosion with his hands.

Brash stared at Serza then turned to stare out at the carnage. He knew SLOB had a lot more to inflict. They were well and truly done for.

Then something extraordinary happened.

"What's happening!" SLOB yelled.

Rotzch came running onto the deck. "There's a problem with the weapons, Lord. The guidance system's gone haywire. They're working on it now."

"Gone haywire? It can't have gone haywire! It's the best system there is!" A large flash drew his attention. "Was that one of ours...?"

One of the generals came rushing in. "We're losing the shield, Lord."

"What...?"

The ship took a hit and alarms sounded.

"We're coming under heavy fire, Lord," Rotzch said.

"I can see that, you bloody moron! Sort it out! Now!"

The resistance was pummelling the craft. SLOB ran forward to see that his weapons were targeting his own ships. This didn't make sense. They'd tested the weapons systems. There was nothing wrong with them. Something was off. This reeked of sabotage. But who? Could there be some die-hard rebels amongst his crew?

He turned to his general. "Change the crews in the weapons sector and on the shield generator. Imprison them for now. And watch the new crews carefully."

"Sir, I don't think it's our men."

"Do it anyway."

As the man walked out, SLOB prepared to take matters into his own hands.

Brash turned to Hendraz, who was staring on astounded. "They're firing on their own craft," Brash said but Hendraz couldn't understand him. "And their shield is down."

"Their shield is down," Hendraz said. "And they're firing on their own craft."

Quenbrarian ships manoeuvred closer, firing like crazy. SLOB's mothership took pounding after pounding. Another of SLOB's ships went up in the distance. Then a third. Many thoughts ran through Brash's mind. Were some of SLOB's crew rebelling? Did he have a problem with his weapons systems? Whatever it was, it was giving him hope. He rushed up to the weapons deck to bolster his crew.

"He's firing on his own craft," Brash called out. "Three of their ships have gone down."

"He's killing his own men...?" Newark asked as he took out another fighter. "Does he hate them too?"

"Is he mad...?" Graham asked.

"I don't know what's going on but the tide's turning," Brash said. "Keep at it!"

As he headed back down, their ship took a hit.

"He's firing on us again!" Johnson yelled.

"Keep your intent, Fraza," Jenna said calmly. "Remember, there's just the power and intent. He's only drawing on his well. We have the whole."

The weapons turned away again. Another of SLOB's ships took a battering. Brash was as confused as the Quenbrarians. *Was* an insurrection going on? Whatever it was, the resistance took full advantage.

"Boytiful, yes?" Serza said, staring at the montage of explosions flickering across the enormous length of SLOB's mothership.

"Yes, beautiful..." Brash could hardly process what he was seeing. Surely, it was just a matter of time before that thing went up.

"Look!" Serza said, pointing.

Two of SLOB's ships went up in close succession. They watched, rapt. It was like a symphony for the eyes.

"We winning now," Serza said, excitement pulsing through him.

"It... looks like it..."

Brash's hope was strengthened by every hit SLOB took. This was how it was supposed to play out. Good triumphed over evil. SLOB was going down.

When SLOB began firing on the resistance again, Brash's surging hope took a nosedive. Not only was SLOB back in action but he was coming back with a vengeance. Good didn't triumph over evil, Brash realised. This was real life and real life sucked!

"Captain," Skinner called, "I have it."

Brash turned and stared at Skinner. "You have it…?"

"Yes, Captain."

"You actually did it…?"

"Yes, sir."

Brash took a few moments to compute that before springing into action. "Right. Serza, get Hendraz to inform the Commander."

Hendraz informed the Commander, who spoke to one of his officers. The officer led Brash, Serza, Hendraz, and Skinner down to the shuttle bay.

The bomb was placed in one of the shuttles. The Quenbrarian officer programmed the shuttle as he spoke to the lead fighter pilot, giving him specific instructions. Checking the flight trajectory, Skinner's amazing brain calculated and set the timer. Brash knew this was a long shot. So much could go wrong but with so many enemy fighters, they had to take the shot.

As the shuttle was deployed, Brash, Skinner, Hendraz, and Serza jumped into a lift and zipped up to the weapons deck to see if this was going to work.

"What's going on?" Johnson asked.

"Just watch." Brash glanced at Skinner. The man was looking down the length of the deck, watching the guns firing. Brash couldn't reconcile this man with the cowardly worm he had once known. He vaguely wondered what it was like to die a thousand deaths. He couldn't even imagine it and for the first time, he spared Skinner a moment of admiration. A moment was all he had. He turned back to the action.

They watched their fighters draw away in unison, the enemy in pursuit. When it happened, it was like a carefully choreographed performance. The shuttle ploughed into SLOB's forces in a glorious, devastating explosion, the effects ricocheting on and on as fighter after fighter ploughed into the fire, creating mini after explosions. Half of the enemy fighters were taken down.

Newark whooped. A chorus of cheers broke out.

"I fucking love you!" Brash shouted, rattling Skinner's shoulders.

"Skinner did that?" Johnson asked.

"Yes. We've levelled the field. Now, annihilate them!"

Brash was on a euphoric high, showering Skinner with praise. Hendraz and Serza patted Skinner on the back, shouting out things in Hellgathen. Brash realised his team really *was* a good team. The best there was. He could barely contain how proud he felt but as they made their way down, his high crashed. A humongous force rocked the ship. Another impact came close behind then another as they struggled to get to their feet.

They entered the flight-deck to see Quenbrarians running all over the place. The Commander was laid-out on the floor, blood pooling around his head. His second was barking orders but the deck was in meltdown.

"What is it?" Brash asked, looking around frantically.

"Everything gone," Serza told him.

"The weapons systems?"

"Everything."

"The shield?"

"Everything."

"The drives?"

"Everything."

"Everything?"

"Everything!"

They were dead in the water, completely defenceless. The only thing keeping them alive were other resistance craft, firing repeatedly at SLOB. Brash knew they were living on borrowed time. It was over. He looked around for Jenna. Where the hell was Jenna? He needed to see her one last time.

Charging out to find her, he saw fires being put out all over the place but he knew it was in vain. Everything had been in vain. They had failed. Their mission had failed. SLOB had won.

"Fraza, I need you to stay with me," Jenna said. "You're blocking it. Get out of your own way. Take yourself out of the picture."

"It's my mind. It's always tortured me."

"I know. But you have to let go and trust something bigger than your mind. You've come so far, Fraza. I need a leap of faith now. You can do this." Jenna opened her eyes and looked at him. "Don't you want to be free?"

SLOB couldn't sustain it. Whatever was causing this was stronger than he was. He'd never come across a power this strong. Where was it coming from? Who was doing this? His god-like status and his dreams of conquering the universe started to crumble before him.

"Seven of our craft have gone, Lord," Rotzch said. "We're still firing on the other three. Should we turn off the weapons?"

SLOB stared at Rotzch.

"Lord?"

"Give me a minute."

He tried again. But nothing was working. It was like his power had dried up. He couldn't stop his weapons firing on his own craft. As he watched another of his craft go up, he could hardly process what he was seeing.

"Should we turn them off, Lord?"

SLOB turned and stared at Rotzch.

"Lord?"

"Turn them off."

Rotzch pressed a button and spoke to the weapons sector. He turned back to SLOB. "The shield is down, Lord. We're taking a battering. The resistance is overpowering us. The main drive is shot. Do we surrender?"

The word wouldn't sink in. "Surrender…?"

"If we don't surrender, Lord, the ship will be destroyed."

His brain felt like it was going to explode. "No surrender!" he yelled.

He stormed off the deck, his mind reeling. The ship was done for. But worse than that, there was someone in this damn universe who was stronger than he was. It couldn't end like this. He had to live to fight another day. With that in mind, he bundled himself into an escape pod and jettisoned the hell out of there. Rotzch, seeing what he'd done, ran back to the deck and opened a coms link in a bid to surrender.

Brash searched frantically. He couldn't find her anywhere. Quenbrarian words echoed down the passageway, followed immediately by the sounds of cheering.

When he got back to the flight deck, a celebration was going on. Jenna and Fraza came in behind him. "What's going on?" Brash asked.

Fraza spoke to Serza.

"The mother ship's surrendered," Fraza told them. "The man gave his name as Rotzch. Rotzch said the Thunder God was no longer on the ship and he had assumed command."

"Surrendered?" Brash asked, stunned.

"Where's SLOB?" Jenna asked.

Fraza asked the question. "Hendraz said an escape pod was jettisoned."

"He's escaped…?" Jenna turned to Brash. "He's escaped!"

"It's not over!" Brash shouted. "We need a shuttle. Fraza, get Hendraz to sort it out quick. And get him to find out the trajectory of that pod."

# Letting Go

The Quenbrarian shuttle swerved to avoid debris as it steered a course to the nearest planet. Hendraz and Serza were up front with the Quenbrarian pilot. The others were in the back.

"I approach him alone," Jenna said.

"I can't let you do that," Brash objected. "He was stronger than you last time."

"Well, he isn't now. Only I approach him."

"Jen-"

"Are you going to trust me or not," she snapped.

"But-"

"Let me remind you that for this mission, you are my team. This is my decision. My call."

"According to Cornelius."

She turned to him, her blue eyes hard. "I'm all this universe has got. We do it my way or not at all."

"Your way? You've been hiding out for the past-"

"I have not been hiding," she said emphatically. "Only I can end this. I approach him alone."

Brash had never heard her speak with such determination and he had never felt so conflicted. If he went with her, it said he didn't trust her. Yet, how could he let her face SLOB alone? He would rather die than do that.

"I know you want to help," she said more softly. "But you can't. Please, Lucas, trust me." Something in her eyes pleaded for his trust.

"Fine," he threw out, staring at the floor.

Jenna turned to Fraza. "I need you to translate."

Fraza nodded.

"I can't believe what happened back there..." Graham murmured.

"He must have had a problem with his weapons systems," Johnson said. "And with his shield too."

"The gods were looking out for us today," Newark reflected.

Skinner was silently pondering.

As the craft entered the atmosphere, the pilot scoured around for the pod. Hendraz finally pointed it out and they touched down.

"He can't have got far," Jenna said. "The air's breathable, I take it?" Fraza asked Hendraz. "Yes," Fraza replied.

"Right," Jenna said, taking a deep breath. "Come on, Fraza. The rest of you stay back."

Brash had never seen her so focused or so brave. This was not the girl he had first met. He realised this was not a girl at all. This was a woman.

The gangway lowered and they all walked down. Jenna turned to them. "What are you doing?"

"Coming out with you," Brash said, staring at her, confused.

"No. Only Fraza and I go out."

"But-"

"Either you trust me to finish the job I came here to do or you don't."

Something in her eyes pulled him up short. Something suddenly clicked in him. Her whole life was in those eyes and he knew, right to the bones of him, that he had to let her go.

Relinquishing control for the first time in his life, he reluctantly nodded. "Be careful," he whispered.

She smiled at him gently. "If anything happens to us, get out of here quick." Her gaze lingered on him then she turned, walking down the gangway. Brash stared after her, feeling like the bottom was falling out of his world.

The crew ran to the front of the craft, watching Jenna and Fraza walk out over the barren landscape. Brash came up behind them.

"You're letting her do this?" Johnson asked.

"Our weapons are useless," Brash said, raking a hand through his hair. "Only she can end this."

Graham looked out, concerned. "She couldn't do anything last time. What's changed?"

"I don't know..."

Newark, for once, was silent. He did not approve of this.

Hendraz and Serza were silent too, realising how attached they had become to the human and the little Kaledian.

The light was blinding. Jenna scanned the land, knowing he was there somewhere, probably watching, waiting.

She drew in a deep breath. She wasn't nervous or scared. The only thing she felt was conviction. "I know the answer to the question you ask," she called out. She turned to Fraza, who was looking at her, confused. She nodded at him and he began to translate. "I know why no-one has ever loved you."

There was silence for a time. A silence so palpable, it seemed to breathe.

Then a dark cloaked figure stepped out from behind a cluster of rocks. His face was impassive yet his eyes betrayed a certain pain. They widened on recognising her. "*You...?*" He stared at her strangely. "Who are you? Did *you* sabotage my ship...?"

"Don't you want to know the answer?"

"The answer...?" he asked, gazing at her curiously. "You know...?"

She nodded.

"Why?" he whispered.

"It was never because you were not worthy of love. Your parents did not know how to love, never stuck up for you. You were never nothing." She took a gentle step closer.

"Get back or I'll kill you," he said, lashing out. Something struck her chest and she stumbled back but managed to stay on her feet.

The crew ran out but Brash yelled, "Stay put!"

"But Captain!" Johnson pressed.

"Stay put. That's an order!"

Jenna moved closer. "You won't kill me because I'm the only one who has ever loved you."

"This is a trick," SLOB spat, his face hardening.

She shook her head. "I could kill you now if I wanted."

"You were no match for me!"

"I know. But I am now."

SLOB's arms pressed to his sides. He couldn't move them. He tried to lash out with his power but he and it were contained in a box. "What have you done to me!" he raged.

"I've blocked your well."

He struggled furiously, trying to wield his power. It wasn't there. He strived relentlessly, like a petulant brat that wouldn't take no for an answer, but it was all to no avail. At last, he stopped struggling, staring at the floor, dazed. Slowly, he raised his head, gazing at her in awe. "You *are* a god..."

"No. There are no gods, just delusions," she said. "Now, are you ready to accept that you are loved?"

"You don't love me! Nobody loves me! Nobody's ever loved me!"

"Well, I do. I love the little boy, Venn, who cried when his father called him an embarrassment; the boy who should have been hugged and loved but who felt completely worthless."

SLOB stared at her.

"Remember how alone you felt, Venn? How ashamed? How worthless? How you just wanted your father to be proud of you, wanted your mother to wrap her arms around you and tell you everything was alright." SLOB's eyes widened in shock. "They might not have loved that little boy but I do."

Fraza stared at her, astounded. "Jenna, he's a ruthless murderer."

"He wasn't then. I'm not talking to the murderer. Please don't interrupt, Fraza. You're breaking the flow."

"What did he say?" SLOB asked, suddenly suspicious.

"He said you're a ruthless murderer." Jenna glanced at Fraza and he reluctantly translated.

"I'm a god!"

"Really? Still? Haven't you figured out yet that you're not a god? Don't you see that your desire to be a god springs from your feelings of worthlessness? You were never a god, just a lost little boy."

He lashed out again but his power remained blocked. Again, and again, he tried but nothing would come. He had nothing. He was nothing. How could he go back to nothing...?

"You were never nothing," Jenna said gently. "You were never worthless. You were a beautiful, trusting little boy. Remember?"

Venn stared at her, a fissure of pain ripping open inside him.

"You were perfect," Jenna said, "just as you were. The fault was not with you. You were deserving of love."

Years of stoppered pain surged up in SLOB like burning magma. He dropped to his knees. "Nobody ever loved me..." he whispered, bereft, clutching his chest. He began to sob convulsively.

Jenna knelt beside him and took his head in her arms. "You've been acting out your pain all these years but now, finally, I want you to know that you are loved."

The crew stared on, incredulous. "Is she hugging him...?" Newark uttered.

Venn sobbed in her arms and she let him. The young child was finally being comforted. He sobbed and sobbed for every hurt, every slight, every injustice... He sobbed for a very long time.

"I have to kill you now, Venn," Jenna whispered, thrusting a knife into his back.

His eyes widened. "You lied," he cried out, broken.

"No," she said gently. "I didn't lie. I love that little boy. Let go now, Venn."

She held him as he died in her arms.

"Fuck me..." Newark mouthed. "She's bloody killed him..."

The crew couldn't make sense of what they had just seen. It was totally surreal.

"That's killing someone in a touchy-feely way..." Skinner murmured, dazed.

Jenna laid SLOB down and got up to walk away. But she stumbled and fell.

"Jenna," Fraza said frantically, leaning over her. "What wrong?"

"He struck me in the chest," she said weakly. "I think it's done some damage." Her eyes were drooping.

"Jenna, stay with me!"

Her head fell back and her eyes closed. Fraza shook her but her eyes wouldn't open.

The crew came running over.

"I think she's gone," Fraza said, almost pleading with them.

"Get out of the way, Fraza," Brash said, pulling him aside, checking her over, desperately searching for a pulse. "There's a weak pulse," he insisted. "I felt it."

Johnson moved in, trying to find it. "I can't find a pulse, Captain."

"Give me some room," he said, pushing her away. He tried again and again to revive her. "It can't end like this!" he said, pumping her chest. "It can't!"

"She's gone, Captain," Graham said sombrely.

Newark laid a hand on the Captain's shoulder. Brash looked up into Newark's watery eyes, his own eyes soaked in disbelief. He stared back at Jenna, unable to take in that she was dead. He stumbled to his feet, backing away in horror. His eyes travelled to the spent form of SLOB. He charged the body, kicking it over and over.

"Let's get him back to the craft," Johnson said, wiping tears from her cheeks.

The Captain's anger turned on them as they tried to lead him away. He lashed out but they steadfastly pulled him to the shuttle. Serza and Hendraz remained there, staring down at Jenna, watching Fraza crying over the body.

"She will to be hero," Serza said softly.

"Yes..." Hendraz agreed, swallowing hard.

# Believing in the Impossible

The Venulians held a special ceremony to honour all those who had died in the fight against SLOB. The whole universe owed them a debt of gratitude. Jenna was honoured for her personal courage in facing SLOB directly. Fraza, with his headpiece on, translated what was being said. The Head told them that Venulians had never heard of humans before but he now considered them to be an excellent race.

"That's a sweeping generalisation," Skinner remarked under his breath.

At the end of the ceremony, the crew went up to receive medals. They were subdued and dignified as they walked down the grass aisle to where Venulians in robes were waiting for them. Their mission was complete. They had done what they came here to do.

Serza, Hendraz and his men were called up next. Then every other serving member of the depleted forces. The whole city had turned out to watch the ceremony, clapping as every medal was awarded.

Brash watched on, knowing that his service was done. He was relinquishing the post of Captain. He didn't know who else he was but he was going to find out. The Venulians had promised to repair the Super Mega HyperDrive in order for them to get home. Brash wasn't sure where home was. He didn't think anywhere would feel like home without Jenna. He had been with so many women but none of them had left a mark on him like she had.

The ceremony was finally over. They were told that evening attire would be provided for the celebratory ball that was to be held that night.

The Venulian ball was held in a large, circular glass-domed room. The ceiling afforded a spectacular view of the ringed planet. Graham and Newark stared at Johnson in her long blue gown. Graham thought she looked like a Grecian goddess. Newark realised there had been a woman in there all along. The men were wearing Venulian evening wear, made three sizes smaller. They had dark breeches and long dark capes. In fact, they looked like they'd stepped out of the eighteenth century. The main body of the crew dreaded the orchestra starting up. When it did, the sounds were sort of tuneful, the orchestra catering for more eclectic taste. Fraza, with his headpiece on, lingered near to Brash as various dignitaries came over to talk to him.

The Quenbrarian woman, whose help Jenna had enlisted, approached Brash. Fraza adjusted his box. "Are you returning to your own system now, Captain Brash?" she asked.

He nodded.

"My officer told me how brave Jenna was."

Brash nodded tightly. The image of Jenna lying on the ground was still emblazoned on his heart.

"We will be honouring you all in Quenbrar."

She bowed her head, smiling graciously as she walked away.

"Why don't you dance with her, Captain?" Fraza said.

Brash turned to look at the vision in the purple gown. He'd been wanting to ask her to dance all evening but he didn't know how he would be received.

Taking a breath, he walked over and tapped her on the shoulder. "Could I have this dance?"

Jenna turned to see a very dashing Captain Brash. There was something different about him but she wasn't sure what it was.

She smiled and held out her hands. "I'll do my best but I warn you, I have no sense of rhythm."

"You don't need any with this music," he said with a mischievous glint in his eye.

As they moved around the room, Jenna tried to figure out what was different about him. In his costume, he looked rather debonair.

"Thank you," she said.

"For what?"

"For letting me go. For trusting me to come back."

"You didn't. You got killed."

She smiled. "Still came back, though, didn't I?"

"You were brought back by Fraza."

"Details."

He smiled. "Any more details you want to fill me in on?"

Her brow creased.

"I have the feeling you've been keeping something from me. SLOB firing on his own ships? His shield going down? That was you and Fraza, wasn't it?"

"Took you a while to figure that out."

"Why didn't you say?"

"I got killed," she said, toying with him.

His arms snaked around her waist. "Why didn't you say before that, or after?"

"You know," she said thoughtfully, "I always wanted to achieve something... and don't get me wrong, I think I've achieved so much these past months. But I didn't realise that I was struggling to be what I already was and why do I need to brag about that?"

"You've lost me."

She laughed. "OK. It didn't seem necessary."

He brushed a hand through her hair. "Did I ever tell you how beautiful you are?"

"My turn," Newark butted in, grabbing hold of Jenna. "Want to see how well *I* can dance?"

The big bundling puppy that what Newark whisked her all over the place. This man was really starting to surprise her. When Fraza had brought her around, Newark hugged her like a long-lost relative. She nearly suffocated. Fraza had to slap him off her. Sometimes you have to die to realise what people think of you. At one time, she would never have believed these people could be her friends. But she had learned to believe in the impossible.

# Epilogue

The lush valley was still there. When they got through the forest, they found the aruks waiting for them.

"Cool, we get another go," Johnson said, excitedly.

"The cute little fuckers," Newark said, stroking a thick black neck.

The city looked just the same. The Erithians were out to greet them as they landed on the grass runway. Jenna looked around for Cornelius. When she saw him, she dove off the bird and threw her arms around him.

"I'm still here," the old man said, patting her back. "And I'm so proud of you. Of you all," he said, glancing at the others.

Llamia stepped forward, smiling that barely-there smile. "You have surpassed all our expectations."

Johnson tried to figure out if that was a compliment or not.

The crew turned as one to see Flint walking over. He looked taller, although maybe that was the way he was standing, with his back erect. When he spoke, he seemed to be inhabiting his body. "Well done," he said, looking at them all surprised. "You... actually did it."

"Come," Llamia said. "Let us feed you. We have prepared a banquet for your arrival."

As much as the crew saw a difference in Flint, Flint saw the difference in them. Jenna was... well, she was swearing for one, but she seemed so much more laid-back, yet confident at the same time. Brash was laid back too. His right ankle rested idly on his other knee and his arm was splayed over the back of Jenna's chair. Flint noted that Newark wasn't goading him and Graham was talking to him as an equal. It was like they had been through a baptism of fire and emerged as different people. Be that as it may, there was something Flint still had to get out of his system.

Cornelius opened the door for it. "Mr Flint has come a long way during his time with us but there is one final thing he needs to do to complete his therapy."

"What's that?" Jenna asked.

"He would like you all, apart from Jenna and Fraza, to line up and allow him to punch you."

They stared at Flint for several moments but when they stood up to volunteer, Flint was visibly surprised. It was enough to restore his faith in human nature. Not enough, though, to prevent him taking his best shot at each of them. After that, they all clapped him on the back.

"You've got some fire in there, after all," Newark said.

"What are your plans now?" Cornelius asked the crew.

"I want to build stuff," Graham said, biting into succulent flesh.

"Ow, that hurt," Johnson complained.

"I want to hang out with Jenna some more," Fraza said and Cornelius raised his eyebrows. He'd already noticed the lack of OCD.

"I want a beer," Newark said.

"I want a woman," Skinner complained. Jenna glanced at him. Had the spell finally broken? Thank god for that.

"And what about you two?" Cornelius asked Jenna and Brash.

"I'm not sure," Brash said. "But I'm not the Captain anymore."

The crew stared at him. It was like having a life-raft swept out from under them. The Captain not being the Captain?

"But you've always been the Cap," Newark said.

"Things change."

"And what about you, Jenna?" Cornelius asked.

"I want adventure."

"Why don't we do that then?" Brash asked.

"I'm in," said Newark.

"Me too," said Johnson.

"And me," said Graham.

Skinner signed up by nodding. Brash realised it was going to take time to shake off the Captain role.

"Flint?" Jenna asked. "You coming with us?"

Flint stared at them. Was he ready for adventure?

"How d'you feel about being Captain, Flint?" Brash asked.

"With one proviso," Newark added. "If he's shit, we sack him."

Cornelius thought Newark had come a long way. He was developing sensitivity. Not long ago he would have used the term, 'we lynch him.' Or words to that effect.

"By the way," Newark said, turning to Cornelius, "now we're heroes and all, d'you think I stand a chance with Llamia?"

"Llamia is from another dimension," Cornelius pointed out.

Newark shrugged. "I'm up for a little head fucking."

Cornelius tried to weigh up if that was a step forward in disguise. Sometimes the simplest people hold the greatest mystery.

Newark sniffed. "After the head fucking, she might try it my way."

Maybe not, Cornelius thought.

He lent back and looked at them all. He was proud of his fledglings. They had become full-grown birds and were about to fly out again. Cornelius had lived here all his life. He had a mind to go with them. Have a little adventure himself.

*****

Printed in Great Britain
by Amazon